Night Terror

J. A. WINRICH

Writer Jaw Books, P. O. Box 356, Ukiah, CA 95482
www.writerjaw.com

Cover design by Mary Ames Mitchell, Mitchell Design

ISBN:0989565009

ISBN-13:978-0-9895650-0-4

DEDICATION

For Stan, David, Tyler and Peyton

ACKNOWLEDGMENTS

Thanks to the Arson Investigators, the Firemen, EMTs, and nurses I interviewed who helped make this book more real. Also thanks to Ana Manwaring of JAM Manuscript Consulting for her editing skills, to my critique groups and the Redwood Writers Branch of the California Writers Club for their support and encouragement, and to Mary Ames Mitchell, Mitchell Design for an inspired cover.

CHAPTER 1

Kathy lay on the bed facing the Queen Anne-style Victorian's bedroom wall. Bright orange flames raced up; the loud crackling hurt her ears. She shut her eyes against the inferno. As she clutched the comforter to her chin, her heart pounded. *Dear God, when I open my eyes, let the blaze be gone.*

She peeked between lashes. The red glow from the clock numbers and the soft green illumination from the hallway plug-in night lights lit the room. Flowered wallpaper—fresh and clean, like the day she'd put the paper up in the bedroom.

No black scarring. No blistered paper. No acrid stench.

No sign of fire.

Wide awake, staring at the wall, Kathy whispered, "Jack, it's happening again." He didn't answer. Without taking her gaze from the wall, she reached across the bed. Her hand patted the cold, empty sheet.

"Jack Hellman?" She glanced around. "Where are you?" Her voice rose with each word.

The telephone rang.

Startled by the loud noise at two in the morning, Kathy jerked back and hit her head on the iron headboard. She bit her lip; the coppery taste of blood seeped across her tongue and slid down her throat.

On the second ring, she reached across the empty space to her husband's nightstand, and grabbed the handset. She put it to her ear and listened.

Screams erupted.

"No, please, not again!" She felt the ache in her heart and wanted to cover her ears. Instead, she stabbed the off button and slammed the phone back down. "Jack?" she yelled. Why was he never around when the arsonist called and played those horrible screams? *God, how much more can I take?*

Kathy threw back the comforter and jumped out of bed, determined to find her husband. She gasped as the summer dampness of the Northern

California seacoast town sucked any warmth right out of her.

The phone rang again. She froze, staring at the machine as if it was on fire and would burn her. A door slammed downstairs. The telephone jingled twice more and stopped.

Jack's voice drifted up from below. She hurried around the bed and quietly picked up the receiver, and heard, "It's a Code Three, possible 10–55. Captain Farley wants his best arson investigator there."

"Where?" her husband asked.

The grandfather clock downstairs bonged twice. Bile rose in Kathy's throat. She fought the nausea until the stomach spasm doubled her over. She gripped the phone tighter.

After the cramping relaxed, she straightened up, dreading the Carsonville Fire Department dispatcher's answer to the location. Why did this arsonist target her? Couldn't he find someone else to torment?

She missed hearing the address of the fire, but heard Jack say, "I'll be there within ten minutes. Have you notified the state fire marshal?"

"Yes, sir. Lovell said the drive would take him several hours to get here." Another phone rang in the background and the dispatcher said, "If there's nothing else, Sir, I have to go."

After the sound of a click, Kathy wanted to say something to her husband, but he hung up before she could utter a word. She slowly replaced the receiver and stood motionless next to the bed, cocking her head to listen.

The minutes ticked off with each beat of the bedroom clock jarring her nerves. The garage door opened, Jack's old Ford coupe rumbled to life, and then tires crunched on the dirt and gravel in the alley.

Alone.

She trembled when she remembered the screams from the first phone call. Pictures of burned, dead bodies flooded her mind, refusing to disappear.

After turning on the bedside light, her breath came in, quick and shallow. Sweat beaded on her brow. Had Jack reset the alarm system?

Something brushed against her legs. Kathy kicked out. Sheba landed on all four feet and jumped up on the bed, yellow eyes piercing. Then the cat twitched her tail and strolled over to the edge of the bed.

Awkward laughter bubbled out and Kathy reached down to pet the tabby's soft orange fur. Sheba purred loudly as if to say, "Don't worry, it'll be okay."

"Sorry about kicking you, but you scared me," Kathy muttered, stroking the cat. She felt her cheeks burn.

"Time to stop this nonsense," she told the tabby, and took a couple of deep yoga breaths to calm her.

The chilly air made her feel like her body had submerged into ice water. *I'll never get used to cold summers along the Pacific coast.* She grabbed her old pink robe off the bed and cinched the belt tight around her waist, feeling a little warmer.

"Come on, Sheba. I can't go back to sleep. How about a warm bowl of milk?"

The cat still crouched on the bed, kneading the sheet into soft tiny mounds.

Kathy drew back the sheer panels at the bedroom window. Jack's car idled at the curb. Why hadn't he left for the fire? Was their arsonist that close?

She bit her lip, scared of that thought. After inhaling deeply and holding her breath for several beats, her heart rate slowed to its natural rhythm. She turned away from the window. The curtains swayed as though a tiny breeze fluttered through the glass. In the hall, she stopped and listened.

Nothing.

The cat padded behind her as she hurried through the upstairs rooms and turned on all the lights.

She descended the stairs, sliding her hand along the polished oak banister, taking pains to avoid that one creaky step near the top.

Downstairs, she roamed from room to room flicking on the switches. At the front door, she triggered both front and back porch lights. A yellowish haze glowed around the house like a halo.

Darkness would not penetrate her now lighted haven.

When she gazed out the front room window, Jack's car was gone. The alarm button by the front door shined green.

"Well, I've done my part," she told the cat. "I can't fight these fires, but I can keep my fear at bay. Come on." The tabby followed her to the kitchen.

As Kathy heated water for lemon tea, she admired the white antique gas stove Jack had salvaged from a barn fire that year she'd miscarried for a second time. The old enameled iron stove had needed cleaning and some repairs, but Jack and she had restored it to its Victorian grandeur. She cherished all of her antiques. Each one told a story.

She sat down in one of the four carved-back chairs at the round oak table, a wedding gift from her folks. Her only inheritance, after the fire.

Cold seeped into her hands. They felt like she'd been rummaging around in the freezer. She wrapped them around the warm mug of tea as her mind wandered back to that first fire. She closed her eyes and willed her shakes to subside.

Fire. Why did it consume her life? Of course, accidental house fires happened all the time. Her parents...

But, then came this arsonist's terrible fires. The thought of this maniac made her shudder again. She hated feeling helpless. So many phone calls, the dreams, too many fires. *Why is this pyro after me?*

Tears formed in her eyes. That's enough. Don't you dare cry!

Early morning darkness blackened the kitchen window. Whether from fear or cold, more shivers wracked her body and she clutched her robe tighter.

The cat rubbed against her legs. "Aw, Sheba, I might as well get ready for Allen today. I'll never be able to calm down if I don't cook something."

During summer break from teaching high school, she taught cooking. Kathy hated the breaks and all that idle time. The ten-year-old from three doors away was her new student. Normally she taught high school age, but Allen really wanted to learn to cook.

Kathy's mother had been an excellent cook and passed on those talents to her daughter. The love of preparing food led her to become a high school home economics teacher.

She stood and walked over to the stove. It brought to mind the one she'd grown up with and her mother had used. If only Mom and Dad were still alive. They were the first... No, she couldn't afford to dwell on those memories.

Kathy gathered scraps of wood and paper from the kindling box. Like when she was a child, she lit them in the built-in trash burner on the side of the antique stove. The comforting familiarity of repeating this simple act made her smile. She moved the teapot onto the top of the trash burner to keep the water warm.

In front of the new white tile counter, she ran her hand across the cracked and broken bindings of the old cookbooks she lined up against the wall. None belonged to her mother. These books came from antique shops.

She grabbed her favorite one, carried it to the table, and pulled out the chair too fast, banging the wainscoting. Her inspection showed no dents on either chair or rail.

Antiques and Victorian houses stirred up images from Kathy's past; both were a part of her. Queen Anne homes were her favorite Victorian style, not only did they remind her of her own family home, but also they were more elaborate and ornate. The patterned shingles, carved fretwork finials and lace-like wooden ornamentation brought Edgar Allen Poe's descriptions of widow's walks and peaked roofs alive for her.

These old houses—one minute she hated them with tears threatening to flood, the next she loved them with broad smiles giving her a bright glow. Jack couldn't convince her to live in any other house.

Lost in her memories, she found herself standing in front of the old stove. "How do I get from one place to another without knowing it?" she asked the cat.

Sheba meowed and swished her tail.

Losing track of herself, going black as she called it, didn't happen often. Only when the arsonist phoned or burned too close—it happened just enough to confuse her. At the stove, she refilled her now empty mug. She couldn't remember drinking the first.

Thoughts of her past and present roiled like the tea water in the kettle. She slid into the nearest chair to copy down her recipe, but instead stared unfocused out the window.

Images of various victims' flashed into her mind. Her palms sweat. She rubbed them on her robe.

Whose house burned this time? 10–55—a coroner's case—someone had died. *Do I know them?*

"Sheba," Kathy said to the yellow-eyed cat, "the arsonist must have followed us again."

CHAPTER 2

I hunker down behind the steering wheel and watch as one by one, the lights flick on. Kathleen's house shines like a beacon in the night, no different than all the other times. Because she leaves the drapes open, it makes it so easy to spy on her.

Too bad I couldn't stay to watch my handiwork. But the need to come here—much greater.

Fear must be coursing throughout Kathleen's body. My skin tingles from the warm, inner glow. There's nothing better than being in total control.

I close my eyes and picture my fire. Perfect timing—like the others. The fire leapt to life at exactly 1:30 A.M. Those hungry flames—I love their varied colors—oranges, yellows, magentas and even blues and greens. They lick higher and higher above the landmark Victorian. The sky glows. Shadows dance.

Fire—it boils through my veins. I listen to the roar of the blaze—screams piercing the night.

I depress the start button with a trembling finger. The Sony tape recorder whirrs, capturing those animal-like screams that I play for Kathleen over the telephone.

She doesn't appreciate those screams, but they remind me of so much. Kathleen always hangs up on me when she hears them. If I'm not careful, those wails will be my undoing!

No, I won't go there and I don't care if she slams down the phone.

Just yesterday, I stood across the street admiring the fine lines of that grand old Queen Anne. That style Victorian holds a special fascination for me.

After studying the house, I cross the street and introduce myself to the family. They were restoring the home to its original glory. I approve their work. They were a pleasant, close-knit family. Too bad they're all dead.

When I think about them it makes me feel as though a woman just wrapped her arms around me. The odor from the fire—a death smell—sweet Death.

My blaze ingests the classical-columned front porch. A round tower perches atop the Queen Anne's far corner, reaching skyward to a peak. It brings up images of my own family home.

As the inferno eats this Carsonville house, I push mental pictures away about one of my first fires, but they assault me.

I'd crept up and threw gas all around the home. I wanted to destroy her. Inside, I splashed gas along the stairway, on furniture and curtains, and outside, threw a match. WHOOSH!

Then later, screams erupted. I ran all the way back to my room, knowing I'd killed her. But it wasn't her!

I watch this Carsonville blaze as flames kindle the bows. The paint crinkles and the slate-blue gabled roof blends with the trim, but soon turns grey. The fire devours it like a child gobbling candy. My mouth waters.

The stained-glass windows explode. Voracious, my inferno leaps hungrily through shards of glass, searching for oxygen.

Yellow flames continue to dance from gaping wounds. Blood surges through my veins. I hug myself enjoying my blaze's beauty.

Chills course down my spine as the fire and the screams bring back the memories to that first one... No! Forget. But I never forget those first screams that run through my mind like passages from familiar old songs.

The wail of fire engines brings me back to my senses. My heart thumps so loud it makes me think of "The Tell-Tale Heart."

I slip behind a thick row of pink rhododendron bushes and watch the first engines race to my work. I have to leave. I sneak away, settle comfortably into the leather seat of my old car parked a few blocks away, and remember to drive slowly down the alley.

It's paramount to keep one step ahead of the arson investigator. Dumb arsonists are caught because they linger too long to watch the firefighters battle their handiwork. That will never happen to me.

I can't stop smiling. After doing my deed, I can dance all day and lift hundred pound weights with one hand.

The initial flickering flames arouse me, but it's the screams from the people burning that send tingles down my spine, electrifying me. The flames, the screams, those aren't the real reasons for setting the fires.

Not even close.

Unlike most arsonists, my main goal is not the inferno itself. What idiot would desire to chase the illusive flame, wondering what it would be like to be consumed by the blaze's heat? No, I can't even fathom why most firebugs have this infatuation with fire. I quiver. No, I'll never have a wish for that.

My fires—to sit here and watch her reactions. The thrill, the risks—soon I will hear Kathleen's screams.

Does she feel safe? Maybe—until she receives the telephone call. Damn, I love those. Her pathetic pleas, questions. The fear. I know her so well—her likes and dislikes; we even share a passion for Victorian houses. She loves to restore them. I love to burn them.

As I watch the house, I reach over to pick my cell phone off the seat. No, I called once. That's enough for now. I clasp the steering wheel. The muscles in my forearms harden.

She should not have done this to me! I'll pay her back for all the pain she's caused.

The longer I refrain from calling again, the more unnerved she'll become. It's so much fun to watch the battle within her.

I have the situation under control. Her time on this earth will soon be gone.

She can't hide. Not from me. We're too close.

When the fire caresses the houses, the teasing, beautiful flames lick the air, I need release. After each inferno, I picture Kathleen, arms wrapping around me, holding and loving me.

Love. To hear her final death screams, proving her complete love for me and no other—that excites me. I can hardly wait!

As the porch light comes on, I know it's time to go. I tear my gaze away from her house. My knuckles have turned white from gripping the steering wheel so tight. I pull away from the curb and I glance over my shoulder at her Queen Anne—one last look. I slowly drive away. Important work beckons me.

I think about watching her and laugh out loud.

Closer, moving closer to the end.

CHAPTER 3

Jack clutched the black, leather-covered steering wheel, gritted his teeth, and gunned the engine. His grandfather's words reverberated in his mind: "Drive slowly or you'll crash this car again." After the two of them had restored the old car, Jack had done what his grandfather told him to do.

He motored along the now congested street in low gear. Five hundred feet from the scene, he jockeyed in between two parked cars, and shut off the engine.

The pain in his leg throbbed and his stomach roiled with the acid building up. Was this their arsonist? His investigation would tell if their pyro had followed them. Or if the phone calls started again. But Kathy hadn't received any. Maybe this wasn't the maniac who tried to destroy their lives.

Flames leaped high into the air from the burning house. They danced and lapped at the sides. Would he find enough evidence to locate where this started?

Jack's main goal was to investigate this inferno and find its origin. But first, like in other small towns he'd worked, he had to help extinguish it. After they killed the blaze, then he could satisfy his curiosity and allay his fear.

Earlier, when the dispatcher gave him the address, Jack almost dropped the telephone receiver. He couldn't believe he was back on this corner at this house again.

A week ago, working his second job as a Carsonville City Building Inspector, he'd met the doctor and his family. The fresh paint odor assaulted him and he felt like gagging, but he held it back while walking through their house. The family was so proud of their restoration work; the smell hadn't bothered them.

The blue tower and stained-glass windows impressed him. Now the flames licked at that tower, and those beautiful colored windows were blown out.

While massaging his aching leg, he muttered, "Great. Just remember, you're the one who always wanted to fight fires." His stomach muscles tightened. He felt queasy. Nothing unusual. This feeling hit him at most fires, but it was worse when it might be their arsonist.

He tore his gaze away from the inferno and searched for someone out of place. He wished he could find one person lurking about, looking suspicious.

This madman burned fires ever closer to his wife and he hadn't been able to stop them. Ten minutes ago, as he left his home, all the lights had brightened the house, looking like a beacon on his street. Kathy had been awake.

Why did she roam the house, flipping on the switches, lighting it up? Maybe it was her way of keeping the fear at bay.

Kathy. When he pictured her, his skin tingled and his heart raced. Should he go home? No, this business needed his attention.

Jack erased her images and concentrated on his work. He snatched the small camera and Sony tape recorder off the seat, but left the cell phone. After jamming the items into his pockets, he climbed out of the car.

The site of the blazing house stopped him for a moment. Flames from the windows reached skyward in pursuit of the sparks floating above. Soon, the Victorian house would be reduced to a burned out shell or totally destroyed, leaving nothing but ashes.

After dispelling intruding memories—ones he could not afford to think about—he grabbed his turnouts from the coupe's trunk. The fire-retardant pants with suspenders folded down over fire-proof boots were always ready to step into, pull up the suspenders, and be dressed in seconds.

He climbed into them, picked up his helmet and grabbed his jacket. Jack rushed toward the heat.

Chaos awaited him.

A firefighter on the roof punched a hole in the shingles and the trapped smoke and heat escaped. Maybe that gave the occupants a chance—if anyone remained alive. Jack replayed the dispatcher's phone call in his mind. 10–55. No one believed that there would be any survivors.

Another firefighter, perched atop the heavy metal ladder from the truck, guided a steady stream of water onto the blazing building. Generators hummed, providing electricity for floodlights that illuminated the staging area.

Jack stepped over hose lines, scattered like so much discarded spaghetti crisscrossing the two intersecting streets. A firefighter sprayed water on the house from the ground.

"Top of the mornin' to ya, Hellman," the firefighter called out over his shoulder. "Took yer wee time 'bout gettin' here!"

The protective helmet covered the man's red hair and freckled face. Jack recognized the fake brogue and massive shoulders and yelled, "Hey, George, I figured you'd have killed this by now. Hurry up."

"Aye me, boy, I'll do that." Struggling to hold the hose, George Everett nodded. Water rushed in an arch at the flames. As the liquid struck, it sizzled and popped. George swung the nozzle. Water deluged a twenty-foot swath across the blazing house.

Other firefighters held hoses spewing water on nearby homes, trees, and shrubs. They attempted to prevent the fire from spreading.

Smoke smell permeated the air. Jack set down his jacket and helmet by a fire engine. After wiping his runny nose, he removed his camera from his pocket and studied the scene.

People milled about; some dressed in their robes, others in coats—all stared wide-eyed at this spectacle. He snapped pictures of the fire and panned to include photos of the crowd, hoping to get lucky.

After a few more pictures, he walked toward the group. A couple of the neighbors glared at him as he approached.

"Excuse me, Sir, did you see anyone or hear anything unusual?" Jack asked a neighbor.

"No, heard the sirens and all the commotion. I live two doors down."

Another man piped up. "You going to save my house? How did this happen?"

"I heard an explosion, but my husband said mind my own business until he heard the fire trucks."

The fire lit their faces. Jack felt the heat and said, "Let's back up a bit." They moved further away, and then he said, "We're doing everything we can to save the neighboring houses." He wrote a couple of notes in his notebook.

"Looks like not enough for that house," one man said. When they heard a popping sound, the man flinched, and said, "Come on, Hon, we can watch from our porch. Let the fireman work."

Three more neighbors told Jack they'd seen nothing. Then he took some additional pictures, jotted down a couple more notes, and hustled back to his gear. He thrust his arms into his heavy fire-retardant jacket and cinched everything tight. The gauntlets on his gloves covered his coat cuffs to prevent the embers from burning his skin.

After settling a breathing apparatus on his back and donning his helmet, he joined Engine Company Number Three.

"Glad you could join us, Jack," one of the firefighters said. "Grab the end of that hose."

They sprayed water, battling a path across the front porch. Jack dogged their heels.

Before entering the burning house, he secured the mask over his face. Fresh air filled his lungs. Within the confines of the hallway, the smoke limited visibility. The heat came through the turnouts.

He still gripped part of the hose and watched the spraying water. Waves of humid heat rolled over him and the other firefighters the minute the water hit the roaring flames. He adjusted his jacket. The sweat poured down his body and the sodden inner clothes clung to him. He thanked God for the protective suit.

Two weeks before, one of the firefighters hadn't protected himself enough. The humidity from that fire's heat caused moisture—scalding steam—to slip into the man's clothes, burning him.

At the open door of the next room, the firefighters held on tight to the hose. They sprayed torrents of water on the blaze until it died down enough for the small band of firefighters and Jack to enter.

Once inside, some of the firefighters chopped holes in the walls with their axes. The constant streams of water flooded the room, slowly killing the inferno.

A rookie ducked when sounds like gunfire burst from various parts of the house. "Hey, kid," Jack yelled, "just aerosol cans and food jars popping."

Victorian homes were the most difficult to extinguish because of their balloon construction. A long time ago, he had learned that this spacing between walls, ceilings, and floors allowed the fire to go straight up into the attic. It spread throughout the house, crawling unseen behind walls and under floors.

Each small room was capable of enclosing its own fiercely burning fire, making it even more difficult for firefighters to control.

One of the men tapped him on the shoulder and yelled, "Come with us. We're going to try to get upstairs."

Jack recognized his buddy Frank Davidson, and followed him and the others up a metal ladder to the second floor. Stepping carefully on the charred, hot wood, he prayed his next step would not drop him through to the first floor. He couldn't afford another injury.

His bad leg held climbing the ladder, but he endured jabs of shooting pain. Don't limp, Jack told himself. If someone saw him, they'd take him off the investigation. He couldn't let that happen.

In the first room, Jack's worst fears came true. Two children lay still in what was left of their beds. He felt his stomach roll. He knew that their small lungs had tried to take in the necessary oxygen, but with the deep breath of super-heated air, their lungs had collapsed.

At an autopsy he'd attended, he'd seen lungs resembling deflated balloons; tender pink membranes forever glued together. He blinked his eyes, dispelling those visions.

Davidson bent down to pick up one of the kids. Jack tapped him on the shoulder and yelled, "No, we have to leave 'em."

"Forget the evidence," Davidson shouted back.

Jack reached out and grabbed his arm. "Can't. They're gone. Might be others alive."

"But—"

"Move. Next room—maybe someone needs our help."

They continued on down the hallway to where they located a man. Probably the father who'd tried to crawl to his children's room. Like the children, he had no chance. His body lay stretched along the corridor, one hand reaching toward the open doorway. Bones protruded through blackened skin. A cloth over his mouth resembled charred paper, adhering to his lips.

The heat would have scorched his lungs before he could help his children. Jack sucked in clean air from his mask, relieved the stench of the burned flesh couldn't get in.

"Can we move him out of the way?" Davidson called out.

"For now, go around. See if anyone's alive."

The firefighters skirted around the body, trying to preserve any evidence and continued battling the blaze. If they didn't kill this fire soon, everything would collapse, and it wouldn't matter where they found the bodies.

In the next room, they discovered a baby had died in its mother's arms; her seared body encircled the infant. Because of trapped gases, the mother's abdomen had burst. The position looked like she'd tried to protect her newborn baby by returning the child to her womb.

Bile rose into Jack' throat; he wanted to take off his breathing apparatus to vomit, but he choked the acidy liquid back down. He couldn't take the risk. Instead, he took several deep breaths of the fresh air from his oxygen mask. Under his breath, he held back more bile, cussed, and went back to work.

Soon after, Jack left the group, staggered outside, and ripped off his breathing apparatus. He wiped the streaming mucus from his nose. Tears, both from the smoke and the gruesome find, ran from his eyes.

Rumors of the bodies spread. Somber firefighters and volunteers trudged about holding nozzles, checking gauges, and switching backpack air tanks.

A few onlookers mingled about, watching. Jack felt like he was being judged.

Hank, an emergency medical technician, administered some oxygen from the large bottles from his rescue unit to the firefighters.

"Here, take this," Hank said, handing Jack another oxygen mask as he rested on the bumper along with two other firefighters. The back of one's coat had burned away, his helmet blistered and melted. The fresh oxygen renewed Jack a bit.

Another firefighter grabbed his backpack. "Sit still. I'll exchange this for you."

"Thanks," Jack said. His voice rasped, and after a coughing fit, he spied Ted Farley the captain in charge.

"Get that line over there. Cover those windows," Farley shouted to his firefighters. The chief, who stood by his red Chevy Blazer, barked final orders and directions.

As the sun struggled to penetrate the fog, flames died into smoldering embers. A few men still sprayed water, making sure no fire remained. The rest of the crew replaced hoses and other gear into the engines and truck.

The quick response time of the firefighters and the new sprinkler system the owner installed had saved part of the structure, although Jack wondered why. The arsonist would be disappointed that his work had not been completed.

"Hey, Hellman," Davidson said, "when you got a minute, the captain wants a word with you." His friend smelled like wet ash. Grime stained his lined face. Moisture dripped onto his jacket from his salt and pepper beard. "Hell of a fire."

"Yeah, it was," Jack said to the retreating firefighter.

The stench of charred wood and burnt flesh filled the air. With gritted teeth, he tried not to breathe too deeply.

George walked up. "Hey, laddy. Heard about the bodies. You okay?"

"No, not really."

"Even through yer soot, you look whiter than me underwear."

"I hate all these fires. They remind me... Oh,..."

"Laddy, something more be bothering you?"

"Not now. I'll tell you later."

"Get it off yer chest, boy."

"You ever see a barn fire?" Jack asked.

"Aye, me boy. So?"

"Our old red barn caught fire in the middle of the night when I was a child. We raised Morgan horses. My folks and I ran out to save them. Dad rushed in and managed to bring out two mares. Mom and I held them while he ran back into the blaze.

"You never forget your first big fire." Jack's stomach churned, but he continued, "Embers glowed like fireflies and flew high into the air. The burning hay made such a roar."

"Aye, me boy. Fires, they be noisy. What happened?"

Images flashed in Jack's mind; he could almost feel the heat from that horrible barn fire. He swallowed. "Dad tried to drag out our prized stallion. Of course, Sir Black snorted, stomped, and fought my father.

"Mom handed me the mare that she held, a horse named Queenie. Funny, the things you remember. Anyway, Mom said, 'I'm going in to help your father.' Jack paused.

"And?" George questioned.

Jack sighed. "I remember holding my breath as she dashed into the burning barn and disappeared through the doorway. Orange and yellow flames danced all around..." He stopped speaking and stared, caught in his memories.

"Don't quit talking now," George said.

"That stallion reared and screamed. Mom and Dad pulled with all their might at the lead rope, but the horse... man, I can still see those wild, white-rimmed eyes, ears pinned back against its head, nostrils flared, teeth bared. Sir Black lunged and struck out with hooves that barely touched the barn floor."

"He kicked them to death?" George asked all traces of his fake accent gone.

"I wish. Sometimes I'd lose sight of them. Flames kept leaping closer. I could just make out their silhouettes through the thickening smoke.

"Queenie nickered and her flesh twitched. The other mare I held took a step backward. Those horses were so scared; I still shiver just thinking about it. Even though I stood near the fire, I remember feeling so cold. I gripped the ropes so hard my fingernails dug into my palms." Jack glanced down at his gloved hands, expecting to see blood dripping.

"Sir Black reared again. My parents tried to get him down. I heard the stallion's wail and my folks' screams blend and become one. It seemed to last forever. Then came an awful loud crack. The roof caved in on them."

"Oh, my God, Jack, I'm sorry, I didn't know." George touched Jack's arm.

Jack shook his head to chase away the haunting images. "Yeah. It was a long time ago."

"Something that traumatic never leaves you though," George said.

"Unfortunately, it doesn't. But I have to concentrate on this fire. Guess I better go find Cap." Jack hurried off.

CHAPTER 4

Jack found the captain leaning against an engine with his helmet under his arm. Farley ran a dirty hand through his salt and pepper hair. Soot smudged his round face and dried mucus clung beneath his long nose.

As Jack approached, Farley rubbed his soot-caked glasses on a dirty bandana. The Cap's eyes looked red-rimmed and watery.

"Sorry we had to call you out," Farley said. "It looks like the work of the same arsonist as before. This pyro knows fires—a Victorian home every other week now."

He finished cleaning his glasses and shoved them back on. Farley wiped beaded sweat off his forehead, leaving a black streak of soot. "This time he killed an entire family."

Jack swallowed and glanced around. Some of the firefighters mingled with the Carsonville police officers. He wanted to stall for time, to gather his wits, so asked, "How many dead?"

Farley held up his hand, displaying five fingers. While speaking, he dropped one finger at a time, beginning with his thumb. "Mother, father, two children, and a baby." He shook his now fisted hand and lowered it to his side.

"Neighbors say they brought the infant home from the hospital yesterday morning. First night at home with their new little daughter."

"Oh, crap!" Jack clenched his jaw. "This maniac is a real sick-o."

"That's the way I see it. Found a kitten cowering behind some rhododendrons. Probably their pet." Farley shrugged. "You got to catch this arsonist. You're the best."

The captain and Jack gazed at the burned out shell. Farley looked beyond him and said, "Finally, our esteemed police detective's here."

When Jack turned around, he saw Detective Steve Burns step from his unmarked Mustang. He wore a black suit and tie and joined the clutch of police officers. They all entered the house.

The detective would have to inspect the bodies to observe their placement. One of them could be the arsonist. Only Jack knew the pyro wasn't among those bodies—only the family had died.

Farley settled his helmet on his head, staring at the smoldering fire. "Paul Lovell should be here any time now. This is the fifth fire since May. Now we have murder besides arson."

"I hope your fire marshal buddy can help," Jack said. "This madman knows his business. Been doing this for a long, long time."

"What do you mean?" Farley asked, raising one questioning eyebrow.

"I'm not sure yet. Let me finish my investigation. I kept hoping it wouldn't be him."

"Do you know who's setting these fires?"

"No, Cap. I only recognize the Modus Operandi. The way he sets these fires is always the same. But, I don't know his name."

Jack walked off in slow, measured steps toward the once-stately home, avoiding the five shrouded bodies and the deflated fire hoses. As the police and coroner investigator carried the bodies to the waiting van, Jack noticed the CSI photographer's pale face. *Glad I didn't have to take those pictures,* he thought.

The smell and images of the black corpses brought the bile up into his throat. Again, Jack battled it down. His injured leg throbbed, but he managed to walk without limping around the once beautiful Queen Anne as he took notes. He waded into the sodden ashes and rummaged through the rubble of what had been a home, filled with life, love, and hope.

A half hour later, Jack heard crunching noises from the wet debris behind him. He continued sifting through the soggy black ash and glanced over his shoulder.

"What have you found?" Burns asked.

"Same MO as before." Jack stood and looked into steel blue eyes. The tall, blond-haired detective dumbfounded him. Burns always dressed the same, no matter what time, day or night. Did the man have several black suits?

"I'm not positive," Jack said, rubbing the back of his neck. "But I think this might be the arsonist that I mentioned when the fires began in May."

"You didn't think it was him then," Detective Burns said. "Holding out on us?" The detective stood with clenched fists, jaw tight.

"No." Jack thought Burns looked like a dynamite keg about to explode. "This might or might not be the same arsonist. There are similarities, but nothing conclusive yet. When I'm certain, you'll have my report. I'll also give you some files on previous fires. I gave some preliminary reports and information to the fire marshal. Lovell's been checking them out, just in case."

Jack couldn't count all the moves he and Kathy had made. City to city, state to state in an attempt to lose their arsonist. How did the maniac know where they were? He gritted his teeth; he didn't want to even consider the answer.

Burns stepped through ashes and paused in front of the burned gas cans Jack had discovered. "Five people are dead. Could you have prevented it?"

"No. Neither could Fire Marshal Lovell or you, Detective, for that matter. This arsonist is diabolical."

Jack bent over and examined a fire trail. "Knows fires. Never leaves a single clue. And, he's not in any crowd scene. None of his stuff is unique; all can be bought at local stores.

"For instance," he held up a piece of twisted, melted plastic goo, "this was probably the igniter. It's assembled from commonly available supplies or a remote-control device like they use for those little toy cars you get for your kids."

After he dropped it into an evidence bag, he said, "The plastic gas cans—bought anywhere. Thousands of these items are sold nationwide. No way to trace him.

"Smoke fills the fingerprints in, if the arsonist leaves any." Jack shrugged. "Besides burning Victorians, there's no common denominator, except he's out to get my wife and maybe me."

"Which is a small little detail you forgot to mention?" Burns' curt voice lashed out. A few firefighters standing nearby gaped at the two men.

"I told Lovell at the last fire! Until I'm sure, I refuse to believe that he's followed us. I mentioned it to you. If you didn't follow up on it, that's your business."

Jack looked toward the street. The station wagon with the fire marshal's logo on it pulled up to the curb. "Excuse me. Lovell's here." Jack turned and walked away, feeling the detective's steel blue eyes bore into his back.

He had not made any friends today. Would it get worse like before?

CHAPTER 5

When the grandfather clock bonged, Kathy jerked her head up off the table, blinking. The kitchen clock's numbers glowed. She'd snoozed for over an hour. Her skin crawled; fears of the arsonist creeping through the house made her jump up.

Crash!

Sheba darted off to a corner, eyes wide, fur standing.

"Oh, for heaven's sakes. Stop this nonsense." Kathy leaned over and picked up the tipped-over chair. She glared at the cat. "I will not act like a frightened animal." The tabby twitched her tail.

Kathy breathed deeply. The light on the alarm next to the back door still glowed green.

At the kitchen sink, she poured her cold tea down the drain, rinsed the mug, and set it in the dish drainer.

"Come on, Sheba." Kathy motioned to the cat. "Let's go back to bed. Can't stay awake anyway." She yawned and walked out the kitchen door after the orange tabby. Sheba raced down the hall and skidded into the living room. Kathy followed the cat into the room, sauntered over to the large picture window, and stared out. She grabbed the floral drapes, but froze with her hand gripped so tight that her nails dug into her palm.

Jack thinks I'm nuts for keeping these drapes open. But she couldn't close them. Why didn't he understand that if she closed the drapes, the arsonist would strike? She looked at the cat. "What horrible thing have I done to deserve this?" When the cat didn't answer, she continued aloud, "Who wants to destroy me?" She gathered her robe tighter.

The cat meandered between her ankles, purring. Kathy sighed. "I guess today we're safe, Sheba. You know this pyro only strikes at night or early morning."

Kathy, feeling like she wore lead shoes, left the front room and trudged up the steps, her gaze never leaving the upstairs hallway. The tabby raced ahead of her and toward their bedroom. Near the top, Kathy remembered to lift her foot over their troublesome, creaky step.

Inside the master bedroom, she caught her reflection in the mirror above her dresser. Red-streaked eyes with dark circles under them stared back at her. She looked down at her belly and massaged the roundness. Her lip quivered and she bit it to keep from crying.

She hugged herself and tried not to shudder. "How am I going to protect this little one growing inside?" she whispered through gritted teeth. Could she carry this one to term? She'd only found out two days before about her pregnancy. The pain of the two previous miscarriages was still raw. She didn't want to think about them.

Sheba sat at her feet, listening.

"Should I tell Jack I'm pregnant again?"

If Jack confirmed these fires were their arsonist's, he would be more stressed out. He was already on edge. They suspected their pyro set these fires.

She looked down at the cat. "That telephone call, we must keep it from Jack for a little while longer. Maybe this fire isn't our arsonist."

She closed her eyes, picturing the scene where she would tell her husband about the baby. He smiled, but the image quickly faded. The next one made her abdomen clench and she patted her belly.

"Don't worry, baby, this will all work out."

The phone call, the silence, the screams. Was their arsonist really here?

Kathy's last miscarriage had come right after hearing the screams from one of those horrible calls. As she massaged her abdomen, she whispered, "I will not let it happen again."

Telling Jack about the baby would be hard. If only she hadn't told Blaze first. But that wasn't her fault. The cat meowed as though she concurred with Kathy.

"You know, Sheba, Blaze came by for a visit right after I returned home from the doctor's office. That stupid grin on my face; my eyes must have twinkled. He knew. At least I made him promise not to say a word until I've had a chance to tell Jack."

That covenant had been hard to extract, but Blaze would honor it. He'd been her brother's best friend; he'd filled the empty space in her heart left after Darrell's death.

Darrell had bright green eyes that always shined with mischief. Even after almost four years, she missed him. Reminiscing about her brother brought more images flooding her mind—her parents and her wedding day. She'd been ecstatic when she married Jack, but the next day had brought terrible misery.

Kathy's reflection in the bedroom mirror dissolved into unwanted memories invading her thoughts. Tears rolled down her cheeks but she inhaled deeply and wiped them away. "Ah, Sheba—family, friends, strangers. Won't this ever end?"

Why couldn't Jack figure out who was doing this? Kathy turned from the mirror and climbed into bed, pulling the covers up under her chin. When should she tell Jack about the baby?

CHAPTER 6

Jack parked across the street behind his neighbor's black Chevrolet. He hunched over the steering wheel. The leather tuck-and-roll upholstery squeaked beneath him as he shifted position. He reached down with one hand and rubbed his leg. He thought about earlier when he'd sifted through soot and ashes at the Victorian house. Burns' anger, his yelling—it brought back Jack's worries. With his free hand, he gripped the steering wheel until his fingers ached.

The nape of his neck tingled. He whipped around in his seat to search the street behind him. No strange cars—no one.

Across the street, rhododendrons, large enough to conceal a person, bordered the sidewalk. Could someone be hiding, watching?

Every light in Jack's house illuminated the windows and grounds. *Why can't Kathy pull the drapes?* That crazy phobia of hers allowed anyone to see everything happening inside.

No amount of neck rolling or scrunching his shoulders back and forth relieved his tension. He stepped out, locked his coupe, and plodded up the rose-lined walkway. The blooming yellow roses smelled sweet, but they didn't make him feel any better. It felt as if he carried fifty extra pounds.

Kathy has a right to be scared. During the dark hours, he understood, she attempted to keep the evil from her sanctuary with lights to mimic daylight. Their arsonist had never torched a house during the day.

Jack limped up the old wooden stairs. Stepping through that charred floor board had been a mistake—could have been costly. He believed the other week's fire had been set by their maniac, even though no proof existed. The phone calls hadn't yet begun.

With the deadbolt key from his pocket, Jack unlocked the secured double locks. He crossed the threshold, turned off the alarm, and then reset it. When he reached out to switch off the outside lights, the telephone rang. He stiffened.

On the second ring, he hurried to the hall phone and snatched the receiver from its cradle. "Hello?"

Silence.

He frowned. "This is Jack Hellman. Who is this?"

"Hello, Jack. Everything okay?"

"Yeah, Bradley, it's early. What do you want?" Jack refused to use the nickname 'Blaze.' He wasn't sure if the nickname stood for an acronym of Bradley Lester Zilence's initials or if 'Blaze' was a metaphor describing his success in forging ahead in life. He suspected it was for something else. Whatever, Jack didn't like the nickname.

"Sorry, I need to talk with Kathy for a minute. Is she up yet?"

"I don't know. I just walked in the door."

"Oh, sorry. Another fire, huh?"

"Yes. Hang on. I'll see if she's awake." Jack dropped the receiver, nicking the small pine table. He rolled his eyes and muttered, "Great. Now Kathy will get ticked at me for hurting one of her precious antiques."

The carpeted stairs muffled his footsteps. He stepped over the third one from the top. *One of these days, I'm going to fix that step.*

He glanced through the open bedroom door. Kathy's black eye mask kept out the bright lights in the room.

She slept curled in a fetal position, under the down comforter, her blond hair draped across her blue satin pillow. The upstairs phone was unplugged. A half-filled glass of water, along with a prescription bottle, rested on the nightstand.

Sheba lay in a ball at the foot of the bed, looked up, and yawned. The cat lowered her head back onto folded paws and closed her big yellow eyes.

Back downstairs, Jack picked up the phone, and said, "Sorry, Bradley, can it wait? Looks like Kathy's taken her pills to get some sleep."

"Pills? She can't take pills in her condition."

"What condition is that?" Jack snapped, wanting to get back upstairs to his lovely wife.

"Well, I, I just meant, meant that she shouldn't take sleeping pills."

"Look, I've had a rough morning. You know that sometimes she takes pills to get to sleep when I have to go out. If this isn't important, I'll have her call you later."

Why did Bradley have to phone and keep him from his wife. Jack's heart rate increased; his chest pounded. He wanted to crawl into bed with Kathy. He needed to hold her, feel her love.

Bradley interrupted his thoughts, and said, "Don't forget."

"I won't. Good night."

"You mean, Good morning."

Jack slammed the receiver down. Why couldn't Bradley leave his wife alone? He ran his sooty hand through his hair. The smoke stench lingered.

He felt the grimy ash, coating his skin. Before he jumped in bed with Kathy, he needed a shower.

After hurrying through the house, flipping off the light switches, he rushed upstairs. First, he turned those lights off and then headed to the master bathroom.

He wanted, no needed, to feel Kathy's soft skin in his arms.

Without her I'm not whole—like a fire without fuel—dead. Only she could make the awful images of what he'd seen at the fire recede and disappear.

After crossing the threshold into their bedroom, Jack stopped and admired her. She wasn't the most beautiful woman in the world, but she loved him. The way her curves fitted against him made him feel on top of the world.

She kept those curves by exercising and always said, "I have to keep fit, otherwise I'll become a blimp." Being overweight ran in her family and it made him happy that she didn't want to lose her figure.

He wanted to grab her in his arms, but noticed his smudged hands. First a shower. He turned off the light, quietly crossed the room into the master bath, and stood before the oval oak mirror.

Two white disks stared back from his soot-covered face. He undressed, pulled the curtain around the claw-footed bathtub, and turned on the faucet. Hot water pounded him as he shut out his feelings and scrubbed at the grime, along with the fire and death odors.

No amount of washing could cleanse him, so he turned off the water. He grabbed the heavy white Turkish towel, swished it across his body until his reddened skin tingled. It felt raw. He still stunk. Even though he blew the soot-tainted mucus from his nose, he never quite rid his nostrils of the stench.

Condensation covered the mirror. He wiped it away and stared at the stubble on his chin. Kathy hated it; would refuse to cuddle if he didn't shave. While foaming his face, he relived their first lovemaking.

His wife had received first degree whisker burns and she had vowed no more. Jack scraped the short black hairs from his face and splashed on some forest-smelling aftershave. The burn on his cheeks and chin reminded him that this minor irritation was nothing like what had happened to that poor family.

He tucked those horrible thoughts into a dark recess of his mind, crossed the bedroom and slipped between cool sheets. He gathered his wife's warm body so that her back touched his front.

"Hmm, that's nice," Kathy mumbled. "You smell like fresh pine. I bet you shaved."

"Of course." Jack whispered in her ear, "I need you." He stroked her tenderly and nuzzled the back of her neck.

Sex was not his first priority; he only needed to hold his wife. Her hair tickled his nose. The lilac scent from her favorite soap drove away the sooty smell and chased away the reminders of fire. He lost himself in her, kissed her soft skin, and caressed her body.

Kathy yanked off her eye mask and whisked off her silk nightgown. It slid from her delicate finger and dropped to the side of the bed. She lay back down and kissed him.

Jack explored her mouth with his tongue. She tasted sweet.

Kathy had not seen the dead bodies and wanted him to make love after he returned from a fire. She always told him he needed the release.

He'd tried telling her how he felt. She didn't understand how a fire affected him. Maybe she was the one who needed sex when he got back from a fire.

The more she stroked him, the more he caressed her. Their lips met again and he held her tight while she moaned.

He grew hard against her soft skin. When she climbed on top of him, he gave in to their joining. The release gave him the exhaustion he sought. Spent, he smiled, and gazed up at her closed eyes.

A smile crossed her face. She lay down next to him and muttered, "Thank you."

Jack rolled over, kissed her eyelids, the top of her nose, and hugged her one last time. Then he turned over and fell asleep.

CHAPTER 7

Kathy flipped over onto her back, then switched to her side, and then rolled to the other side. A half hour after their lovemaking, unable to get back to sleep, she crawled from between the cool satin sheets. She scrunched her toes on the Persian carpet and tiptoed to the bathroom. As the morning sun beat down on the Victorian's clapboard siding, the house moaned, protesting the change in the outside temperature.

The warm spray from the shower cascaded down her taut body. The fragrant lilac lather allowed her hands to slip over her skin, where she lingered on her slightly bulging belly. Nothing Jack would notice, but she knew, and smiled, feeling happy.

After turning off the water, she stepped out of the tub and toweled dry. She wiped the steam off the full-length mirror and turned from side to side. What am I going to look like at nine months?

When thoughts of the two previous miscarriages popped up, she buried them away. After pulling on her jeans, she buttoned the tightening waist, and slipped into a T-shirt.

Her husband rolled over. She froze, not wanting to wake him. His breathing continued in a slow steady rhythm. After studying him for a minute longer, she sneaked by the bed and went downstairs to the kitchen. Sheba dogged her heels.

The cat darted toward the back door and meowed.

"Okay, okay, I'm coming." Kathy reached down and scratched the tabby behind her ears. Sheba purred, weaving between her legs. Kathy keyed in the code to shut the alarm off and opened the back door.

"Don't be gone long now." The cat scurried outside and wiggled through a hole in the fence that led to the alley. The haunting sound of a distant foghorn echoed Kathy's feelings. She closed the door.

When the brass teapot whistled, she made herself a cup of herbal tea. She heard meowing and let Sheba back in. At the refrigerator, Kathy rummaged through the contents to fix Jack something special for breakfast. He loved her breakfasts, and after one of *their* fires, she felt he needed replenishing. Their fires—what a cruel joke.

Her stomach flip-flopped, drawing her attention to the little life growing within. From all she had read, her attitude had tremendous affect upon the developing fetus. These fires and the pressure made it difficult to remain calm.

How can I tell Jack? She'd promised not to get pregnant until he'd solved these particular arson fires. Her tummy protested. She murmured, "Hush, I'll feed you in a minute."

"Feed who in a minute?" Jack asked.

Kathy jumped, grasping her husband's hands as he encircled her waist from behind and gently kissed her neck and shoulder.

"You scared me. I didn't hear you come in. Why are you up?"

Jack squeezed her a little tighter. "Because I missed your warm, luscious body next to mine." He spun her around. When he cupped her face, tingles started in her toes and ran up her legs. He gazed into her eyes.

Slowly leaning down, he kissed her. She wanted to throw her arms around him, but didn't. Then he pulled back and studied her face. "Don't change the subject. Who were you going to feed if you didn't know I was standing behind you?"

Kathy's cheeks burned. *Quit blushing!* She averted her gaze from her husband's penetrating stare and concentrated on the curly hairs on his bare chest.

The baby—she couldn't tell him yet. "You shouldn't listen to a woman's ramblings," she said, batting her eyelashes. "Especially one who has just left the man she adores alone to sleep. Quit eavesdropping like an old woman."

Sheba bumped up against them, purring loudly.

Jack looked down. "Of course, you have to feed your buddy."

Kathy smiled and kissed the tip of Jack's nose. She elbowed him in the ribs and grinned. Her pregnancy would be discussed later.

Jack was preoccupied with the fires and hadn't noticed anything about her; it needed to stay that way. After last night's fire and telephone call—not the right time to tell him. *Why am I afraid to tell him about the call?* If she did, would it make it real? Would he go crazy about the baby?

"Hey, I'm not like an old woman," Jack said, leering at her with twinkling eyes. "I proved that earlier this morning. The only thing you muttered then was 'Oh, Jack, oh.'"

He placed his hands on her shoulders and held her at arm's length. "Honey, is there something you're not telling me?" He tilted his head and his eyebrows scrunched together.

The clock in the hallway ticked.

"Don't be silly," Kathy said, shoving a stray hair behind her ear. "What do you want for breakfast?" Turning around, she escaped her husband's grasp and leaned down to continue her search of the refrigerator.

The cat sat nearby, flicking her tail.

She wished she could ask about the fire. Long ago, they had agreed not to discuss them. She shuddered.

Jack pulled her up, turned her around to face him, and hugged her; the point of his chin rested on the top of her head. The hairs on his chest tickled.

"I don't care what we have for breakfast," Jack said. "Let's skip food and go back to bed." He stepped back and wiggled his eyebrows up and down a couple of times, leering.

She laughed at the gleam in his eyes. "No, we can do that later, but right now I'm famished. Let's fix something together."

"Sure, why not." Jack released his grip and walked to the cupboard.

Kathy removed bacon, green onions, mushrooms, eggs, and cheese from the refrigerator to make an omelet. She also grabbed some bread for toast. After setting the items on the counter, she asked, "What coffee flavor are you having today?"

"Not sure." Jack grinned. "Something with Vanilla Roast."

"Hey, Mr. Coffee Guru. As much time as you spend browsing through those coffee bean catalogues, I'd think you'd come up with something more exotic."

"Just 'cause the guys call me guru at the station, you don't have to pick up on it," he said, smiling. He searched through several of his three-pound coffee bean bags. He grabbed two different flavored bags, mixed the beans into equal amounts, ground them, and then added them to the French press.

Kathy went about making breakfast and when she broke the third egg into a bowl, the aroma of fresh brewed coffee wafted about the kitchen.

As her husband set a plate on the oak table, the telephone rang.

Kathy froze, staring at the ringing machine. What if it's him? She bit down on her lower lip and fought down the acid in her throat. Her heart raced.

If it was the maniac caller, it would be the first time Jack would be with her when he called. *Please be the arsonist.*

Before her husband reached the phone, she yanked the black receiver from the wall. "Hello?"

"Hi, Kathy. How's my favorite cook?"

She sighed. "Fine, Captain Farley. You need to speak to Jack?"

"Yes, if he's awake."

"He's right here." Kathy handed the phone to Jack and turned her back. Why couldn't it have been their arsonist?

Other police departments had tapped their phone, so Jack knew about the calls. Sometimes she felt like even though he knew, he didn't believe. *Is that my insecurity?* Privacy was important to her, otherwise she'd have him record all incoming calls they ever received. Some of the calls were too personal and she hated that idea.

At the counter, she whisked the eggs into a frothy mixture. The swooshing of the whisk relaxed her. She smiled and thought about the baby. Everything would be all right once the baby was born.

She poured the omelet mixture into the frying pan; the liquid popped and sizzled when it hit the hot surface.

Jack hung up. "I have to go downtown."

Kathy spun around, holding the spatula in the air. "Now? But breakfast?"

In three steps, Jack stood in front of her and placed one hand on her shoulder. "No, not now."

He smiled, cupped her quivering chin with his other hand, and sniffed. "Boy, breakfast smells good. Are we ready? I'm starved."

From the kitchen doorway, the cat meowed. Jack tilted his head toward the tabby. "What's wrong with your pal?"

Sheba sauntered through the kitchen, her tail swaying like the pendulum in the grandfather clock.

Kathy caught a whiff of the bacon's greasy aroma. Bile rose into her throat, she covered her mouth, and ran for the bathroom, almost stepping on the cat in her haste.

Down on her knees, Kathy hugged the white porcelain commode with one hand. She held her hair back with the other and threw up.

A few seconds later, Jack rushed in, knelt beside her, and held her head. "Honey, what's the matter? This is the flu, right?"

Kathy heaved and heaved again. Her husband's voice sounded so worried. She felt worse for not telling him. When her stomach settled, she stood and gripped the back of the tank until her legs quit trembling.

At the bathroom sink, she splashed cold water on her face and rinsed her mouth with a cool minty mouthwash. Gazing in the mirror, she saw the pulse throbbing in her throat. "I guess the smell of food didn't agree with me."

"Tell me it's the flu," Jack said as he ran his hand through his dark hair, looking puzzled.

Kathy clasped his hand, led him back into the kitchen, and guided him down onto the chair at the table. "I want you to listen."

Jack pointed toward the bathroom. "Tell me... No, you're not!"

"Yes, I am," she said, placing both hands on his shoulders and staring into his dark, concerned eyes. Clearing her throat, and with a half-smile, added, "Dad."

"Dad?" Jack questioned his gaze boring into hers. "My ears are grimy from last night's fire. I thought you said, Dad."

Kathy looked down at her tummy and patted it. "I did. Soon my belly will get a lot bigger."

Her husband sat wide-eyed. His mouth opened as if to speak, but he snapped it closed.

She knew he didn't want children—at least not until after he caught the arsonist. He cocked his head and got a vacant look on his face. The tick-tock of the grandfather clock broke the silence.

She watched him open his mouth slightly. One eyebrow raised, but he still said nothing.

What are you thinking? Was he picturing all the dead bodies and all the people who had burned? Their arsonist was catching up to them. Not the time to begin a family. "Well, don't you have anything to say?"

"You're sure?" Jack managed in a low, somber voice.

"Yes. The doctor confirmed it," Kathy said. "There's no doubt about it. The rabbit definitely died." She closed her eyes and pictured Jack holding the new infant in his strong arms, gazing down at his newborn with love.

She remembered that time when he'd picked up the neighbor boy after he'd fallen from his bike. Jack had bandaged the kid's knee and sent him home. The little boy laughed all the way as he pedaled his bike.

"I've been so caught up in these fires." Jack pulled Kathy onto his lap and stared at her stomach. "I haven't paid you much attention. You don't even show."

Faded blue jeans, snug against her body, hugged her as a second skin. She visualized the wheels turning in her husband's mind. How could he not say something about her pregnancy? When the silence stretched on, unbidden tears flowed from her eyes. They dripped off her chin onto her T-shirt. *Must be the hormones.* She sniffed, brought the back of her hand up and wiped both eyes.

"I know I promised and we didn't plan this," she said. "Timing is off, but sometimes God knows best."

"No, it's not the right time. We agreed not to have kids 'til after I catch him. I think he's followed us here. Have you received any telephone calls yet?"

"I think he's here, too." Kathy ignored his question because she was afraid—but of what, she wasn't certain. "But I can't help being pregnant. You kind of helped with that."

She caught herself chewing on her lower lip—a habit that caused a red bruise. Her husband looked troubled.

Images of their deceased loved ones invaded her thoughts. She shifted on his lap a bit, and said with a smile, "Besides, I'm happy about it. We'll have a family."

Jack closed his eyes and sighed. When he glanced up; his eyes gave away his true feelings—uncertainty, anger. He said, "I know it's not your fault; but, this *is* a bad time. How far along are you?"

"I'm past three months. You should have seen all those pregnant women waiting to see the doctor. He's new to the area. I like him. He and his family are renovating an old house. He told me he used Carsonville Electricians for the wiring like we did."

Her husband placed his hand on Kathy's tummy, moving it over her stomach, gently probing and stroking. He whispered, "I'm going to be a father. Now I have to protect and worry about two. Wish my grandfather was here. He'd be a big help and know what to do."

Jack's face looked pale. Kathy said, "Grandpa Hellman did a great job of raising you. I trust you." She smiled broader and patted his cheek. "You'll figure out what to do and everything will turn out right."

Kathy covered his hand and kissed the top of his head. "Oh, Jack, I know you'll make a great dad. Please say you're happy about the baby."

She hoped he could see the sparkle in her eyes and not the dull ache that had been hidden deep inside for so long. She wanted this baby. Didn't he?

"Honey, this is great," he said. "But I'm not ready. Maybe I'll never be." Jack hesitated. "What about a miscarriage?"

"I'm further along this time. I have a good feeling. This one will make it."

"Okay." Jack smiled and kissed away the last few teardrops. Pulling her close, he found her lips.

She pushed back from the long kiss, catching her breath. "Oh, no you don't. Let's eat breakfast."

"You're hungry?"

"Well, I'll have a piece of dry toast while you eat."

She slid off his lap and went to the stove. No flame on the burner. The uncooked egg mixture and bacon were cold. Jack, ever conscious of fire, must have turned the gas off before rushing into the bathroom.

"Don't you have to eat for two?" he asked.

"Of course not." Kathy stood at the stove, looking over her shoulder. "Besides, I'll eat later."

She turned on the gas. With her back to her husband, she continued talking and cooking breakfast. "Dr. Graves said I'd be a bit queasy. He moved into a house on E and Boone Streets.

"You'll like Dr. Graves. His wife is going to have a baby any time now. She might have already had it."

Kathy popped the bread into the toaster and flipped over the omelet and bacon. With her back still to him, she asked, "When do you have to leave to see Captain Farley?"

"After… after, um, breakfast."

She turned around. "Is something wrong?"

"No… No, I'm… I'm just stunned."

She set his omelet down in front of him and sat across the table with her toast and hot tea. Throughout breakfast, she kept glancing at him. "You seem nervous. Is it the baby?"

"No, sorry." He inhaled his omelet and put his fork down. "Gotta run. My mind is on other things. I'm sorry. I can't talk about it right now. We'll talk when I get home."

He hurried around the table and kissed her on the cheek. "I'm glad you're pregnant. I love you. Everything will be okay." He hesitated, patted her abdomen, and then left.

She hurried after him to the front door. When he started to rush out, she said, "That's it? I just get a chaste kiss?"

He turned, took her in his arms, and kissed her with passion. At the bottom of the steps, he stopped and looked like he searched for something.

"What are you looking for?"

"The paper."

"Try the bushes. Might not be here yet. Why?"

"No reason. See ya."

She waved as he drove off. Why did Jack want the morning paper? He was never interested before. She closed the front door and leaned up against it. Her stomach threatened to convulse again. *Oh, please, God, she prayed, let him be happy about the baby.*

CHAPTER 8

I sit, gripping the steering wheel, every muscle in my body tight, ready to explode. My gaze remains glued to the front of the house. It's a risk to sit watching for her during daylight hours, but today, I can't help it. A brief glimpse of the terror within her—I need to see that.

I wait, but when Kathleen doesn't appear at the window, disappointment floods me like cold water rushing from a fire hydrant. I've got to go. Can't draw suspicion.

My fantasy about her terror satisfies me for now. Later, I'll witness her fear. I glance in the rearview mirror. My smile looks like a grin I used on Christmas mornings when opening presents as a kid. I know Kathleen sits by the phone, waiting, afraid her house is next.

Let her anxiety build.

I close my eyes and imagine her on the final night. Her blue eyes wide with fright, cloud with confusion at seeing me. Yeah, she'll beg, plead, but nothing she can say will change anything. I taste her terror on my lips, run my tongue along them.

A fine line exists between love and hate. I've loved her so much for so long and for what? Now I hate her.

A car rumbles by. I open my eyes; the driver glances in my direction. I quickly avert my face.

"I hate Victorian homes," I snarl, focusing on the old house once the car has passed. This Queen Anne, trimmed with chocolate brown, smiles down and mocks me. I'll get my revenge though. Why does Kathleen always have to live in a Victorian?

I study her house. Bay windows have a cozy niche to sit, probably have hiding places beneath the seats. This Victorian home is a reverse copy of its neighbor.

Kathleen's decorating reflects traditional interior design and furnishings. I imagine those old-fashioned heavy brocade drapes framing the windows burning from my fire. Thank you for not closing them. I can watch everything going on inside—almost. If only the hedging were strong enough to support me, I'd climb up and see her in bed.

The perimeter Cape Honeysuckle hedge along the side of the house grows in profusion. It provides ample coverage when I sneak around during the night. One time I tried spying during the day, but the bees are attracted to the flowers and I got stung. A hummingbird darted in among the fluted blossoms, annoying me as it sucked out the nectar, taking away the life force just like she does to me.

Last night as I drove through the graveled alley behind the garage, I scraped one of the garbage cans. As I got out inspecting my car, a cat meowed loud. Then I heard something coming. Scared me; thought I was caught. Turned out to be a bulldog. He chased the damn cat away and the night quieted down. I didn't know how I would have explained my presence to the cops. Maybe the cat that night was Sheba.

I hope these fires end here with this Queen Anne. I want to destroy her, all that she holds dear, especially her damn, precious Victorian house.

Why does she ruin everything between us? Our lives were full, before him. When she got close to him, everything changed. Our tight bond disappeared. I miss the closeness; her love is different now. He changed everything.

And that thing growing inside of her! It has to go. I need to step up my timetable. She can't have a baby. No, I can't allow her to have that child.

Children—memories of my own childhood surface.

Underneath the bleachers at high school, this kid is about to punch me in the face when she appears.

"Leave him alone, you big bully," Kathleen screams at him. She throws a soccer ball at the kid and he runs away. When she asks me if I'm okay, I only nod. She pats me on the shoulder and then she hurries off.

I push the memories aside and stare at her house. A yellow fire hydrant guards the corner. It won't matter with my type of incineration. The Queen Anne will burn to the ground, along with anyone inside, before firefighters can attach their hoses. I'll make sure of that.

That doctor's house—lucky. If the firefighters hadn't arrived so fast and the doctor hadn't installed a sprinkler system, the two-story would have caved in. The home would have been totally burned with nothing left but ashes—the way I like it.

I feel giddy. Kathleen doesn't have a sprinkler system.

I'll use more fuel on the next Victorian. I can't risk any more mistakes. No owner or any fighters will save my next choice!

After pulling away from the curb, I drive down the street and hum along with a snappy tune on the radio. Kathleen's last, dawns a day closer every day, and soon I'll conclude this five-year ordeal. It's almost July 10th. A long time to wait, but it's been worth it.

Now, I need patience. At a stop sign, I push back a few locks of hair that have fallen over my eyes. Maybe her day is here. However, prolonging her agony a little while longer might prove to be fun. I drum my fingers on the steering wheel. Perhaps a close friend first?

I'll have to stop for the morning paper. The headlines—they'll thrill me! I smile. The more Kathleen suffers, the more I'm excited. Possibly one or even two more fires before her reckoning day.

The pulp mill whistle startles me back to the moment. It's ten o'clock; my boss waits for me. I hurry downtown and maneuver my car into my usual parking place. I strip off my black leather gloves and place them beside me on the bench seat. I suck in a deep breath, switch personas: it's time to go to work.

CHAPTER 9

In the kitchen, Kathy stood at the counter. *Why would Jack want the paper?* She thought about it for a few minutes more, then marched through the swinging door, down the hall, and opened the front door.

She couldn't spot the Daily Bee. She ventured to the edge of the porch. *Our paperboy has such a bad aim,* she thought. The paper had landed behind the bushes. No wonder Jack didn't see it.

Kathy hurried down the steps, dug behind the rhododendron, snatched the paper, and pulled off the rubber band on her way back inside.

As she shoved the front door closed behind her with her foot, she opened the paper, and froze.

The headlines—Doctor and Family Die in Arson Blaze.

Kathy leaned back against the door and read: Dr. Graves, his wife, two children and newborn baby...

That's as far as she read. She slid down the door, hugged her knees to her chest and sobbed. Her doctor and his family all destroyed.

That's why Jack had grown quiet when she'd started telling him about her doctor. He'd recognized the name. No wonder he wanted the paper. That's the fire he'd been to last night. *God, he didn't want me to know I'd gotten my doctor killed.*

She thwacked the paper onto the floor and yelled, "That's it. I've had it. I'm going to find out who you are if it's the last thing I do!"

Her great arson investigator husband had a problem with this one. He'd solved every other arson fire he had investigated. Why couldn't he solve these?

Jack has handled this by himself long enough. She felt like she hid in a corner like a frightened animal, cowering as she lost friends, loved ones.

I should break the rules, talk to Jack. No, she couldn't do that. He'd be against anything she wanted to do because of the baby. But, this had to end. She would figure out another way.

The cat strolled over and butted her head against Kathy's legs and purred. While petting the tabby, Kathy said, "Sheba, we're going to solve this." She stood and marched into the kitchen to make a potato salad. Cooking helped her think.

Something nagged at her mind, but she couldn't quite grasp what. She set the boiled potatoes aside, and then pushed through the swinging kitchen door.

Before she reached the staircase, the telephone rang.

On the second ring, she picked the hall phone receiver up and said, "Hello."

Silence.

"Hello? Who is this?"

Someone breathed heavily, but no one answered.

Then, "Hello, Kathleen. Did you enjoy the fire?"

Her heart beat faster and her ears rang. The only person who called her 'Kathleen' was Darrell—her dead brother.

Silence extended on the line, but the hallway clock ticked, mocking the silence. She slammed down the receiver. It rattled in the base. She hugged herself and tried to control her shivers.

Why did the voice sound like Darrell's? The voice shook her up so bad, she froze, couldn't respond. If she was going to solve this, she needed to get tougher.

The telephone jangled again. Kathy stared at it, took a deep breath, and snatched the receiver up on the next ring. "Who is this?" she yelled.

"Kathy, it's me. What's wrong?"

"Thank, God, it's you, Blaze." Kathy pushed back a strand of hair with her quivering hand.

"Talk to me," Blaze demanded. "You and the baby okay?"

"Yes, I'm... we're fine. Where are you?"

"Where do you want me to be? You need me?"

Kathy laughed. Some tough woman. She relaxed her shoulders and used her yoga breathing to stop the trembling. She took another deep breath. She hated herself for dumping her problems on Blaze.

Ever since her brother's death, Blaze had always been there for her. Oh, Jack had been there for her, too; but Blaze sensed her moods better.

She reminisced about the previous telephone call, and her resolve.

"Hey, you still on the phone with me?" Blaze asked. "I called first thing this morning. Did Jack tell you?"

"No, he must have forgotten."

"Bet he didn't tell you on purpose."

"Stop that! You know Jack's been busy." Kathy sighed. "He's had a lot on his mind."

Sheba sat on the floor at Kathy's feet. The tabby licked her paw, and then wiped her face with it, repeating the procedure several times. The cat appeared to ignore Kathy, but she felt the cat's yellow eyes watching her every movement.

"Jack said you'd taken some sleeping pills last night," Blaze said.

"No." Kathy softened her voice, thinking about the little life growing inside her.

"But Jack said you had a bottle of pills by the bed."

"Yes, they're always there. The baby's fine." Kathy smiled and rested her hand on her soon-to-be swelling belly.

"Did you tell him?"

"This morning." Kathy closed her eyes and pictured how Jack had looked and acted.

"Well, what happened?"

"Nothing." Kathy blinked a few times and shifted the receiver to the other ear. "Jack says it's the wrong time, but what time is a good time? He'll make a great father."

"Why?" Blaze asked. "Because he didn't have one?"

Kathy looked heavenward. Both men tolerated each other for her sake. She never understood why they disliked each other. It even went so far that each suspected the other might be the arsonist. But she knew that wasn't true.

The love she held for each of them differed. Blaze was like the brother she'd lost. Kathy prayed that the baby would pull them together as a family.

"Blaze, don't say things like that. It's not fair. Jack's grandfather took his father's place. My husband will make a good dad."

"If you say so," Blaze said. "I just want you to be careful. Jack's under a lot of strain. You know I think he might be—"

"Blaze, no—"

"Oh, hell, he told me about the fire."

The grandfather clock's ticking amplified.

Blaze cares for me so much. Kathy knew he hadn't found another friend like Darrell. She bit her lip, wondering if she was his only family. He didn't talk about relatives, except when he'd told her that his parents had moved away after his graduation. *Come to think of it, I never did meet his folks.*

"You going to hang up on me?" Blaze asked.

"No. Sorry. By the way, you never answered me," Kathy said. "Where are you, anyway?"

"I'm calling from the front seat of my new silver Toyota Camry, driving toward Carsonville, heading your way. I'll stop by and you can fix me something fabulous to eat. I'm starved. I'll be there in about twenty minutes or so." He hesitated. "Sorry about the fire. You okay?"

"Fine. We'll talk about it later. So, you broke down, ditched your old clunker, and bought a new car?"

"Hey, it's no junker, but a classic like your husband's. I kept it. Too many good times in that car to part with. Wait 'til you see the Toyota, though. She's a beauty."

"I can hardly wait. I'll expect you shortly. I'm making a potato salad and will whip up something to go with it. I made some macaroon cookies for Allen."

"Who's Allen?"

"My new cooking student who's coming this afternoon. If you're good, you may have a couple of cookies. Drive carefully." Kathy hung up, feeling chilled. Blaze sounded tense. Probably worried about the fires coming closer.

At the kitchen sink, Kathy sliced the cooling potatoes. The telephone rang. She grinned. Blaze—after every conversation he always had to call back because he'd forgotten to tell her something.

She grabbed the receiver. After tucking it in between her ear and shoulder, she continued slicing potatoes and said, "Hi, Blaze. What did you forget this time?"

Silence.

She frowned. "Blaze, is that you?"

Nothing but loud breathing. Then—screams.

The knife slipped, cutting her finger. The potato and knife fell to the floor. The phone dropped from her shoulder. Panic welled up and spread through her faster than a wild fire in heavy winds.

She gathered her courage, picked up the receiver, and yelled, "Who are you? Why are you doing this to me?"

Silence.

More heavy breathing.

Kathy banged the telephone onto the wall receptacle. It rattled, fell down, dangling at the end of its cord, and swung against the wall. She fumbled the phone and managed to set the receiver back in the holder. Blood dripped from her cut finger and smeared the wall. Cold seeped into her bones, making them ache.

The telephone rang again.

"Stop it!" she yelled. *I hate when it rings, but if I'm going to solve this, I have to get a grip and have courage.*

After the third ring, she picked it up.

Dial tone.

In the bathroom, she bandaged her finger. She stared into the mirror and wondered who that frightened woman was staring back with blood on her face. *That's enough!* She would not be afraid. She had to figure out who was after her.

Kathy washed up, closed her eyes and locked her fear away in its usual place. When she opened her eyes, the woman she saw now appeared more familiar. *Be brave and think this through*, she told herself. How hard could it be to find the arsonist?

Back in the kitchen, she scrubbed the blood off the wall. She picked up the knife and potato, washed up, and continued cooking.

Later, as she placed the potato salad in the refrigerator, the doorbell buzzed.

Kathy peeked through the peephole in the front door and flung it open. "Glad you're here." She hugged Blaze. "Come on in."

He took a step back and pointed. "Don't you want to see my new car?"

"Oh, Blaze, it's beautiful," she cried as she peered out over the porch railing, eyeing the shiny new Camry at the curb.

They walked down the steps toward the new Toyota. Kathy glanced around, searching for strangers. A few familiar cars were parked along the street, but Blaze and she were the only people in view. Inhaling a deep breath, she slowly blew it out, and smiled as she admired the car.

"Isn't she sleek?" Blaze asked. "Look at that interior. Gets great gas mileage."

Kathy nodded. An unfamiliar car came around the corner. She tried to memorize the license plate numbers. "Let's go inside."

Halfway up the walkway to the front door, by the blood-red roses, Blaze grabbed her arm.

He spun her toward him and held her at arm's length, studying her. "You're jumpy. What's wrong? The fire bothered you that much?"

"Of course." Kathy sighed. "Guess I should be used to them by now." She waved her hand to dismiss the topic. "Let's go eat. I'm hungry."

Blaze clasped her hand and held it up. "What did you do to your finger?"

Kathy wrestled her hand away. "Cut it slicing potatoes." She hurried into the house. Blaze followed.

He sat across from her at the scarred oak kitchen table and chewed a mouthful of salad. His gaze never left hers. Kathy bit her lower lip and remained silent. Blaze cocked his head; his gaze still locked onto her every movement. She chewed on her lip and glanced at the wall where the telephone hung.

It rang.

She jumped. The pulse in her neck throbbed; feeling like it would burst through her skin. Her throat tightened to where she could barely swallow.

Not again. Kathy blinked and glared at the ringing phone. Her body felt weighted down by a hundred pound sack of potatoes. Blaze was here with her, so she needed to straighten up and answer the phone.

"Aren't you going to get that?" Blaze asked, as he shoveled another bite into his mouth.

"Yes, of course." If it turned out to be the arsonist, this time she'd have a witness to the call. With a silent prayer, she picked up the receiver. "Hello?"

"Kathy, where've you been? You had me worried."

"Hi, Jack," Kathy said, sighing.

"Are you all right? You haven't gotten any phone calls yet, have you?"

"I'm fine. Blaze is here for a bite to eat."

"Oh, no, I forgot to tell you he called."

"You had other things on your mind," Kathy said. "You okay?"

"Yes. Just wanted to let you know I'll be late. Be home by six. Sorry, but I gotta go."

Kathy hung up and sat down. "That was Jack."

"I couldn't tell," Blaze said, his voice sounding flat. When the silence dragged on, he asked, "They've started?"

Kathy scraped her teeth across her bottom lip. She created another bruise, but couldn't help herself. She pounded the table. "Yes!"

Tears slid down her cheeks. She felt like a fool being this emotional and couldn't seem to get herself under control. Her hormones had gone out of whack when she conceived both times before.

Blaze reached across the table and covered her hand. "Why didn't you tell Jack?"

"I can't right now." She pulled her hand back.

Blaze walked around the table and lifted her to her feet. He encircled her with his strong arms.

She couldn't stop the tears and sobbed on his shoulder. Blaze stroked her hair and held her close. Kathy sniffed. His Brut aftershave smelled strong. She loved the smell, reminding her of better days.

He gripped tighter and said, "It's okay."

"I've never understood these fires," Kathy said, pushing back and gazing up into his face. She wiped away more tears, grabbed a tissue from the box on the tile counter, and blew her nose.

"He called just before you did. It's stupid, but it sounded..." She took a deep breath. Blaze's green eyes were wide; his stare bored into her. "It sounded like Darrell," she blurted out.

Blaze scrunched his eyebrows together. "Darrell?"

"Yes." Kathy nodded. "I know that's crazy. It can't be him, but he called me Kathleen. No one uses my full name, except Darrell. After you called, the phone rang again." She sighed. "I thought it was you again, but it wasn't.

"I'm so sick of this. Now, it's not just Jack and me. We have the baby to worry about."

Blaze pulled her back into his embrace and hugged her to his chest. She listened to his heart thumping wildly. "Kathleen is your name," he said, "and Darrell is dead. Did it sound like Darrell's voice or just because he called you Kathleen?"

"I don't know." She bit down hard on her lower lip and let out her breath slowly. "It must have been the Kathleen. That bothered me."

"I've heard Jack call you Kathleen."

"He does that when he's angry. And, it wasn't him!"

"Maybe it's time we called Jack, or even Captain Farley? Let someone know."

"No!" She pushed away. "No, we can't now that Jack knows about the baby." She shook her head; her hair whipped around and hit her in the face. "Maybe I won't get any more calls."

"Kathy, once they start... you know..." Blaze shrugged.

"No. Jack's good at arson investigation, but somehow this one has him stumped. I've avoided this too long. I can no longer hide my head in the sand."

"About time," Blaze said. "Let's tell Jack."

"You don't understand." She wadded the front of Blaze's shirt in her fist and glared at him. "Jack will make us move. I'm tired of moving." She enunciated each word slowly and said, "You will not tell him, yet."

A twinge in her gut gripped her; she reached down and massaged her abdomen. *I will not have another miscarriage!* She couldn't go through that again.

She inhaled deeply, and then exhaled with determination. "I have to remain calm, especially now that I'm pregnant. I'm sick and tired of running. I want this to end. I promise, if he calls again, I'll tell Jack."

Blaze's shoulders drooped. "Okay, we'll do it your way."

Kathy forced a smile. "Now, do you have any free time this afternoon?"

"Why?" Blaze tilted his head and raised an eyebrow.

"Because after Allen leaves..." She hesitated. Blaze might not like the idea of her getting involved in investigating any more than Jack would. She'd have to do this on her own.

"You were saying?" Blaze asked.

Kathy quickly changed ideas. "I have a few hours free, and, well, Uncle Blaze, want to look at baby things?"

"Baby things? Oh, my, God, Kathleen, how can you even consider such a ludicrous idea? This maniac is burning people and getting closer to you. It may even be your own husband, and you want to go shopping for baby things?"

"Don't say that! Jack is not doing this. What's the matter with you?" Kathy stepped back. "Aren't you happy that I'm pregnant?"

"Sorry, thought you weren't going to be an ostrich. Pull your head out of the sand," Blaze said in a calmer voice. "I'm glad you're pregnant. But, I'm worried about you having another miscarriage. It's not the time to go shopping for God's sake."

"I'm just trying to lead a normal life."

"Your life is not normal." Blaze looked at his watch. "I have an appointment. I better go." He spun around and pushed through the kitchen door.

The back swing almost crashed into Kathy as she ran after him. The vehemence in his voice surprised her. She reached out and grabbed his arm.

He never broke stride as he looked over his shoulder and said, "Under the circumstances, I think you should wait for baby things. With this arsonist and all..." He didn't say anymore.

She released her grasp. "But—"

"I know." Blaze yanked open the front door and hurried down the steps. Kathy rushed after him. Blaze slid inside his car, turned, and glared up at her.

His anger astonished her. What had set him off? Good thing she hadn't told him about her real plans.

Allen walked up beside her. "Hi, Mrs. Hellman. Cool car, Mr. Zilence," he said, looking at the Camry.

"So you're her student, Allen. Thanks, kid. See ya, Kathy." Blaze slammed the door, revved the engine, and peeled off, tires squealing.

"Wow, what's his problem?"

"Never mind, Allen," Kathy said, wondering the same thing. Could Blaze be that worried about another miscarriage? He knew how upset she'd been over the last two. "By the way, how do you know Blaze?"

"Blaze?"

"Mr. Zilence," Kathy said as they walked up the path to the house.

"Oh, he sold us some insurance last week. Dad got me a life policy that will somehow pay for my future college education. Some way to save money."

"Then are you about ready to learn how to feed yourself when you're old enough to go away to that college?"

He made a face and glanced around. "Not so loud."

Kathy laughed. "Oh, okay. Come on in. I made cookies. You may have one before we start."

"Think they're as good as mine?"

"If they're not, you can teach me."

Allen sat at the kitchen table, munching a cookie, while Kathy placed the necessary chicken recipe ingredients on the counter. Before he took another bite, Allen said, "Mr. Zilence sure has a neat car, but not as good as Mr.

Hellman's. Now that's cool and old. I just saw him drive by a little while ago. Wish we had a car like it."

"Jack's at work, Allen. Unless he had an inspection, you didn't see his car."

"Is Zilence your brother?"

"No, he's like one though. He and my brother were best friends."

"Where's your brother?"

"He's dead."

"How? Oh, sorry. Probably shouldn't ask."

"That's okay. He died in a fire."

"Do you miss him?"

Kathy patted Allen's head. "Very much. He was a little younger, but I helped raise him and we did a lot together. He was very special."

"Didn't you hate him just a little? My older brother and I fight all the time."

"No, Darrell and Blaze, er Mr. Zilence, used to follow me around. Tormented me, but I knew they were just teasing. Embarrassed me whenever they could."

"How?"

"Well, when my husband and I got married, they refused to wear tuxedos. I had to beg them. Also, they wanted to wear their baseball caps."

"To your wedding?"

Kathy smiled. "Yes. Had a heck of a time convincing them not to wear those things. Darrell wore his cap everywhere. Practically lived beneath his Detroit hat. He had long blonde hair and wore it in a ponytail. The tail stuck out the hole in the back. He used to tell me the 'D' on the cap stood for Darrell and not Detroit."

"Did he wear it at your wedding?"

"No. He loved me and wouldn't do anything to hurt me. Besides, Mr. Zilence convinced him not to wear it. Darrell brought it to the church and wore it at the reception though. Mr. Zilence didn't."

"Brothers can be strange."

"Is yours giving you a hard time?" Kathy asked.

"Yeah. If he finds out I'm taking cooking lessons from you, I'll never hear the end of it."

"Well, I'm sure you guys will work it out."

Allen shrugged and looked unconvinced. "Just don't tell him I'm taking these lessons."

Thirty minutes later, Allen's hands were covered with batter from dipping the chicken. "By the way," he said, "I forgot to tell you. Mom's getting a new kitchen."

"She's remodeling that lovely old-fashioned kitchen?"

"Yeah, she's not like you. She hates old stuff, wants to be modern. New dishwasher, trash compactor. She's using the same electrical company you used for rewiring. There's this cool electrician, wears his baseball cap backwards when he works. He lets me help. Anyway, that's what I'm going to be when I get old enough."

"I thought you wanted to be a chef?"

"That's just so I can eat."

After they'd removed the chicken dish from the oven and tasted it, Allen grabbed a few cookies. He rushed off to his baseball practice.

CHAPTER 10

Kathy watched Allen jog down the street from the open front door. Before closing it, she spotted the Thompsons out for a stroll with their dog and their two grandchildren. Joanna waved to Kathy, turned to her husband, and spoke. He, the grandkids, and the dog walked away while the short, gray-haired woman, who never sat down for more than a minute, shuffled up the walkway.

In their mid-sixties, the Thompsons had bought a large Victorian house a few blocks over from Kathy. Joanna wanted to open a bed and breakfast place, so the Thompsons were renovating the old house.

Joanna and Kathy had become friends. This friendship gave her pleasure. They shared the same passion for Victorian homes and antiques. They spent many hours together scouring antique stores on Second Street for just the right pieces.

Kathy held the door open.

"Hello, dearie." Joanna marched up the stairs.

"Come on in."

"How are you holding up? You must feel awful."

"What are you talking about?" Kathy asked.

"The fire last night."

"Let's go back to the kitchen," Kathy said, sighing. "We'll get a cup of tea."

In the kitchen, Kathy poured two cups and brought them to the table.

"You knew them didn't you?"

"Yes. Dr. Graves and his entire family. Jack couldn't tell me after he learned Dr. Graves was my doctor."

"Your doctor?" Joanna questioned.

"I'm pregnant. Just saw him."

"Oh, dearie, that's wonderful you're pregnant. I'm so sorry about your doctor. Anything I can do?"

Kathy sat back. Maybe Joanna could help. How could she convince her though?

"Is there something else wrong, dearie?"

Joanna was a good friend and always called her dearie. Would she help if she knew the story?

"It's just these fires. I've lost so many friends and family."

"Oh?"

"I never told you about my parents. They were such wonderful people. You remind me a lot of my mother."

"Why thank you. What happened to them?"

After taking a deep breath, Kathy said, "I had a grand wedding day. Mom sewed a satin dress with a long lace train. It's sealed up in the back of my closet.

"My brother Darrell and his best friend Blaze, you've met him, were ushers. They were so handsome."

"Sounds nice. What's this have to do with your folks?"

"After the church wedding, Darrell tucked my train into the old Ford coupe Jack and I have now. We all headed for the reception to stand in line to greet our guests."

"Did you have many friends there?"

"Yes." Kathy blinked. "As a matter of fact, I just remembered one of my girlfriends had needed an escort. Funny, the things you remember.

"I was surprised she brought my old boyfriend. She told me later that he'd insisted on bringing her. Anyway, unfortunately Jack and I changed our honeymoon plans."

"Why unfortunately?" Joanna asked.

"Originally," Kathy said, ignoring the question, "Mom and Dad were to relinquish the family Victorian home to us. But, we rented a cabin on the other side of the lake and changed the plans. We didn't tell anyone except for them and my friend Susan.

"I can still see the smiles on Mom and Dad's faces as we bundled them into the old rumble seat and whisked them off to their home. The last time I saw them alive."

"Oh, I'm so sorry. How'd it happen?"

"A horrible fire. The home burned to the ground. Poor Blaze and Darrell thought it was Jack and me. I remember holding Darrell as he cried. He took it hard. We all did."

Kathy still felt the anguish that had gripped her that night and pictured the look on Darrell's face. The happiest day filled with tears of joy had turned into the saddest night with sobs of unendurable sorrow.

"Five more days and it'll be our fifth anniversary. A year after losing Mom and Dad, I lost Darrell to another fire. I hate fires."

"My, gosh, that's so awful," Joanna said.

"It gets worse," Kathy said. She spoke about all the other fires. "We've moved so many times to try and outrun this arsonist, but somehow, he manages to follow us." She also told Joanna about the telephone calls.

"And now he's here in Carsonville," Kathy said. "If we don't stop him he'll burn lots of these beautiful old Victorian homes in this seacoast town, besides my doctor's. And now, he's killing people, again. I can't let that happen."

"I'm sure Jack's doing his best."

"Yes, but you don't understand." She fought back tears. *I will not cry!* "We've been doing this for a long time and Jack hasn't solved anything yet." Kathy hesitated. She couldn't tell her about her doubts, her nagging suspicion, or even Jack's. "Maybe a fresh perspective would move the investigation to a faster solution. Will you help me?"

"Of course," Joanna said. "But how?"

"I'm not sure, but shopping relaxes me and I can think better."

"I thought it was cooking that did that."

"Yes, but shopping does too. How about you?"

"I love to shop, dearie. Let's go"

Half an hour later, the two women strolled along the sidewalks, browsing in Carsonville's section known as Old Town. Kathy looked up and down Second Street. "I just love what they've done down here."

Antique stores and restaurants wore new faces with a vintage look. Bricks lined the sidewalks. Each window dressing depicted the past. A few of the brick buildings had been remodeled on the inside to serve as offices. At the north end of the street stood the magnificent Eureka Mansion.

At the center of historic Old Town, Kathy and Joanna gazed around the little brick-lined park from the raised gazebo. People milled about. Kathy pointed to a woman huddled in her faded red wool coat and orange stocking cap atop her head. "There's that well-known bag lady on her usual bench."

The bag lady chatted with some derelict in a baseball hat.

"Look, there's Max." Joanna waved. The old man tipped his black top hat in acknowledgment. Then he helped a young girl up on to the seat of the old-fashioned carriage. Wally, the 16-hand gray-spotted gelding, stood patiently, blinders covering the sides of his eyes.

"Isn't it nice, dearie, that Max and Wally have a job with the Old Town Carriage Company? He enjoys driving the tourists through Old Town and along the waterfront."

"Yes. A shame about his wife."

Joanna nodded. "He'd have wasted away after her death if not for his job. He's moving in to the bed and breakfast when it's finished?"

"He'll help around there?"

"Yes, he's a good handyman and he'll still have time to work with the tourists."

They left the park and wandered inside one of the antique shops. At the back in a dark corner, Kathy rummaged through the scattered and stacked furniture. "Joanna, come look at this crib. It's perfect."

Joanna squeezed between two overstuffed chairs and looked the bed over. "Needs cleaning."

The dust-covered crib had chipping brown paint. Kathy sneezed. "Of course, but when I refinish it, you won't recognize it. It's perfect for the new nursery."

Kathy purchased the crib and found an old dresser to restore. She arranged to have them delivered late that afternoon.

After Joanna helped Kathy put the other small items they'd found shopping away in the nursery, they said their good-byes. As her friend toddled down the walkway, Kathy tried to discover a way to investigate these arson fires. A plan formed. When it developed further, she'd talk with Joanna about it. She watched her friend turn at the corner, and waved.

At least now Kathy had help. She could do something about the arsonist. Joanna was a good friend; a better sport.

Kathy walked into the house just as a young man wearing a Dodger's baseball cap like her husband's hurried around the same corner as Joanna.

CHAPTER 11

Jack parked up across from the fire station. The bay door stood open, exposing the firefighters as they bustled about, getting ready for future fires. Jack locked his car and headed into the melee.

The freshly washed red and white engine, along with the ladder truck, glimmered in the reflected light. After every fire, the firefighters' work continued at the station. They refueled each vehicle and washed them to remove embers that might damage the paint. Two firefighters hovered like bees around the hive, toweling dry the magnificent machines, not only to keep busy, but also to prevent spots that dulled the luster.

Other co-workers washed the soot from the cloth hoses and hung them on racks in the tower to dry. They pulled out the hard rubber hose and stretched it to full length. After cleaning it, they'd rewind the hose back on the reel.

"Hey, Hellman, what's the word on the investigation?" Davidson asked.

"Don't have anything yet."

The scent of Davidson's Old Spice aftershave triggered memories of Jack's grandfather. Davidson leaned against the fire pole, holding a clipboard, containing an inventory list of all fire equipment. He checked to be sure all of it had been collected from the Graves' fire.

He placed ticks next to axes; shovels; spanners, which were used to connect the hoses to the hydrant; and other equipment listed on the inventory.

Davidson stopped marking and questioned, "You have nothing?" He shook his head. "That's not like you."

"Hey," Jack said, running his hand through his hair. "Give me some time to investigate. I just woke up."

"Yeah, right. You mean you just finished with your old lady." Davidson snickered and walked off, tucking the pencil over his ear.

"Hey, keep a civil tongue about my wife," Jack called out.

Chuckles and hoots pealed from some nearby firefighters. When Jack glared at them, they wiped the smirks off their faces and continued washing their personal gear and hung them to air dry.

The breathing apparatuses still had grime on them. "Instead of dissing my wife, rinse those off," Jack said, pointing. "And fill the tanks with fresh air." He muttered under his breath, "That'll keep them busy," and walked over to George.

Jack's friend poured fuel into the portable generators they had used to illuminate the Graves' house last night. George nodded to Jack. "Aye, laddy, don't mind them. No leads yet?"

"Not so far."

"Well, don't worry, me boy, you'll figure it out."

George's attempt at the brogue always made Jack laugh. The man was third generation Irish/Scots, but he'd been born in, and had never left, Northern California. That didn't stop George from using the accent though.

Jack's mirth was short-lived. If these fires belonged to their arsonist, not much would be found. No hard pieces of evidence had appeared so far. This maniac's style had been easy to identify, but that's where it ended. Lots of leads that led, well, he hated to think where they led. Most of them dead ends.

The pyro managed to get into the house, either through a window or by jimmying a lock on the old-fashioned door of the Victorian houses. With an igniter and gasoline, he set the place ablaze. The firefighters found all of the inside doors open at each fire.

The house filled with flames, smoke, and intense heat that didn't leave much of an escape route for the victims. Fed by the oxygen-rich air beyond the open doors, flames sucked into each room, consuming all in their path.

"Why don't people think about fire protection and escape?" Jack asked, turning to George. "After all the lectures we give, most people still don't protect themselves from fire."

"Guess they rely on smoke and carbon monoxide detectors," George mused. He finished filling the generators.

Jack pictured his arsonist's fires. The intense flash from those fires, caused by the instantaneous igniter, rendered the detectors useless. His victims never stood a chance.

"Yeah," Jack said. "They get smoke alarms, but very seldom furnish escape ladders in a two-story home. Those ladders are found at almost any hardware store."

He rubbed his chin. Even if these fire victims had ladders, this maniac destroyed them, and people never prepared for a jump out of a second story window. Correct landscaping could help soften the fall and provide an escape. Jack figured people hated escaping out of a second-story window, even if they could make it to the opening. That's why he'd set up his house and lectured on its importance as well as having fire drills. *And,* he thought, *like my grandfather always said, "Practice makes perfect."*

"I guess some people just don't think," George said and shrugged his massive shoulders. Aside from his fake brogue and a big frame, George's face had been bashed in numerous times. He kept in shape by sparring with a partner. Broken noses came with the fun.

"True, it is too bad they don't think," Jack said. "Guess I better go see Cap. Later."

Through the reinforced glass door that led into the reception area, he saw no one lingering at the counter. The two office workers were at their desks.

Jack shoved the door open and crossed the threshold onto the carpet. He stopped at the counter. "Hi, Gloria," he said to the older woman. "How's everything?" He enjoyed chatting with the two secretaries and besides, his nerves bothered him, so he stalled before going to the captain's office.

Gloria, a stout woman, sat as straight as a drill sergeant at her computer keyboard, clicking away. She had worked for the fire department ever since Captain Farley's rookie days. Gloria stopped the rapid movement of her fingers, peered down her long nose over her granny glasses at Jack. "He's waiting for you." She resumed her typing.

Her secretarial assistant changed with the seasons.

Young girls enrolled in the Carsonville High School work experience classes or immediately post-graduation seemed more interested in the firefighters than the menial office duties. Unable to recall this one's name, Jack smiled at her.

She smiled back, and said, "Too bad about Dr. Graves' family." She shuffled papers on her desk and continued talking, unable to look Jack in the eye. "I heard he was a good doctor."

Gloria looked over at her, and without missing a key stroke, said, "Don't you have some filing to do, Christina?"

The young girl blushed. She stood, turned around, and yanked out the metal gray drawer. Gloria peered over her glasses, hit the print button and started typing again. She tilted her head toward the captain's office. "Don't make him wait too long."

Just then, Captain Farley stepped out from his office. He held his door open. "Jack, come on in." The cap's voice sounded tired.

"Good-bye, ladies," Jack said, and walked into Farley's office. As he passed the captain, Farley clapped him on the back, then followed him in and went around the desk to his chair. Three black leather chairs sat in front of Farley's desk. He pointed to the middle one. "Have a seat."

"Thanks, Cap." Jack sunk into the soft chair that sat directly in front of Farley. The leather uttered a complaint as air gushed out from the cushion. He'd expected to see the police detective and the fire marshal, but guessed they'd not yet arrived.

Distracted, he gazed out through the window. If he told his story to this man, would he lose his job? *I can't afford that now that Kathy is pregnant.* But he owed Farley. Would the captain stand by him? Sometimes he felt so alone. Maybe it was time to try for help.

"Are you all right?" Farley asked.

Jack shifted under his boss's piercing gaze. Wrinkles furrowed the captain's brow. "Yes, Sir, just tired."

"I'm exhausted, too. An arson fire every other week since May. That's cause for us all to be wrung out. This family's death has caused an uproar with residents. Calls are coming in already. We'll be hounded with more by nightfall. The press is calling nonstop.

"What do you have to tell me?" Farley asked. "Clues? Ideas?" The captain sat back in his dark leather chair, placed his hands in a pyramid beneath his chin, resting his head. He waited.

Jack sat rigid but met his boss's gaze, noting the man's concern. Cap and he had become close. At times, Farley acted almost like the father he'd been cheated out of. The captain treated him like a son. Jack hoped their relationship would survive what he had to say. "Well, first I have a story to tell you. Guess I should have told you a long time ago. I hoped I'd outrun this arsonist."

"I wondered when you'd get around to telling me."

"You know about it?"

"Word gets around." Farley shrugged and continued, "Especially when one firehouse dumps its main arson investigator, and others have made similar attempts. Our chief insisted we investigate." Cap leaned on his desk.

"Besides, I don't suggest we hire anyone without checking them out thoroughly first. At that time, the chief agreed with me they were only unfounded rumors."

Jack sighed and slumped back into the comfortable leather chair. He flexed his fingers and grimaced. "Guess it's about time I told you. You should have said something. I'd have spilled my guts sooner."

"Figured you'd get around to it when you were ready."

"Yeah, well your friend Lovell has a few reports on these Carsonville fires and some similar ones. I'm not sure where to begin, but this particular arsonist seems to follow Kathy and me. He sets fire to houses—always Victorians—and gets closer and closer to our home."

He studied the captain and continued, "We try to outrun him, packing up and moving, but no matter where we go, he finds us. After this last fire,

I'm almost certain he's here in Carsonville. I can feel him in my bones. The third house..." Jack shrugged. "He's getting too close to us again."

"How long has this been happening?"

"About four years."

"Four years!" The captain stammered, "That's, that's..."

Jack nodded. "It sounds like a long time, but after we move, the fires don't begin right away. We settle in, then fires start every couple of weeks—like here. When he gets too close, we move.

"I've tons of material on this one pyro. He uses the same MO. No solid clues. I've hundreds of case pictures with no one particular person hanging around to watch his handiwork. State Investigators and I can't get a handle on him. They just seem to be glad when I leave their state. Cap, I'm not the only one who's clueless." Jack massaged his neck.

"Four years," Farley repeated, shaking his head. He removed his glasses and pinched the bridge of his nose. Laying his spectacles down on a stack of paper, he peered into Jack's eyes. "And?"

Jack told him about Kathy's parents' fire. "We were supposed to be at the home, but rented a cabin along the Lake Pend Oreille shoreline. It's a huge glacier-formed lake in Sandpoint, Idaho where Kathy grew up.

"Her folks stayed home. I'll never forget my wedding night. Only person besides Kathy's folks who knew about our change in plans—her best friend and neighbor, Susan.

"At three in the morning, pounding came on the cabin door, then yelling. I recognized the voices. Made me furious. I figured Kathy's brother Darrell and his best friend Bradley had talked Susan into some sort of wedding prank. Kathy spent a lot of time with her brother, and Bradley always tagged along. They were all very close. The two boys tormented Kathy like brothers do. But, when I opened the door and saw their faces, I knew something horrible had happened.

"It was so sad the way Darrell fell into his sister's arms. He kept sobbing and repeated over and over, 'I'm sorry, they're gone.'"

Jack glanced up. The captain sat ram-rod straight as he listened to every word. "I'll never forget the look on all their faces," Jack said. "Kathy held her brother trying to comfort him, not knowing what had happened. All Bradley could do was stand and stare at my wife. His face was as pale as her negligee. When I asked what happened, Bradley managed to croak out, 'Fire. It started at about one-thirty this morning. Your parents...' He'd raised his arms, flipping his hand, and continued, 'The whole house destroyed.'"

Jack closed his eyes, still feeling the pain of that night.

"Was it arson?" Farley asked.

"Yeah," Jack said. He opened his eyes and nodded. "I've no idea why or who?" He ran his hand through his hair and shook the memories away.

"That's not the end though. Exactly one year later, Kathy's brother Darrell burned in his apartment, a studio in a converted Victorian house. They saved the rest of the home, but, Darrell and his room went up in smoke."

He sighed. The clock on the wall ticked away, breaking the silence. "At least that one was accidental. God, how I hate Victorian houses."

Jack leaned forward, placing his face in his hands and muttered, "We moved to Colorado a few months after his death. That's where these arson fires began.

"Like I said before..." He paused and looked at the captain. "Each fire involves a Victorian house, but not everyone entails deaths. This pyro always saves the pets. Haven't a clue to his or her identity."

"Her identity?" Farley asked. "I thought most arsonists were men?"

Jack sunk back against the cool leather of his chair and pushed away thoughts about his wife's peculiar blackouts when she stared into a flame. Ignoring the captain's comment, he continued, "This arsonist starts on the outskirts of town, working his way closer to where we live, like we're the bull's-eye on a target."

"What about the police or even the FBI?"

"They've tracked down thousands of leads—all going nowhere or in the wrong direction. You know most of the evidence a firebug leaves behind is destroyed, making him the hardest criminal to catch. And this one is real clever."

Jack thought about all the previous fires and how he couldn't find enough evidence. "Never any traceable fingerprints. Smoke fills them in or he uses gloves. I don't think he hangs around long enough to be photographed like most arsonists, unless he's the master of disguise. And, the telephone calls can't be traced to a particular suspect."

Leather creaked as Farley leaned forward in his chair, eyes brightening. "Phone calls? What phone calls?"

"He phones our house. Unfortunately, I've never been there when he's called. Kathy says there's silence or heavy breathing on the other end of the line. Sometimes he plays horrible screams, but still says nothing. I don't know why he's doing this."

"Why can't the calls be traced?"

"This arsonist knows electronics."

"How do you know that?"

"When the police do tap our line, they find his calls route through an electronic relay at pay phones or he uses throw away cells." Jack shook his head. "Seems to know exactly when we have tracers on him. Most pyros get off on the fire, but I think this one enjoys tormenting my wife."

"Why?" Farley asked.

"If I knew that, maybe I could guess who, but I haven't a clue. Kathy's never done anything to anyone that I know about; she's suffered the tremendous loss of her entire family. Now she tells me she's pregnant. I don't know if I can deal with that. How am I going to protect her? Them?"

"Maybe it's someone you know?"

"I've thought of that. From Colorado we moved to Nevada, then Rancho Verdes in Southern California, and now here."

"Anyone relocate near you?"

Jack didn't mind Farley's questions. He appreciated help and looked forward to other's input, especially from Cap whom he had great respect.

Farley befriended Jack and Kathy when they moved to Carsonville. Jack believed the captain was lonely since his wife's death. Kathy said he reminded her of her father. She helped the captain rearrange his furniture and taught him to cook a mouth-watering lasagna, a mean pot roast, and prime rib that melted in your mouth. Kathy liked the captain. So did Jack.

"Well?" Farley asked. "Anyone come to mind?"

"Bradley Lester Zilence. I have my suspicions," Jack said, "but if you'd seen the three of them together after Kathy's parents died... Her brother named them 'The Three Cats'; Cougars slinking through the land, conquering the world. D. Cougar and his 'kitty kats,' Kathy and Blaze."

"Blaze?" Farley asked.

"Bradley's nickname. He says kids started calling him 'Blaze' in school because his initials are B.L.Z." Jack's mind flashed on the file he had on him safely locked in his desk at home.

"Kitty kats, uh?"

Jack refocused on the present. "Yeah, Cap. Darrell considered himself the leader of the pride, being the original Cougar. Kathleen, that's what he always called my wife, was now a Hellman, and Bradley was an honorary 'kat.' Poor Bradley. He's the one that found Darrell."

"Found?"

"Yeah. He had to call Kathy. At first when we arrived at the hospital, he made it sound like Darrell had crashed his car, but then he told us that Darrell had burned.

"Kathy freaked." Jack would never forget the look on her face and her whispering, "Not again?"

"Poor girl," Farley said, shaking his head.

"When I asked Bradley what happened, he explained they'd been at a party, drinking too much as usual." Jack sighed. "After the folks died, Darrell and Bradley were party-animals. I had to bail them out of jail a couple of times. Darrell drank more than Bradley did. We tried to get them to stop.

"Bradley explained that Darrell had driven home alone. He'd worried about him and went over to see that he'd made it okay. When he arrived,

Darrell's apartment had flames and smoke billowing out the windows. The firefighters arrived shortly thereafter and contained it to his room alone. Saved the Victorian, but couldn't save my brother-in-law.

"Bradley had run upstairs and identified Darrell before they brought him outside. When we arrived at the hospital, he begged me not to let Kathy look at Darrell's face. The kid was white," Jack said, remembering Bradley had handed Kathy Darrell's watch and ring. He hadn't wanted them to get stolen.

"After Darrell's death," Jack continued, "Bradley became more like a brother to Kathy than ever. His company reassigns him, but not always to the same town as us. On occasion, sometimes he's transferred before we even move. Kathy would never believe Bradley—an arsonist?"

"What do you believe?"

Frustrated, Jack ran his hand through his hair again. "I don't know. Why? Not sure of a motive. They're like brother and sister. Drives me crazy. Sometimes I think he loves Kathy a little more than a brother should."

He felt jealous. He shouldn't, but the green monster raised its ugly head when he pictured Kathy smiling at Bradley. "He's the only one, besides me, that's always around. Lovell has copies of my reports on these last four Carsonville fires and copies on some of my other similar unsolved cases. Maybe he'll come up with something."

"Well, Jack, I don't know what to say. Except, now, murder is included, and our esteemed police detective is furious. Says you're holding back information."

"Not true, Cap. I mentioned this arsonist to Burns in May. At that time, I didn't know if it was my pyro or not, and I'm still not positive. No phone calls that I'm aware of have started. Besides, two years ago, he burned down a Victorian next to the firehouse where I worked.

"We were all out at a fire—not one of his. All the firefighters, including the state fire marshal and the police worked hard on that case. One of my friends died. Each department discovered nothing. The chief asked me to resign. Said he couldn't justify the risk." Jack watched Farley, looking for any sign of dismissal.

"I'm sorry they wanted you out, but I can see their point." Farley looked him straight in the eye. "As a matter of fact, our fire chief is rather anxious."

The captain held up his hand for Jack to remain silent. "I've convinced him to let me handle this. Don't disappoint me."

"Sir, five fires. Now, this family murdered. I found out this morning it was Kathy's doctor. I couldn't even tell her."

Farley stood and walked around the old mahogany desk. He moved aside a stack of papers and perched on the edge. "Look, are you sure there've been no telephone calls. Are we sure it's your arsonist?"

"My gut says it's the same 'person,'" Jack said.

"Person?"

"Politically correct phrase." Jack half-smiled and raised one shoulder in a half shrug. Two years ago he'd come home unexpectedly and discovered Kathy standing over the burning trashcan in the center of the kitchen floor. She'd been immobile, not attempting to extinguish the flames. Her eyes had a distant, glazed appearance, and a slight smile toyed with the corners of her mouth.

"Kathy," he'd hollered. Only after the second yell had she responded. In the meantime, he'd smothered the fire with the lid.

She'd asked in an agitated voice, "What? What happened? Why's the trash on fire?"

The captain's repeated question about the telephone calls brought Jack back to the present. "Kathy hasn't mentioned any. Until she receives the first call, I'm never positive it's our arsonist. I always hope and pray it's not."

Farley nodded his head. When the intercom buzzed, he reached around and picked up the receiver. "Yes?" After a pause, he said, "Thanks, Gloria. Send them in."

The captain hung up, leaned forward and placed his hand on Jack's shoulder. "Paul and Burns are here. We're going to give you all the help you need this time. Let's sift through the ashes. Look under every stone. Don't rule out anyone, and I mean anyone."

CHAPTER 12

Jack looked over his shoulder. Fire Marshal Paul Lovell strode in to Farley's office behind the police detective. Burns took the furthest seat, while Lovell settled into the chair on the other side of Jack.

The fire marshal reached out his gnarled hand to shake. Jack was careful not to squeeze too hard as the old man's crippling arthritis looked painful. The strong grip surprised him. He figured the man ignored the pain.

Lovell smiled; his tobacco-stained teeth emerged from between his wrinkled lips. "Jack, I'll get right to the point. You've been after this arsonist for a long time. Have a better fix on him than us. Those reports—interesting reading. However, something caught my eye. Either you can't face it or don't see it 'cause you're too close."

With the back of his hand, Lovell wiped spittle from his chin, wiped it off on his pants, and continued. "Now that Detective Burns here is significantly involved, I think we need to discuss this."

The detective brushed an imaginary piece of lint from the sleeve of his black suit. Burns glared, and said, "From what Lovell says about your reports, I guess you carry a string of unsolved arson cases with you." He raised one eyebrow.

Before Jack could open his mouth to say something, Burns blurted out, "And, wherever you go, more develop.

"Some suspect you might even be setting these fires; but I haven't had the privilege of reading all your data. Why don't you enlighten me?"

Jack balled his hand into a fist and gritted his teeth. He turned away from Burns and looked across the desk at Farley. His skin tingled as he imagined Lovell's gaze boring into him and hoped Cap would at least keep an open mind. *Burns suspects me and probably the old fire marshal feels I'm guilty or...* Except for the squeak of Jack's leather chair as he squirmed, it was so quiet he could hear the ticking of his wrist watch.

Farley didn't say anything.

Finally, Lovell said, "If I may." He reached down and pulled out a legal pad from his charred leather briefcase.

Jack couldn't stop staring at it.

The fire marshal chuckled. "Yes," he said, "this briefcase went through a fire couple year's back. But it's my favorite case, so I cleaned it up as best I could. Still use the thing, 'cause my late wife gave it to me. I couldn't bear to part with it."

Jack shifted in his chair and nodded.

Lovell glanced over his legal-sized notepad. He looked up at the captain, who nodded and said, "Get on with it."

Burns sat, tapping his foot, and waited.

"Like I said," Lovell continued, "I found a few things. You're probably aware of them, but I thought we might start with a review."

"Like what?" Jack asked. He couldn't keep quiet any longer, fearing what was coming.

"Did you know the victims?"

Here it comes, Jack thought, but said nothing.

"Your own records state you visited the victims' home one week before each fire."

Jack bolted from his chair. "Yes, I did. So?"

"Sit down," Farley ordered. "I didn't know you'd been there a week before. Each and every fire?" he questioned Lovell.

Burns leaned forward, smiling. The detective produced a notebook from his suit pocket and flipped it open. He clicked his silver pen and scribbled some notes.

"Since the beginning," Lovell said. "Each victim had been visited by three people. Jack, who'd been the building inspector. By the way, do you always take a second job as a building inspector wherever you live?"

"Yeah, if the town is small enough and it's allowed. I need the extra money."

Before Lovell could say anything more, Burns said, "I want to see your records of visits regarding all building inspections you've done since May."

"I'll get you a copy," Jack said. "But you'll find that with each fire, I inspected every place a week before. And, there are many other houses I've visited that have not burned."

"I'll check that out." Burns wrote a note.

Lovell cleared his throat. "When I found out you'd been to each home, I asked myself who else would have access to the victims' houses? Of course, the obvious—the mail carrier. But, they usually don't go inside. Besides, these fires are scattered throughout the town, so there's more than one mailperson involved." The fire marshal coughed and took a deep breath. "So, I wracked my brain. Repairmen have access."

"Look," Jack said, glaring at the old man, "I've been all through this. Oh, hell, so have others. Nothing's new."

"I'm sure you've reviewed the information hundreds of times. Why don't you let me continue?" Lovell squinted at the scrawled chicken scratch Jack could see on the notepad. "Then it hit me," the fire marshal said. "What about insurance? Doesn't each of the victims have insurance?" Lovell looked up from his pad and his gaze bored into Jack.

Jack scowled back as his foot tapped a steady beat against the floor.

"I imagine the owner's would've at least had some home insurance," Farley commented. He picked up his glasses and twirled them in his fingers, then put them on.

"Yes, Ted, they did," Lovell agreed. "In fact, the same company insured each of them. The house on E and Boone was insured the end of May. All the Carsonville houses that this particular arsonist has burned were insured within the last few months." The fire marshal kept staring at Jack as he talked. "Appears one man insured them all. He had access to their homes, just as Jack did."

"Are you going to keep us in suspense?" Burns asked, not blinking an eye. "Or don't you know who this man is?"

"Jack," Lovell asked, "you have any ideas?"

"I've checked everybody out."

"I understand." Lovell nodded. "Who's Bradley Lester Zilence?"

Farley looked at Jack. "Kathy's friend?"

Jack ran his hand through his hair. "Well..."

Burns jumped out of his chair. His face turned red and he yelled, "You know this guy?" He leaned down over Jack's chair and gripped its back. "First, you make light of the arson fires so I don't check them out. You're the hotshot arson investigator. I figure you can handle it, so I put a rookie cop on the case. He just follows up on your reports. Besides, I have other crimes to solve. Now, I hear I should be investigating you and maybe some guy by the name of Zilence."

"Wait a second," Jack said. "Calm down. I have files—"

"People are dead." Burns straightened up and stared. "Who cares about files?"

"I do. You'll see. Lovell has seen some of them."

"Yes, but I don't have any," Burns said.

"They're locked up in my desk at home," Jack said. "I'll go get them."

"Why don't you call Kathy and have her bring them down?" Farley asked.

"Because I don't want Kathy to know about them," Jack said. "One is a very thick file on Bradley. She wouldn't be happy about that."

"Does your wife control all of your investigations?" Burns asked as he sat back down in his chair and glared.

"No," Jack said, "but this one—"

"Should be no different," Lovell finished for him. "You're good, Jack. Too good for this. Just what is holding you back?"

"It's complicated," Jack said. "Maybe I am too close to this one."

"And?" Lovell asked.

"Shit, now come the trust issues. Whenever the department finds out I've inspected the victims' house a week before, all the firefighters become suspicious. The looks, the rumors take off as fast as a fire in dry grass. So, I quit my job, and Kathy and I move. The arson fires—they always stop. Then after a time, they begin in the town we've moved to. No evidence points to me, but heavy suspicion."

"So let us help you this time," Lovell said.

"From what Jack tells me," Farley said, "he's had lots of help before to no avail."

"This time might be different if you don't move," Burns said.

Jack took a deep breath. "Lovell, maybe you're right," he muttered, running his hand through his hair. "Maybe it's time to let someone else take over, Cap."

Farley glanced over at the fire marshal and the detective, then back at him. "Look, Jack, I said I believe in you."

Burns snorted. Jack squirmed under Lovell's studied gaze.

"Save it, Cap," Jack said, holding up his hand, warding off any further remarks. "I've been through it all before. No evidence, but lots of suspicions. Trust is gone. Doubts fester. Maybe it is me." He stood and paced the office.

"Maybe I'm setting these fires, and I don't even know it. Some of the papers I have in my files are on me."

He halted from strolling back and forth, and leaned against the wall. "Lovell, you haven't come up with anything new."

"It's time we put an end to these fires," the fire marshal said.

"Don't you think I know that?" Jack stepped away from the wall and grabbed the back of his chair. His knuckles turned white. "And, you can bet when I move from here, there won't *be* any more of these fires.

"Everyone here will be convinced it was me, because, soon, they'll start up in the town that I move to. Cap, if you don't mind, I'd like to call my wife, tell her to start packing. I guess it's time to move on." He headed for the door.

Before he reached it, Burns said in a cold, calculating tone, "I wouldn't, if I were you."

Jack stopped and turned. "No offense, Detective, but better officers than you have checked me out. Either I'm too clever, or it's not me. Either way, there's been no indictments, no clues. Everyone seems to be relieved when I move, not only from the town, but from the state."

"Maybe it's time to quit running," Farley said. "Look, you're making it difficult. I'm sure you've been all through this before and it must be very frustrating, but we need some answers here. Work with us, not against us.

"Let's get all your files to Lovell and Burns so they can check out your data. A fresh perspective is always helpful. Maybe they'll come up with something?"

Jack hated the pleading tone in his captain and friend's voice. Maybe this time would be different. "Okay, fine. I'll try to wait 'til one of them comes up with a better plan, unless this arsonist gets too close."

"Fair enough," Farley said. "Maybe we can get the detective to tap your line, so when the telephone calls start, we can try and trace them."

"Phone calls?" Burns asked, looking at Jack.

Farley motioned toward the seat. "Jack, please sit down." The captain explained the calls.

"Yeah, we'll tap your line now." Burns scribbled a note on his pad.

"Kathy hates the phone taps," Jack said. "Likes her privacy. Besides, there's still a minute chance it's not our arsonist. We're never certain until the calls begin. So far, I haven't heard of any."

"Don't you have caller ID?" the detective asked.

"Yes, but it doesn't help, what with all the blocking systems," Jack said, hesitating. "Like I told the captain, this arsonist knows electronics. He taps into other numbers, goes through pay phones and uses throw-away cells. Trace all you want or check the incoming calls—it'll turn out to be another dead end and a waste of time, and money. Kathy really doesn't like it."

"So don't tell her," Burns said. "We'll tap into the line when she's out of the house. I don't need your permission. I can get a court order."

"Fine." Jack nodded. "Tap the line. First, I'm going down and check out last night's fire again. Then, I'll get the files and bring them in."

CHAPTER 13

Kathy drove to the fire station. Before she parked, she spotted Jack's Ford pull out. She followed him.

They cruised slowly down E Street, passing many majestic Victorian homes that lined each side. *I wonder,* Kathy thought, *if Jack still has those tourist maps for the historic homes?* When she sent for them, she knew she wanted to live in the quaint seacoast town. Jack tried arguing with her not to move some place that had so many Victorian homes, but she fell in love with Carsonville and couldn't help it.

Not the wisest decision she ever made. Especially since their arsonist always burned Victorian homes. Jack hated them, but she refused to let this pyro get to her.

She gripped the steering wheel harder as she pictured the Eureka Mansion in town going up in flames. Would anyone forgive her when they found out she brought this arsonist to town if that Italianate/Queen Anne landmark burned? Those multiple Gothic towers, turrets, exquisitely hand-carved gables and friezes, with finials on every roof cap, would no longer guard Humboldt Bay like a sentinel.

Of course it's not the houses that count, she thought. Would anyone forgive her when they found out she'd been responsible for bringing this crazy person here?

A burned out shell of a home was up ahead. Kathy slowed and pulled over as Jack parked in front of the house. The smell of lingering smoke hung in the air. This was where Dr. Graves and his family had lived. Many times she'd driven by this old once-beautiful place. What a shame.

Should she talk to Jack now?

Kathy watched as he pulled on his boots, crossed the sidewalk, lifted the yellow crime scene tape, and ducked underneath. Would he want to move again or would he stick around this time?

She spotted the slight limp, before her husband corrected his gait. Now was not a good time to talk. Let him investigate Dr. Graves's fire. He kept files of the arson fires locked in his desk and didn't know she knew. One day she'd watched him studying those thick folders and when he put them away, she saw where he hid the key.

It was time for her to get involved. Help put an end to these horrible night terrors. Maybe she couldn't talk to him now, but she could go home and do some research.

Kathy stopped at the post office to get their mail before going home. Inside her house, she carried the envelopes to Jack's study. This way if for some reason he came home, she had a reason to be there.

Papers littered his desk, along with pencils and pens. She didn't like things to be untidy, so after placing the bills down, she straightened his desk top.

The center drawer was locked as well as the file drawer. *That's odd,* she thought. No matter, she knew where the key lay hidden. She lifted up the pencil holder. No key.

Jack must have moved it. Kathy thumbed through stacks of papers and looked under the flower vase. She even picked up the telephone.

Where was the key?

She eyed the heavy lamp. When she lifted it and looked underneath, she found the key taped to the bottom. What did Jack have in his desk that he didn't want her to find besides the files?

Kathy unlocked the center drawer, pulled it open, and saw nothing unusual. As she reached inside, moving some papers around, she accidentally hit the play button on his tape recorder.

"Hello, Kathleen," boomed in her brother's voice. Kathy jabbed the stop button, and eyed the machine.

Her finger trembled, but she pushed play again. The recording continued, "I know you're not home right now, but I just wanted to call and tell you I'm glad we have each other. I love you. God, I wish Mom and Dad were still here. I miss them so much."

She poked the stop button. Sheba appeared at her feet, purring loudly. Darrell had left that message right after her folks' funeral. She and Jack hadn't arrived home yet. He must have saved it, preserving her brother for her because he knew how much she had loved Darrell. She closed the center drawer and locked it back up.

Next, she unlocked the file drawer and as she pulled out the files from the big drawer, she hesitated. *What makes me think I can figure this out any better than my husband?* She blew out her breath and shrugged. She had to try. She would not run away again, or be terrorized. *And, I refuse to lose this baby!*

Before opening the folders, she dialed Joanna. "Can you come over? I need your help?"

"Be right there, dearie."

Kathy left the stack of files on the desk and went to the bathroom. Before she returned to the study again, the doorbell rang.

She hurried to the front door, peered through the peep hole, and yanked it open. "Hi, Joanna. Come in."

"What's up?"

"You said you'd help me with these fires. I need copies made of Jack's files so we can study them."

"Have you talked with him?"

"No." Kathy held up her hand to ward off any comment from Joanna. "I'm not going too. With me being pregnant, he'd think it would be too much for me."

"Is it?"

"No. I'm a lot stronger than anyone thinks. This time I'll carry the baby to term. We will not move again."

"Well," Joanna said, "let's get to it."

CHAPTER 14

Jack studied the burned house. His gut rumbled and ached. He rubbed his temples, wishing the pounding would quit. After making the decision to stay, he had to put everything into solving this case—even if it meant working long hours.

He flicked the button on his Sony recorder. The machine whirred and he listened to last night's notes.

Burns had taken the two melted gas cans and a melted, twisted ball of plastic to be analyzed. Those items would lead nowhere, but it was the detective's job to check them out. At least Burns would be busy and maybe keep off Jack's back.

As he sloshed across the charred, wet wood, his leg throbbed. He ignored it and managed not to limp.

The point of origin was at the bottom of what remained of the stairs. Why did the arsonist always start his fires in the same place?

Jack snapped a few pictures, and then recorded his observations and thoughts. If the staircase hadn't collapsed, he could have tracked the fire by following the trailers up the steps.

A metal ladder lay on the floor. He picked it up and leaned it against the second floor hallway. As he climbed, each step groaned, protesting his weight. Even though the firefighters had braced the second floor, he could fall through with one wrong step on the weakened wood. When working in a burned house, he spelled careful with a capital "C," not wanting another accident.

The damaged surfaces along the hallway told him a story. As he studied the burn patterns, he blocked out pictures of the dead family he'd seen only a few hours ago. His concentration had to remain on how this fire started. It was up to Burns to discover who to arrest for the murders.

In each room, Jack examined the remaining windows for cracks in the glass to determine the heat's intensity.

Back out in the hallway, bent down on one knee, he prepared to measure the depth of charring in the wood, when a rasping voice said, "You're still here; not getting the files?"

"Yeah," Jack said, without moving. "I figured you'd show up sooner or later. It's your job, too." He looked up and saw Lovell's frown. "This is more important to me than the files."

The fire marshal wore his gray hair short above a weather-beaten face. He said, "Look, I'm sorry that this is happening again and you didn't like what I had to say."

Jack snarled, "You haven't told me anything I haven't already thought of, or acted any different than the others."

"How come you've never approached this Zilence character?" Lovell bent over and copied Jack's figures onto his legal pad.

"What makes you think I haven't?" Jack stood and eyed Lovell, after again recording the information.

"Ted says your wife loves this man like a brother. After reading part of your file... I don't think you'd allow yourself to believe it's him."

"No, I want to suspect Bradley, but I can't." Jack stepped down the hall, stopped at a charred hole in the wall, and pulled out wiring. He inspected the strands and followed them down the burned hallway. "Besides, different police departments have checked him out. No proof of anything."

He sprayed doorknobs with an ultraviolet spray, searching and hoping for fingerprints, not expecting to find any. He stopped. "You know, like I said before at the meeting, I even wonder if it's me sometimes."

"According to the copies of your files, others have wondered the same thing."

"No one's ever found any evidence." Jack looked back over his shoulder. "Maybe I'm too clever?"

The fire marshal raised an eyebrow. "No one's that clever."

Jack turned back to a doorknob while Lovell stepped closer and peered at the knob. The spraying produced no fingerprints. Jack moved aside and studied the fire marshal.

Lovell nodded his head back toward what used to be the stairway, and said, "The cone of scorching is down there, marking the point of origin."

"Yeah, I know." Jack sighed. "This fire isn't new to me. Same patterns as before."

The fire marshal ran his hand along the bumpy wall. "Lot of alligation here."

Jack reached out and felt the knobby wood. The fire had made it look like an alligator's hide. He grimaced. "This poor family never had a chance. I didn't know this was my wife's doctor. She's pregnant. Now I have two to protect."

"You're not alone." Lovell clapped Jack on the back. "Your past work on other fires proves you're one of the best investigators I've seen in a long time. We'll figure this particular one out."

Jack spun around. "But I'm not good enough. This guy's been after us for too long. If I could just..." He rubbed the back of his neck, turned around, and followed the burn pattern back down the hallway to where the stairs used to be.

He made some quick pencil drawings on his pad, and then descended the metal ladder. At the bottom, he watched the fire marshal climb down, steps groaning. Lovell's foot slipped. He started to slide. Jack dropped his pad and grabbed the side rails.

Lovell slid down. His yellow pad fell, just missing Jack by inches. The old man's gnarled hands tried to grasp the ladder, and just before crashing into Jack, those hands found their grip. Lovell regained his footing and climbed down the few remaining rungs without further mishap.

He shook his head. "It's a good thing I'm retiring soon."

"Those rungs are wet and slippery. Could have happened to anybody." Jack picked up his sketchpad, along with the yellow pad and handed it to Lovell. "Have you talked with Farley about what he saw when he arrived on the scene?"

"Yes," Lovell said. "He was on the first engine, but the captain didn't see anyone lurking around. A few people out in their pajamas, but nobody suspicious."

"Fits the pattern." Jack sighed. "No one stands out in the hundreds of photos I have. No fingerprints—not even a partial."

He followed Lovell's gaze to his hands. They both wore those throwaway latex gloves to keep from leaving their own fingerprints at the crime scene.

"Can you tell me anything that's not in your files?" Lovell asked.

"No, everything's documented—even the false leads. I even have copies of police and FBI reports. So many experts have tried. Leads go nowhere." Jack snapped a few photographs of the downstairs with his small camera.

"Well," the fire marshal said, "what little evidence we have will go to the lab. Detective Burns is involved now. You know who his prime suspect is?" Lovell coughed and stared at Jack.

"Yeah, I know." Jack nodded, and said without averting his gaze, "I wish him luck."

The fire marshal turned and the two men headed out of the structure. "Get those files to us as soon as you're through here," Lovell said. "If you think of anything, contact me. Especially if your wife gets any of those telephone calls."

"I hope she doesn't. There's always a slim chance—"

"Have you gotten a psych analysis?" Lovell asked.

"Yes, I'm heading there now. Then I'll get the files."

As they walked outside, a few TV and newspaper reporters accosted them before the men could reach their cars.

"Arson Investigator Hellman, is it true you're familiar with this arsonist?" a young reporter shouted out.

Jack held his hand in front of his face, avoiding the lights of the camera. "No comment." He hated saying that, but those were his orders.

Lovell gripped Jack's arm and propelled him toward the station wagon.

Another reporter yelled, "Has this pyro followed you and your wife from Rancho Verdes? Why's he after you?"

Jack wondered how word had gotten out so fast. Then he sighed. *Thanks, Detective.* Burns didn't like him; he was the detective's prime suspect. Didn't Burns know that if he had reporters following him around it would hamper his investigation? Or maybe the detective figured he couldn't set fires if reporters tailed him.

Lovell threw his boots in the back of the station wagon. "You reporters back off. We have no comment."

"Oh, come on, Fire Marshal Lovell, what's your take? This family died a horrible death. Public needs to know what's going on?"

Lovell spat on the sidewalk. "There was a fire. We're investigating. When we know something, there'll be a press conference. If you hinder our investigation, it won't help the public. Now back off."

The fire marshal climbed in behind the steering wheel of his car.

Jack leaned in and Lovell said, "Stay on top of this. We'll get him this time. I feel it in these old bones." He smiled a tobacco-stained grin and then drove away.

The minute the station wagon departed, the reporters shouted at Jack: "Is it true you know who this arsonist is?" "Do you have any leads?" "Come on, can't you give us something?"

He shoved passed them. "You heard the fire marshal. No comment." Jack got into his old Ford and locked the doors.

The reporters pressed in close to the car and yelled, "Hellman, does your wife know this guy?" "How come he's after you?" "Are you trying to kill your wife?"

He sat in the driver's seat, stretched his fingers, and then clutched the black leather steering wheel, ignoring them. *A very good question.* Was he trying to kill his wife?

CHAPTER 15

Kathy took the papers from Joanna. She put them in the copy machine in Jack's study and then handed the originals back to Joanna to put back in the folder. The grandfather clock in the hallway ticked like a metronome keeping the pace of the copier. It bonged on the half hour and hour.

Each time Kathy heard a noise, she jumped, afraid Jack had come home. What would he do if he caught her?

After Joanna and Kathy copied all three of Jack's thick files, she locked the originals back in Jack's desk and taped the key back under the lamp.

"How about a cup of tea, Joanna?"

In the kitchen, they sat down with the copies on the table.

"Where should we start?"

"You take this file. I'm not ready for it yet."

Joanna read the label out loud. "Bradley Lester Zilence, aka Blaze. Isn't that your friend?"

"Yes. Jack has to look at him. He's always around."

"What am I looking for?"

Kathy shrugged. "Hopefully you'll catch something odd. Compare the reports. See if anything stands out that's different or maybe even the same. I'm not sure."

"I feel like James Bond."

"Funny, I don't remember him going through paperwork. Hopefully we won't get into any trouble like he does."

They sipped their tea and read. The thick file on Jack shocked Kathy. "Why does Jack have one on himself?" she asked, not expecting an answer.

Joanna said, "Not sure."

Kathy didn't respond, but kept running her finger over the words, reading.

About two minutes later, she said, "I don't believe this. Jack saw a psychiatrist."

"Wouldn't he want a psych analysis?"

"Oh, you're right. Says here Dr. Vince Madison is a consultant to the fire department."

"Well, dearie, does it give an evaluation of what to look for in an arsonist?"

Kathy read a few pages. "Yes, here it is. Ninety percent of the typical arsonists are white males ranging in age from teenager to senior citizen."

"Well, I'm a senior citizen and no arsonist. Neither is my husband," Joanna said with a wry grin.

"I was pretty sure it wasn't your husband," Kathy said, smiling. She appreciated that Joanna was trying to ease the tension. "Says here, they're usually social misfits, loners, and they're alcohol or drug users." Kathy smiled wider. "So, I guess that does let you out. It also states, pyros range from professional to derelict and they usually have a criminal history. They're also convicted frequently of less serious crimes and have usually served a sentence."

"Jack's never been arrested, has he?"

"No, neither has Blaze. As far as I know, he's never been in trouble."

Joanna looked down at her folder and tapped it. "Then you know about his parents?"

"No." Kathy shook her head. "I've never met them."

"And you never will. They're dead."

"Dead?" Kathy's mouth dropped open. She blinked a few times, not believing her ears. "When?" she asked.

"When he was a young boy and lived in Denver."

"That can't be."

Joanna studied the report. "Says here his father had left paint supplies too close to a heater and the Victorian they lived in caught fire. If you're friend hadn't gone downstairs for something to eat, he would have been killed like his parents and two older brothers."

"Oh, my God. I had no idea."

"Did you know he's also insured every home that's burned?"

"What? He sold them fire insurance?"

"Not always for fire. Some were for life, some home, some health, but each victim was insured in some way by your friend."

Kathy felt nauseous. "No wonder Jack has a file on Blaze. Keep reading."

On the folder Kathy had, she noticed Jack had made a note in big red letters. 'Split personality?' What could that mean?

"Well, dearie, I have to go fix dinner for my family. Can we continue this later?"

"Yes, of course. Joanna, thanks for helping me." Kathy gathered all the papers and slipped them under some towels in the bottom kitchen drawer.

"No problem. You might peruse Blaze's file when you get a chance. There's something about the insurance forms that bother me, but I can't quite put my finger on it. Maybe with your fresh look..."

"Okay, I'll check it out."

"Don't worry, dearie, we'll figure this out and hopefully no one else will get hurt."

CHAPTER 16

When Jack pulled away from the Graves' fire site, a few reporters followed. Those guys were relentless. He didn't want the newshounds to follow him home. Kathy didn't need the aggravation. He couldn't believe his wife was pregnant again. Would she carry the baby to term?

If his luck held, the press wouldn't discover where he lived for awhile. He never listed his phone number and he used a post office box for all mail. When the reporters found out his address, they'd be parked out front and start hounding them. He couldn't have that.

A couple of the persistent paparazzi followed, but he lost them by taking alleyways and back streets. When he felt sure no reporters remained behind him, he drove to his destination and parked in front of the renovated brick house.

The rose bushes lined the walkway up to the steps and smelled sweet. The fragrance of the blossoms reminded him of happier times, and his own walkway. Dr. Vince Madison's engraved plaque hung above the doorway. A bell tinkled when he opened the door and entered.

The waiting room had a long plaid couch and an oak end table filled with month-old magazines. No one waited there. The young receptionist sat behind a computer desk. Her red fingernails stopped hitting the keyboard as she looked up and smiled. "May I help you?"

Jack handed her his arson investigator card. "Does Dr. Madison have a minute? I need to ask him some more questions about a case."

"He's with a patient right now."

"Could you ask him? It is important."

The bell tinkled. He turned around. A young, blond-haired man, wearing a red shirt, with a notepad in his hand, walked in. Jack recognized the reporter from the ones who'd accosted the fire marshal and him back at the burned house.

The young man fired out a question. "Hellman, is it true you could have prevented these fires?" Without waiting for an answer, the reporter continued, "Why is this arsonist after your wife? And, can you tell me why you're here?"

"Unless you have an appointment," Jack said, "wait outside. I'm working on a case. I have no comment."

"Just answer a few questions."

"I said, no!"

The receptionist stood. "Is there a problem?"

Without looking at her, and keeping eye contact with the young man, Jack said, "No problem. This reporter is leaving."

"Reporter? We can't have you in here," the receptionist said. "Our patients... there's a privacy policy. No reporters. Please leave."

Jack stepped toward the young man. The reporter watched him, but held his ground. Jack glared.

Finally, the man smiled at the redhead and said, "Sorry." He looked at Jack. "I'll wait outside for you, Investigator Hellman."

"Tell any others to wait outside, also," Jack said, "or I'll have them arrested for trespass."

"You can't do that."

"But I can," the receptionist said, placing her hands on her hips and glaring.

The reporter nodded and closed the door.

After he left, Jack turned to the receptionist. "Sorry. He's a little overzealous. Hopefully, no one else will come in."

The receptionist raised an eyebrow and sat back down. "Just one minute." She picked up the telephone and pressed a buzzer. "Dr. Madison, I'm sorry to bother you, but Arson Investigator Jack Hellman is here. He says it's important he speak with you.

"Also, there are a bunch of reporters outside the building. One tried to come in, but we sent him scurrying away." The receptionist nodded. Then, she said, "I'll tell him."

The receiver clicked into its cradle. The receptionist said, "Dr. Madison says if you'd have a seat, he'll have time to see you between appointments."

Jack sat down, picked up an old copy of "Field & Stream" and flipped through its pages. Every now and then he'd look up and catch the receptionist staring at him. The last time he caught her, she smiled, bent her head back down, and typed furiously.

The looks were starting. *Damn, I can't stand them!* They made him feel like an exotic specimen under scrutiny. He lost confidence and worried he wouldn't measure up. He had to ignore them. Maybe he wasn't good enough. He'd solved many cases, why not this one? He continued thumbing through the magazine.

Five minutes passed before Dr. Madison opened his door. Dressed in khaki pants, polo shirt, and a sports coat, the doctor walked across the waiting room. He reached out and gripped Jack's hand hard when they shook. "Investigator Hellman. Nice to see you again. Come on in."

Jack followed the doctor into his office and lowered himself into the straight-backed chair, avoiding the leather couch. The room reminded him of a library instead of an office. No signs of another occupant. The previous patient must have exited through the back door.

"Dr. Madison," Jack said, "last night the pyro struck again. Killed five people—"

"Yes, I read about Dr. Graves in the morning paper."

"My wife's pregnant. It was her doctor. I don't know that there was a connection, but I'm scared."

"I'm sorry." Doctor Madison pulled off his spectacles and laid them on an opened book, its pages turned to a chapter on sibling rivalry. When the doctor noticed Jack's interest, he moved his glasses and closed the book.

"Are you sure this is your arsonist?"

Jack shrugged. "The MO is too similar to ignore, but he hasn't started calling my wife yet. My gut says it's him."

The psychiatrist leaned back in his chair. Silence stretched between the two men as they studied each other.

Dr. Madison peered deep into Jack's eyes. "Do you want to ask me something?"

Jack ran his hand through his hair down to the back of his neck and rubbed. After fidgeting, he cleared his throat and blurted out, "What I want to know is, could I be doing this and not know it?"

"Possibly."

Several seconds of silence passed. Jack asked, "Could you expound on that?"

"Well..." Dr. Madison picked up his wire-rimmed glasses from his desk and placed them on his long nose. The doctor shoved his chair away from his desk, wheels clicking on the hardwood floor, and stood.

Books lined wall to wall shelves, floor to ceiling. He scanned the titles, brushing his finger over the binders of each book. He halted, finger pointing at a title. "Here it is."

Dr. Madison rested his backside atop his metal desk and held the black leather-bound book open. He leafed through the pages. They fluttered one after the other until he found a certain passage and read for a few minutes, lips moving, no sound.

"Yes, yes, this is it." The doctor tapped the page.

"What? What do you think?" Jack asked. "Do I have a multiple personality or am I schizophrenic?"

Dr. Madison glanced at Jack. "Don't mix them up."

"What's the difference?"

"Schizophrenia is a disabling brain disease."

"So, do I have a split personality?"

"The term is Dissociative Identity Disorder."

"Doc, I don't care what they call it, do I have it?"

"Have you had a stressful life experience?"

Jack leaned forward, scrunched his eyebrows together, and said, "Yes." Could he finally be getting an answer?

The doctor waved his hand through the air. "Not to worry, most of us have. However, to have more than one personality, there must be a life threatening trauma before the age of seven. You'd display antisocial behavior. Your brother or sister would not have been abused—just you."

"I don't have any siblings," Jack said. "Could I still be doing this?"

Dr. Madison shrugged. "Offhand, from what I've seen of you, I doubt it. That's not a hundred percent guarantee, just my impression."

Jack sat up straighter in his chair, wanting this man to tell him it couldn't possibly be him. "Why?"

"Like I said before, you show no outward symptoms. You love your wife. What reason would you have for harming her?"

"I don't know. Maybe my 'other side' has a reason."

"Possibly," Dr. Madison said. He stood and walked back to his chair. He sat looking at Jack.

"Maybe I'm jealous?"

"Jealous of whom?"

"Bradley?"

"Are you?" The doctor leaned back in his chair. "Isn't that the man you said your wife calls 'Blaze'? Isn't he like a brother to her?"

"Yes."

Dr. Madison studied his watch. "Well, then—"

"Please, don't act like all the others. None of them believe anything's wrong with me."

"Other than you have terrible guilt feelings."

"That's the truth." Jack squirmed in his seat. He wanted to know for sure. "Are you positive it's not me?"

"Not one hundred percent, but it's highly unlikely. Can you say for certain, this is your arsonist?"

"Touché, doctor." Jack reached up to run his hand through his hair and stopped. He hated the habit. "Dr. Madison, I'm at my wits end. My wife's pregnant."

"Yes, so you said."

"I'm not sure how I feel. I mean I want children, someday; but, there's a killer after her. I don't have a clue to his or her identity."

"You believe this person might be a female?"

"At this point, I don't know what to believe. I need your help on this."

"I'd help if I could."

"Would you? Even if you had to betray a client?"

"It would not be betrayal. My patients know that I report crimes and I take steps to prevent others from apparent danger."

"Would you report a pyromaniac?"

Dr. Madison pushed his chair back and stood. "Of course, I would." He glanced at his watch again. "I'm afraid I have someone waiting."

"Do you suspect someone?"

"If I suspected one of my patients to be a clear and imminent danger to others, I'd report the person."

"Doc, this is important. He or she is good at this job, been doing it a long, long time."

"I'll help you all I can. However, if you want to explore yourself further, make an appointment with my secretary." He pointed to the office door, then the back door. "Your choice."

Jack looked from one door to the other. He stepped in one direction and stopped. For some reason he thought of that opened book on Dr. Madison's desk. He spun around and left without seeing the waiting patient.

Why had he gone back to Dr. Madison? None of the other psychiatrists had been able to help. Who was this arsonist? The motive eluded him. He listed his possible suspects—too short, and the names, too intimate.

The reporters spotted Jack as he walked around the corner. The young man who had entered the office hurried up to him before he reached his car. "Can you tell us why you're here?"

"Sorry, no comment," Jack said.

Another reporter asked, "Is Dr. Madison working with you on this case?"

Head down, Jack kept walking. A man jammed a microphone under his nose. "Did this same arsonist burn homes in other towns where you lived?"

Jack recognized the reporter from Rancho Verdes, California. For a brief moment, he wondered if he'd ever seen him at any of the other fires. He shook his head and said, "I'm sorry. I'm under orders to say 'no comment,' while the investigation is still going on. You might get answers from Police Detective Steve Burns or Fire Marshal Paul Lovell."

Reporters followed him to his car, shouting questions as he climbed in and drove off. A few reporters tailed him.

He drove around town to ditch them. When he didn't spot any of their cars, he headed home. He took a few back alleys and doubled back one more time, to be sure.

When he walked inside the house, Kathy didn't greet him like she usually did with a kiss and hug. Instead, she sat on the couch in the living room, staring out the window.

He walked over and sat beside her. "Honey, what's the matter?"

She glared at him. "Why didn't you tell me about Dr. Graves?"

Jack gritted his teeth, reached over, and clasped Kathy's hand. She winced.

He noticed the bandage. "What happened to your hand?"

"I cut my finger slicing potatoes. Don't change the subject."

"I'm sorry," he said, gazing into her troubled eyes. "I didn't know how to tell you. Your news about the baby... My head reeled with sights and sounds that terrified me. Then you talked about Dr. Graves being your doctor...." Jack spread his hands wide and shrugged.

"You should have said something."

"How could I tell you?" He reached out and put a stray hair behind her ear. "I knew it would hurt you too much."

"God, I'm not that fragile. I'll admit this pregnancy has my emotions in turmoil, but I'm stronger than that and you know it."

"I'm sorry, you're right. I took the coward's way out. But, if it is our arsonist, you should have gotten calls—"

"Oh, Jack, Dr. Graves and his family. That poor little baby." She brought her knees to her chest, wrapped her arms around them, and peered up at him. "We have to do something."

"Yes." Jack nodded and patted her hand. "This time we'll stay and see it through. I think Farley will help us."

"Really?"

He smiled. "Yes, really."

Kathy threw her arms around him. "Oh, that's great."

He hugged her tight. Then he pushed her away and said, "Look, I've got some work I have to do in the office. Then I have to run back to the station. Won't take long."

"Okay," Kathy said.

In his office, he reached for the key under the lamp. Something looked different. Then he noticed the mail on his desk. Kathy must have gone to the post office.

When he opened the file drawers, his folders were not in the same order. Had Kathy searched them? He glanced at Bradley's thick file and found a short brown dog hair. How could a dog hair fall into his folder? He thought of Chaco, the Thompson's chocolate lab. Did Kathy know about these? Would she enlist Joanna's help? Too many questions, not enough answers.

Jack gathered the files together and walked out of the study. He smelled Kathy's cooking, but he didn't go to the kitchen. He'd ask her about the files later. He left the house without saying goodbye and drove to the station. His thoughts turned to the meeting with Dr. Madison. Could Bradley be the arsonist? *Could I?*

CHAPTER 17

I stand behind the rhododendron near the window, peering through the darkness. Foggy mist swirls around with fingers weaving in and out among the rooftops, sliding across the town.

Nothing moves.

When I punch the button on the side of my watch, the Indiglo lights up the dial. My perfect time. The date will surprise them. The firefighters have grown used to an inferno every two weeks, but I can't wait that long now. A surge of power wells up inside me. I have the control.

I can't stop snickering. I throw my hand over my mouth and when my snorts subside, I look around to make sure my sounds haven't traveled. After listening for a few more minutes, I jimmy the old window lock, shine my light deep within the room and open the window part way before slithering in through the crack. The room is familiar since I've been here recently. My job makes it easy for me to case homes, to note their layouts—get to know the occupants—or victims.

The big brown dog meets me in the kitchen. A low growl emanates from deep within its throat; lips curl back and reveal sharp teeth. Then the mutt tilts its head and studies me. It knows me and isn't sure if it should bark or not.

Ever since that one dog bit me, I come prepared. I toss the steak. The dog sniffs at it, looks up and cocks its head again. Then its tail wags in full recognition and gobbles the meat. The only noise in the house comes from the chomping and the whirr of the refrigerator. Minutes tick by.

I don't move, but watch the mutt eat. Soon, its legs weaken and it drops to the floor, eyes closed, tongue hanging out.

The dog is heavy, but I manage to lift it up, carry it outside, and set it down onto the grass by a bush. Before walking away, I pat the sleeping form.

With my two five-gallon gasoline cans that I'd set by the back door, I enter the house again. The igniter rests in the can setting on the bottom step.

Upstairs, I scurry along the hallway with the other gas can, checking rooms, leaving doors open. A loud snore stops me in my tracks. When I'm sure it's safe, I retrace my steps and leave a trail of gas that follows me down the carpeted steps as I hurry to the bottom.

After splashing volatile liquid throughout each room downstairs, gas fumes fill the air. I vanish out the back door, slip behind a large rhododendron bush far enough away, yet close too, and depress my thumb on the button.

The Queen Anne erupts in flames. The neighbors on both sides have left for their annual vacations. I checked out the people across the street—they're deaf. They won't notice a thing until the firelight or smell of smoke arouses them.

I hover behind the red rhododendrons for protection. Seconds click off. Then, above the roar, screams penetrate the din. I feel my face tighten as my smile spreads wide, then wider. I jab the record button on the Sony tape recorder and listen to shrill cries piercing the night.

Ecstasy! Warmth from those screams pulses through my veins and brings orgasmic spasms that shudder down my body—like always. Release. I sigh with contentment and open my eyes.

That old woman should never have helped Kathleen.

Darkness highlights the yellow and orange flames, all shrouded in foggy mist. Fire laps at the wood structure while the black smoke soars high in the air, darkening the fog. I picture horror movies.

The screams die away. I shut the recorder off and secure it back in my pocket. I breathe deeply and savor the smell.

A light flickers on in a house down the street. Sirens wail. I'll have to leave soon, but I watch for a minute longer, enjoying the fire's heat, proud of my careful and consistent work. No pay, though the perks make me happy.

I relish the upcoming telephone call; my grin broadens. Kathleen sleeps only a few blocks away. Maybe even dreaming about the baby. Damn pregnancy! She's making me move faster than I want. My joy vanishes. She makes me do this—it's all her fault.

Pay more attention to detail, I admonish myself. No mistakes before I finish.

An old man from down the street, dressed in a robe, his hair tousled, has come outside.

It's time.

When I take one last look at my handiwork, a long sigh escapes my throat. I worm my way through the shrubs to the back alley—all quiet.

Dressed in black, feeling invisible, I saunter down the quiet, deserted, gravel lane, and listen to approaching sirens. Dogs howl. I look over my shoulder. A halo of fire lights up the misty sky.

I've left no clues behind—except death. They might wonder why; but I know the reason. I grit my teeth.

The car door squeaks as I shut it with agonizing slowness not wanting to attract attention on this street. As I pull slowly away from the curb, a cat darts in front of me. I slam on the brakes, barely missing it. Trembling, I sit at the wheel as I watch it race off into the dark. Tears roll down my cheeks and glancing heavenward, I mutter, "Thank you, for letting me miss the cat. It might have been Sheba."

I stay for a minute longer, getting my emotions under control. The advice to drive slowly echoes in my head. I cruise down the street.

Now, to make that phone call.

A block from Kathleen's house, I pick up the cell phone and punch in the number. Perfect timing—I know she's alone. It rings three times before Kathleen picks up.

"Hello," she answers sleepily.

I push play.

CHAPTER 18

When Jack stepped across the threshold of the back door, the cat darted in. Sheba spun around, and with a twitching tail, glared at him. He didn't like the cat's unspoken accusations.

Ignoring the tabby, he turned around and slowly closed the door, barely hearing the click of the lock. He punched in the alarm code, made sure it armed, and then walked across the kitchen floor, almost on tiptoes. He didn't want to wake up Kathy.

As he opened the swinging kitchen door into the hallway, Sheba skittered out and around it. Jack smiled. He knew where the cat headed—they both wanted upstairs to the woman they loved. At the bottom of the stairway, he ascended two steps.

The telephone rang.

He squeezed the oak banister, pushed the button on his Indiglo watch, and frowned. It couldn't be him again. The time was right, but the day was too soon. He rushed to the hall phone and grabbed the receiver. "Hello?"

"Jack Hellman?"

The dispatcher's voice again. "Yes," Jack said, dreading what Tom had to say.

"Sir, I think we have another roast."

Jack stiffened. That firefighter's term sickened him—burned, dead bodies—images that he detested. The smell of human flesh—the worst part of a fire. Jack swallowed back a gag.

"It hasn't even been a week yet," Jack said. "Where?"

The dispatcher told him the address on Celeste Street.

That address took his breath away. He knew that house. "That's only three blocks from here."

"Yes, we know. Captain Farley sent George Everett over to watch your house. The captain wants you at the fire ASAP."

"Right."

Sheba bolted back down the stairs and rubbed up against Jack's black Levi's.

"I'll be there as soon as possible." Jack hung up, shaking his head. Why so close? The telephone calls always started before the arsonist burned this close.

He glanced up the stairwell, wondering if Kathy hadn't told him. Maybe he should go ask her.

He hesitated. He said he'd be there as soon as possible. He didn't have time to confront Kathy now; he had to get to the fire.

Jack hurried to the back door, put in the code so it would reset, and rushed outside. The door clicked behind him. The house was locked and alarmed.

Inside the garage, the squeak of the green coupe door sounded so loud he heard it over the howling dogs. Jack made a mental note to oil the hinge, and backed the car out.

The bulldog that always hung out in the alley ran at his tires. Jack headed for the stop sign and waited. In the rearview mirror, he saw the dog standing in front of his garage, still barking.

The streets appeared deserted. A red Chevy blazer, with the Carsonville Fire Department logo on the side, turned the corner. He recognized the red hair, waved to his friend, George. Jack fished his tape recorder out of his pocket and placed it on the passenger seat next to his cell. The three-block drive over to Celeste Street took only a couple of minutes.

Fire engines and a ladder truck already surrounded the Queen Anne. Men and women in turnouts ran around, hooking up more hoses, checking gauges on the engine and fighting the fire. Water shot from nozzles. Flames popped and sizzled.

He'd just examined this Victorian house a week ago. The Thompsons's bed and breakfast place was almost finished. Electricians had replaced the wiring and the plumbing had been redone. They'd discussed a sprinkler system, and it would have been installed next week.

Joanna Thompson, using Kathy's ideas, decided to redo each room in a different theme. Kathy helped her pick out furniture and decorate.

How could Jack tell Kathy about this one? She'd been angry with him for not discussing the doctor, but she'd been pacified when he'd said that he just couldn't, afraid of the hurt she'd feel over the deaths.

Kathy treated this friend almost like her mother. This would be a thousand times worse.

Jack climbed out of his car. Farley stood off to one side yelling orders. The unit first on the scene was always in charge. The captain glanced up, waved and hollered, "Over here."

Hoses zigzagged across the road. Jack maneuvered around, stepping over them and walked toward Cap. Jack's gaze never strayed from the magnificent fire, which instilled him with both awe and fear.

Barn fire—his parents' death. He had to concentrate on the work ahead. Those memories wouldn't help.

Jack stopped at the captain's side.

Farley leaned over and said, "We can't save it. Neighbor three doors down says he's pretty sure the owners, a Mr. and Mrs. Thompson, are home. No one's outside, except their dog."

"Where is he?" Jack asked, looking around for Chaco.

"Neighbor couple of doors down took the poor thing over to his house. Found the dog lying by the shrubs. When the lab came to, even though drugged and wobbly, it kept trying to run into the burning building."

Farley said, "Guess your arsonist likes pets. We find them outside the burning house, safe, yet the people die. Why not kill the pets, too?"

"I don't know." Jack shook his head and shrugged. "Maybe he's a PETA member." He dispelled the memory of Sir Black's shrill wail. Relief flooded him that Chaco was restrained; he feared the lab might run over to him. The dog had followed him all through the house on inspection day.

"Cap, the timing's off. Maybe this isn't my arsonist."

"Only you can tell us." Farley bellowed out an order to one of the firefighters. Then he said, "However, we found the dog outside. Neighbor said it lived in the house."

The captain glanced back toward the roaring fire. "It'll be several hours before you can get in. We tried a rescue, but like the other times, failed. Heat's too intense. He added more fuel so it's hotter. Must have upset him the other house didn't burn to the ground. I sent Everett over—"

"Yeah, I saw George. Thanks."

"Does Kathy know the arsonist's this close?"

"Don't know," Jack said. "I was downstairs when I got the call. Didn't wake her. She'll be okay. This maniac never sets more than one fire at a time."

"But he's changed his time schedule," Farley said.

"Maybe it's not him."

"Or he got careless. Get to work." The captain slapped Jack on the back and hurried over to an engine to talk with another firefighter.

The fire chief pulled up in his Chevy Blazer. From where Jack stood, he spotted the man's scowl and deep furrowed lines on his brow. The chief still gripped the steering wheel. He eyed Jack, raised one eyebrow, and then turned toward the fire, staring.

Jack followed the chief's gaze. After this fire, how long would he have a job?

Pushing that thought away, he remembered Kathy had told him that the Thompsons had their two grandchildren visiting. Maybe they'd gone home. He couldn't remember if the Thompsons had rented out any rooms yet. They had Chaco, but their cat had died about a month ago. Only one pet to deal with.

Last week when the Thompsons had shown him the dining room, they both had beamed, proud of their restoration work. They'd pasted up old-fashioned wallpaper by themselves. Mr. Thompson had put up an oak chair rail at the standard height of three feet, six inches from the floor, separating the two different patterns. Jack knew the exact height, because the old man had measured it for him.

Joanna and Kathy had scoured the antique stores on Second Street for the furniture that would best fit in each room.

Jack watched for a moment as the firefighters battled the blaze. Then he grabbed his camera out of his pocket and photographed the people milling around. He also took a few pictures of the fire to study later.

After clicking a few more shots, he climbed into his turnouts. Then he snapped his jacket, pulled on his gloves, and stepped in behind Davidson, helping hold a hose.

Water sizzled onto the flames that leaped from the window. The liquid turned to steam. They sprayed the next window, fighting the inferno as best they could, slowly smothering the fire.

Engine Company Number One firefighters clambered inside the Victorian house through a lower-floor window, and dragged their hose behind them. Jack followed.

They sprayed the water from side to side and doused the flames. Steam hissed. One firefighter started a chain saw. The whirling blade ripped through the walls, opening them to get at the fire that crawled up the inner walls to the attic.

The screeching sounds Jack heard were nails being ripped out as the firefighters tore off the lap siding. Another long, early morning stretched on. From the looks of the inferno, Jack doubted there would be anything standing.

The fire was too intense to battle their way deep inside. They were near the stairs when Jack heard creaking and groaning. The Engine Number One Leader yelled, "Back! Back outside. It's going to cave in!"

The firefighters rushed out. As Jack dashed through the opening, the roof and second floor collapsed, embers flying, hitting the back of his jacket.

"Crap!" Jack yelled as a firefighter batted at his back. "That will make it harder to find any bodies." They would have to search through burned junk to find any trace of the Thompsons or their grandchildren.

An hour later, when the fire had almost been put down, Jack took a breather.

Davidson, covered in soot and barely recognizable, tapped on the window of Jack's car. "Hellman, what are you doing?"

Jack put his tape recorder in his pocket and laid his cell on the seat. The door creaked as he opened it. "Thanks for coming to get me. Just getting my notes together while the impressions are fresh. Looks like we've got it under control."

"Yeah, no thanks to you."

Ignoring Davidson's comment, Jack studied the scene. Burns, dressed in his usual clean black suit and tie, pulled up and parked behind a fire truck. "Hey, Davidson, how long do you think it takes the detective to get ready?" He nodded in Burns' direction.

Davidson shook his head and walked off. Jack frowned. A week ago, or even a few days ago, Davidson would have laughed at what he'd just said, if nothing else, to relieve the tension. The rumors were spreading; the suspicion starting, even to his friends.

When the flames died and only sodden smoking debris remained, Jack searched in the area where he figured the bedrooms had been. He discovered the charred remains of four bodies, two of them smaller.

The grandkids had not gone home.

The stench made him nauseated, and he fought the bile down. He motioned for the detective, Burns' men, and the coroner investigator.

Jack stood off to one side and watched Dr. Loretta Mayhill sift through the ashes. Before the photographer came over to take some pictures, Jack noticed him plug his nose with Vick's Vapor Rub. Dr. Mayhill never used it because it could hide other smells that might be important to her findings. Jack didn't use it either, but wished he could.

After several photographs and measurements, the blackened corpses were placed in four individual body bags, carried over to the waiting van, and loaded inside.

Burns took out his notepad and scribbled notes while the officers talked. A couple of times, the detective glanced in Jack's direction. They locked stares. Dr. Mayhill climbed in her van and sped away to the morgue.

Jack trekked through the debris. He hated the smell of burnt flesh. It permeated his nose and reminded him of his parents. But like the coroner, he couldn't mask the smells because he needed to be able to differentiate among odors to determine the type of accelerant.

He pictured the deceased, which triggered thoughts of Kathy. His shoulder muscles tensed. Was she okay? He hoped George kept a close eye on the house.

"Over here, Jack." Farley stood close to where the front door of the house used to be.

The captain knelt down by some charred pieces of wood, which appeared to be part of a staircase. "The point of origin," Farley said. "This fire was started like all the others. If the stairs were still standing, I bet we'd find trailers going up the steps and along the hall."

"Probably."

"The accelerant—gas again," Farley said. "Only this time lots more. I'd say it's your guy all right. No mistakes this time."

"Looks that way. I'm going to go to the perimeter and then work my way in." Jack walked back out and around the old foundation recording what he observed. He put the Sony in his pocket. With the house mostly gone, he'd find no point of entry. Just once, he wished this arsonist would make a single, fatal mistake. Then, he'd nail his ass.

Neighbors stood around in clumps, some fully clothed, and others in pajamas covered by coats. Jack clicked off more photos, including more shots of the crowd. Later, when he would download all the photos onto the computer, he'd compare these pictures with the ones he'd taken when he first arrived. Maybe he'd get lucky, but he doubted it.

He searched the point of origin and snapped photographs of the melted gas cans. A few firefighters stood around, watching him. When he made eye contact with one of them, the man quickly looked away. The others refused to look him in the eye. They whispered among themselves. "You guys got a problem?" Jack asked, knowing they suspected him as the arsonist. Why not? He had reservations about himself.

"Okay, guys step back," Farley ordered. "Let Hellman do his job." Everyone moved away. At one point, the fire chief and Cap got into an animated discussion. Every now and then, Jack saw them glancing in his direction.

From the back of the destroyed house, he stared. The fog turned everything grey, like his mood. Lovell drove up in his station wagon. Burns walked over to the fire marshal as he climbed out of his car. The detective yelled and pointed toward Jack, but he couldn't hear their conversation.

Lovell waved his gnarled hands, looked over to where Jack stood. Burns followed the old man's gaze. All three men stared at each other. Jack refused to look away. This had happened before. *Don't look away. Show no fear.* Burns glanced at the fire marshal. Lovell lowered his gaze and walked toward the front of the ashen lot where the front door should have stood.

The fire marshal knelt at the point of origin. Jack walked up beside him. Lovell said nothing.

Jack wandered a few feet away, trying to trace the burn patterns on pieces of charred wood. His mind drifted to Kathy again. *Hope you're still sleeping.* He doubted it was true, but wanted to believe she had no idea he sifted through the ashes of another family they knew only three blocks away.

A dog barked. *Don't let that be Chaco.* If the neighbor released him, the lab would race up to him. That would start all kinds of questions he didn't need right now.

"Well, what do you think?" Lovell asked, coming up from behind. "Is this the work of your arsonist?"

Jack dusted some debris from his gloves. With the back of his hand, he wiped sweat from his brow. "Sure looks like it. But..." he hesitated.

Burns walked over; the soot swirled around his pant legs with each step. It latched on and stained his suit with shades of gray.

"I don't understand it," Jack said. "The MO is here. Everything points to him, except for the phone calls. If it's him, he should have started them by now."

"Sure your wife would tell you?" Burns asked. "Maybe she's afraid to."

Jack ignored him and turned to Lovell. "Why would she be?" The minute he stated his question, he knew. The baby.

Lovell cocked his head and lifted his eyebrow. "Jack, what is it?"

"Of course." Jack couldn't believe he'd been so dense. "I wasn't thinking straight. She's pregnant. I'm not sure she'd tell me this time."

"Maybe there's more to it," Burns said.

"Hey, Detective, I know what you think—"

"Yeah." Burns took a step closer. "What's that, Jack?"

"Listen you two," Lovell said, stepping between the two men. "We're here to stop these fires and senseless deaths, not to start our own fireworks. Detective, are the wire taps in place?"

"Yes, they are."

"And?" Lovell asked.

Burns glared at Jack. "You tell me."

Jack shook his head. "Like I said, I don't know of any phone calls. Do you?"

"Look, this isn't a contest," Lovell said. "If you know something, Detective, tell us. Otherwise, maybe Jack should check with his wife. See if she's had any calls."

"Good idea." The detective adjusted his tie.

"I'm only three blocks away. I'll drive home and ask."

"Why not phone her?" Burns asked.

"Brilliant. Let's scare her to death while we're at it," Jack said.

"Will your wife be up?" Lovell asked.

"Probably, usually. I don't know for sure."

"Then, why don't we all drive over and ask?" Burns suggested.

CHAPTER 19

Kathy tossed and turned. The fire crept up the wall. *Not again. I'm sick of these night terrors.*

She opened her eyes. The fire leapt up to the ceiling and she watched the flames devour the wallpaper.

After blinking a few times, the fire disappeared, but the smell of smoke lingered. Then came the sirens. They sounded so close. She sat up in bed and reached over to get Jack's attention.

His side of the bed was empty. She jumped out from between the warm covers. *Oh, my God, is the house really on fire? No night terror.*

The phone rang.

Where's Jack? She crawled across the cold, deserted space and snatched up the receiver.

Screams.

She hung up and yelled, at the top of her lungs, "Jack, where are you?" She felt so cold and the fear ran through her. She couldn't move.

No answer. "Damn you," she admonished herself, "don't just stand here, move!" She ran out into the hall and down to the nursery.

No flames.

No smoke.

A door slammed. Kathy started to yell, but the telephone rang again. The night terror still gripped her. She heard talking downstairs. She gasped so loud, she thought Jack must have heard her. Before the horror seeped from her body and she could open her mouth to call out, Jack left again. *There's another fire.* It must be near because the smoke smell of her dream still lingered.

Sheba strolled over to her and twitched her tail. Kathy snatched up the tabby, turned on the light, and raced back down the hall to her bedroom.

She flipped the switch, lighting the room. The silver comb and brush on top of the dresser caught her gaze as they glistened. Both lay on a lace doily.

All three items reminded her of the ones her mother used in the old family home.

Thoughts about her mother morphed into images of that first fire like picture fragments from an old movie. *Oh, God, someone else is burning.*

Kathy put the cat down, took a deep breath, and slipped on her pink robe, exhaling loudly. She wriggled her feet into her slippers, and raced through each room, turning on all the lights. Sheba loped after her. From an upstairs window, Kathy noticed the fog had an eerie orange glow. Flames shot high into the air. She jumped back from the window as if afraid she would be burned. "Oh, my God!" she whispered, covering her mouth with her hand.

She hurried downstairs, Sheba's paws pounding behind her. The porch light brightened the entry. Kathy peered through the window. A red Chevy Blazer with the Carsonville Fire Department logo on the side sat parked across the street. Jack must have been worried if he sent a car over to watch the house.

Unconsciously, she placed her hand over her stomach to protect her growing baby. The fires had never been this close before. Sheba purred and rubbed her slippers. Kathy reached down and scooped up the tabby. As she hugged the cat to her body, she stroked the soft fur, wondering about this fire.

The telephone rang.

Sheba leaped out of her arms, leaving an angry scratch on her forearm.

Kathy covered her ears. She wanted to let the phone ring without answering it. With her new resolve, she stared at the menacing machine drawn to it like she'd be with flickering flames of a blaze. She stomped toward the phone and grasped the receiver.

The ringing stopped.

Kathy closed her eyes. She felt like vomiting. These calls, she'd handled them better in the past. She turned on all the lights downstairs, illuminating each room.

In the kitchen, she withdrew the photocopies from a drawer where she'd hidden them—a place she knew Jack would never look. Blaze's reports lay on top.

She sat down and read.

Sheba jumped up in a chair and watched. The cat's tail twitched in time with the ticking clock, distracting her. Mesmerized, Kathy stared at the tabby. Visions of her parents watching her and Darrell open Christmas presents. She, babysitting her brother, teaching Darrell to fish, to ride, like her parents had taught her. Why had they died?

When Jack found no answers, she had turned to Blaze, discussing it with him for hours. Blaze had no answers either.

To dispel the memories, she went back to reading the insurance forms that Blaze had sent back to Illinois. Joanna had said that something bothered her about these reports. The cat plopped down on top of the paper.

"Sheba, move."

Kathy shoved the cat away. *What had Joanna found?*

The cat butted her arm with its head, purring. Kathy petted the cat and tapped the report in front of her.

"What's this?" she said aloud.

The cat's paw stomped on top of the paper. Kathy pushed Sheba away again and leaned forward to peer at the report.

The telephone rang.

She glanced at the clock, reading four A.M. Jack rarely called her from work, but since the fire was so close, she eased her chair back. At the telephone, she lifted the receiver from the wall and listened before saying anything.

Silence.

She jammed the receiver onto the receptacle.

Kathy took a deep breath. Back at the table, she grabbed the papers on Jack. She continued reading from where she'd left off when Joanna was with her. Her shaking finger glided down the page and she flipped to the next one. She sucked in her breath as she read Jack's note. "Oh, my, God!"

The cat darted off the table.

Kathy couldn't believe what the report said. Jack had never told her. Oh, she knew his parents had died in a barn fire, but she never knew exactly how it had started.

Jack had been reading earlier out in the barn and had left the lit lantern too close to a hay bale. It had ignited. He'd been responsible for the fire. Why hadn't he told her?

The phone rang again. She snatched it up and screams exploded in her ear.

She hung up. She swallowed the fear that threatened to bubble up and out. *My God, Jack and Blaze both burned their parents.*

When the phone rang a third time, she hesitated, but answered it. "Who is this?" she yelled.

A muffled voice said, "You're next, Kathleen."

Kathy screamed and slammed down the telephone. More screams echoed in her mind. She covered her ears to block out the horrible cries of pain and desperation.

Pounding came at the front door. Then, incessant banging. "Kathy? Kathy, are you all right?"

She ran from the kitchen to the front and checked through the peep hole. She was about to fling the door open when she remembered the alarm. After punching in the code, she opened the door.

"Oh, George, it was him." She balled her hands into fists and bit her lower lip.

"Him? Who? You were screaming. What happened?"

George shook her gently. He looked over his shoulder at the street behind him. Then through the open door, his gaze darted around the house. Kathy knew no one was in the house, but she chewed on her lip, fighting for control. *So much for being brave.* She had to get a grip. She let George guide her further back inside. He shoved the door closed with his foot.

Kathy inhaled, counting to five as she did so. She blew out her breath. "I'm sorry. Those screams were so hideous."

"Yes, your screams scared me, too. What was the problem?" George steered her over to the settee. "You need something to drink?"

"No, I can't," she said, automatically placing one hand over her abdomen.

"A glass of water?"

She shook her head, practicing her Yoga breathing. *Get it together, you stupid woman.* Being pregnant sure screwed up her hormones. Tears threatened to make her feel even more foolish, but instead, she bit her lip harder.

"Sorry, George. This is not me."

George nodded. "What happened?"

"It was him. I know it was."

George knitted his eyebrows together. "Him? Who?" He glanced around the deserted room.

"The arsonist," Kathy said. "When the phone rang, I picked it up. Oh, God, it was horrible—all those screams." Tears flowed down her cheeks. She couldn't stop them.

"Be right back." George hurried toward the kitchen. Kathy heard running water, and he brought back a glass. "Here, drink this. Are you sure you're okay? Do you need a doctor or anyone?"

"A doctor? Who would you call? Doctor Graves is dead."

"I can have paramedics here within minutes."

"No! No, it's all right. I'm shook up, but I should be used to it by now." She sipped the water and watched the cat.

Sheba sat on the arm of the settee and swished her tail like a pendulum on a clock. Ears forward, the cat appeared to listen intently.

"Used to it?" George questioned, raising his eyebrows.

"This maniac follows us. Each time the fires get too close, we move. Somehow, he seems to know where we are. First, he teases us by setting the horrible infernos across town. Then they creep closer and closer to our home. Eventually, I receive these telephone calls." She paused to sip more water and clutched the glass with ice-cold hands. They only shook a little now.

"You don't have to tell me."

"No, it helps to talk." Kathy brushed some hair behind her ear. "Anyway, first, hang-ups. Then, heavy breathing. Finally, he records screams and plays them over the phone." She trembled. "Who would do such a thing?"

"I don't know, lass, but me and your hubby, we sure be finding out for yer."

Kathy tried to smile. Leave it to George to try and defuse the tension with his fake accent. She gazed out the window and said, "These arson fires have been baffling Jack for a long time. This one's only a few blocks away, isn't it?"

George hesitated. She turned and faced him, waiting for his answer. Finally, he cleared his throat and said, "About three blocks, I'm afraid."

His accent disappeared. A chill surrounded Kathy like the Carsonville fog engulfed houses. A bleak coldness seeped into her core.

"But don't worry," George rushed on. "I've been right outside. No one has been around. You're safe."

"Safe? He never burns more than one house in a night," she muttered. With a heavy heart, she stood, trudged toward the kitchen, but stopped. "Did you say three blocks?" *Joanna Thompson,* she thought, *lives only a few blocks away.*

"About that."

"Do you know the exact address? Is it on Celeste?" Kathy's knees shook and she felt like she might crumble to the floor.

"I'm not sure of the exact address. It's somewhere over there."

Don't let it be Joanna. Kathy had to believe that. Surely, Jack would call her if it was her friend. She went into the kitchen.

George followed.

For once, Kathy didn't feel like fixing anything, but asked anyway, "Want some coffee, George? Won't take a minute to put on a pot."

"Sure, if it's not too much trouble."

He sat down at the table across from where Kathy had sat earlier. She saw him trying to read the papers.

She straightened them up and put them in a neat pile upside down. "Jack hates paperwork, but I don't mind. How about you?"

She turned her back on George and grabbed the electric percolator. After filling it with water, she poured in three scoops of Folgers, not taking the time to grind beans like Jack did, and plugged it in.

George laughed. "Yes, my wife does a lot of the paperwork for me."

Kathy pushed thoughts about Joanna, Blaze, and Jack back into that safe place in her mind. To forget the raging fire a few blocks away, she asked, "How is Linda?"

"Me wife's doing well. And, the wee babe's due in a bit. We're looking forward to the arrival." George's face lit up at the mention of the upcoming event.

"This will be your second?"

"Aye. We already have a wee lad. Now I hope we've a lassie on the way with red auburn hair like me wife's—not like me unruly red."

Kathy forced herself to laugh. Like Jack, she loved it when George put on his imitation brogue. One day, she hoped he would make it over to Ireland and Scotland where his ancestors were from.

"What about a sonogram?"

George's eyes twinkled. "We had one of those, but decided we didn't want to know the sex. We'll be surprised. By the way, Jack told me about you. Congratulations."

Kathy smiled and patted her stomach. "Thanks, I'm not due 'til late December."

George grabbed his coffee mug with his large freckled hands. He sipped the fresh, hot brew. The orange tabby paced the floor. "Jack excited?"

"I think so. I'm not sure. He says he is, but sometimes I can't tell with him." She shifted from one foot to the other. "Of course, with this business, it's not the right time."

"Most men never think it's the right time. I said the same thing to Linda. Of course, I couldn't be more thrilled. I'm sure Jack is, too."

Kathy nodded. She leaned against the cabinet, her leg touching the drawer where she wished she could have shoved the paperwork.

While George drank his coffee, Kathy fidgeted.

"Well," George said, "thanks for the brew, but if you're feeling a tad better, I best keep watch outside."

Kathy walked him to the front door. She touched George's sleeve. "Thanks."

He pointed at his car. "I'll be right there if you need me."

"No, I'll be fine." Kathy smiled. "Guess I'll go cook up some cinnamon rolls. I won't be able to sleep."

"Can you make extra for the firehouse?"

"Of course. Don't I always?"

"Eating sure has improved since you and Jack arrived. Between his flair for exotic coffee and your cooking skills, we've all gained a few pounds." He patted his rounding belly. "Thanks for passing on your great recipes."

Kathy watched George until he climbed into the red Blazer. He waved at her. She waved back, shut the door, and recoded the alarm.

Back in the kitchen, she flipped over the reports. *How screwed up would I be if I was responsible for burning my parents?* Kathy wondered. Could she be that wrong about Jack or Blaze?

No, she knew them too well. She had to push thoughts about them being the arsonist out of her mind.

She decided to make the cinnamon rolls she'd promised to George. She grabbed what she needed to whip them up. When the rolls were in the oven, she sat down and re-read about Jack's parents and then turned to Blaze's insurance reports.

Two hours after George left, Kathy took the cinnamon rolls out of the oven and put them on the counter to cool. The telephone caught her eye. *Every time I resolve to figure out who this arsonist is,* she thought, *the phone rings and I lapse into fear.* How did the pyro know to call when she was alone? Sometimes, his timing was impeccable, like right after Jack left.

Kathy yawned and closed her eyes. She jerked them open and stared at the paper. She couldn't remember what she'd read earlier and read the same page twice. When it still didn't make sense, she stood and said, "Come on, Sheba. Let's go up and take a cat nap."

She scooped up the tabby and cuddled the cat in her arms. Purring broke the silence of the house. Kathy climbed the stairs as she stroked Sheba. *I hate those phone calls. Just once I wish Jack would be home when the arsonist called.*

CHAPTER 20

Blaze had finagled a transfer from his employer to the college town of Arcata, about a twenty-minute drive north from Carsonville. He rented a small Victorian house, with a large red brick fireplace and a mahogany mantel, reminding him of the house so long ago. It suited his purpose.

Although it was the middle of summer, Blaze piled sticks and paper in the fireplace and built a fire. Orange flames sucked the chill away from the early morning. While staring at the fire, he smiled. He leaned back in his brown leather recliner chair—his favorite piece of furniture because Kathy picked it out.

Next to the chair, the telephone rested on a table with a lamp. He placed his hand over the receiver and then brought it back. Too wound up to go to bed, he'd fallen asleep many times in this comfortable chair, his bed too big and lonely at times. Tonight had been one of those times.

Should he call again? He could still feel her soft beautiful body next to his, the way her silky hair flowed through his fingers. Memories of her floral scent still lingered in his nostrils. He smiled wider. Love, like watching a sunrise, filled him with warmth. His body tingled all over. Blaze remembered how her eyes lit up; she came alive when she smiled. She felt so good in his arms. She belonged with him.

He watched the flames of his fire and let his mind wander. He soon forgot about his love, and focused on another fire. He'd never even told Darrell about that night so long ago. Blaze's father had been angry for something not done and yelled at him to go to his room.

I'll never forget stomping off. Blaze sighed and remembered his awful words he'd muttered. "I'll fix you." He could still hear the loud slam of his bedroom door.

He closed his eyes and let the picture play out.

After his family had fallen sound asleep, he slipped out of his room. His dad was restoring an old house in lieu of the rent. On the Victorian's second story, paint materials and other building supplies were stacked along the wall, near to the gas heater, ready for painting the next day. Blaze used the paint stir sticks for kindling, and he built a fire on the bare hardwood floor in the hallway. His parents were such sound sleepers, nothing but a bomb going off would wake them. They were usually drunk by the time they fell into bed and heard nothing until they stumbled out of their room in the morning.

Blaze shook his head. He didn't want to relive this, but the old movie played out. If he hadn't gotten hungry that night, he wouldn't be here now.

He decided not to let the fire on the floor go to waste. A marshmallow roast sounded fun. After hurrying downstairs to the kitchen, he dragged a chair over to the cabinet where his mother kept the marshmallows. He climbed up, and as he reached out to grab the bag, the upstairs exploded. The chair rocked. He crashed onto the hard, cold tile floor. Somehow, he picked himself up and found himself outside.

Screams paralyzed him. Dazed, he stood listening to them. Then he recalled the burnt matches that were in his pocket, thankful he'd taken care to pick them up. His dad would have beat him if he'd found out Blaze had built a fire in the hall.

The firefighters encountered him outside, staring transfixed at the leaping, yellow flames. The place burned to the ground, all lost, including his family. The arson investigator had stamped "accident" across the case file. Figured his father had left the paint supplies too close to the heater. How lucky, young Bradley Lester Zilence had gotten hungry and come down to the kitchen or he would never have escaped. Blaze had convinced himself that it had happened just that way.

The kids at his junior high school had known his passion for playing with matches. He could still hear their taunts. "Hey, there goes Blaze. Got any matches on you? Burned anyone lately?"

He told himself the nickname stood for his initials, B.L.Z., and because he always forged ahead in life.

Thank God, his foster parents had moved away from Denver. Luckily, somewhere along the road, they'd argued and driven off, leaving him at a gas station. No one returned for him. They'd been killed in a car crash.

Ever since, he'd been on his own. Whenever he needed a set of parents, he created them, making up stories why they weren't around, changing his handwriting and forging a signature. No one ever asked enough questions or insisted on meeting his folks for him to get caught; therefore he managed to slip through the cracks of bureaucracy. He became tough and hard-headed living on the streets. It was difficult for him to trust.

Stopping in Sandpoint, Idaho and meeting Darrell Cougar changed his life. He adopted a new family. Mrs. Cougar always gave Kathy cooking lessons and invited Blaze to eat with the family or take some food home.

Mr. Cougar played baseball with Darrell and him; Darrell's father also took them on campouts. Kathy treated Blaze like another brother: drove them to school, took them to the movies, and even gave away some girlish secrets. Blaze could walk in the back door any time without knocking.

Then, Jack came along, always calling him Bradley. He hated that name. Blaze shrugged, dispelling some of the memories, lifted himself up from the chair, and poked the logs on the fire. He settled back into the comfortable leather seat and put his feet up. He reached over and pushed the play button on his video recorder, as well as the record button on his voice recorder. Images from the movie flashed across the screen: Darrell, Kathy, and him.

"Kathleen," Darrell yelled. She splashed him with water. Darrell pointed. "Your next." Neighbors walked by and Darrell yelled, "Hello. Did you enjoy the fireworks last night?"

Blaze continued to watch the summer scene of years past. He smiled. He missed his friend. Restless, he stopped both tapes, rewound them, and switched them off.

Flames danced and crackled in the fireplace. Sweat beaded his forehead. He toyed with the idea of putting the fire out before the neighbors woke up and noticed. In the middle of summer, they might think him odd for having a fire. Instead, he reached for the nearby telephone. He drummed his fingers on top of the receiver. He pictured her face. He played with the black voice recorder by the phone.

Blaze picked up the receiver and dialed her number.

CHAPTER 21

Jack, Lovell, and Burns turned from the Thompson fire and headed for their cars. Camera flashes temporarily blinded Jack. The police secured the reporters behind the line while firefighters bustled about doing their job. But as soon as the men crossed the yellow tape out into the street, they were inundated with questions by the reporters: "Is this fire arson?" "Is this the same arsonist who killed Dr. Graves and his family?" "Have any suspects?" "Jack Hellman, do you know who's doing this?"

Burns held up his hand. When the questions subsided, the detective said, "We're in the middle of an investigation. As soon as we have solid answers, we'll give you some information. Please, stay behind the line and give the firefighters and the police a chance to work."

At his car, Jack climbed in. Lovell and Burns went to the detective's car. Reporters yelled, "Where are you going?" "Is this related?" Some reporters ran to their own cars and followed as the three men drove off.

While driving the three blocks to his house, Jack thought about taking off to ditch the reporters. He didn't want to lead the vultures to his home. But he knew Burns would pull him over not understanding. That would cause an unwanted scene.

Jack parked across the street, wishing he could give the reporters a false lead as to which house they might be going to. He climbed out of his car, walked to the sidewalk and stood by the side of his house. Burns pulled up behind Jack's car. A couple of cars stopped in front of them and across the street. Reporters rushed out, slamming doors. Jack shook his head. *Crap!*

The reporters cried out: "Who lives here?"

"Why are we here?"

"Is this related?"

When the detective and Lovell joined Jack, Burns again held up his hand until the reporters quieted down. "We are investigating these fires, notifying next of kin, and getting statements. Your story's back at the fire. There'll be a press conference later this afternoon. Let us do our jobs."

A few of the reporters left. Jack led Lovell and Burns past the remaining reporters and the yellow fire hydrant on the corner. They progressed up the front walkway. Jack noted that the remaining reporters at least had the decency to stay by their cars and watch.

"Thanks, Detective, for not telling them anything."

"Did it for your wife, not you."

Jack swatted at one of the bees that buzzed around the roses. Before entering the door, he turned and waved to George. His friend waved back, started the fire department's Blazer, and drove off.

Inside, Jack punched in the code, shutting the alarm off. He flicked the front porch light off and entered the sitting room. He turned off those lights as well. The detective and fire marshal followed him. Lovell said, "Excuse me—"

"Whenever I'm called out at night," Jack said before Lovell could finish, "after I leave, Kathy turns all the lights on."

A muffled voice from upstairs drifted down the stairwell, breaking the silence. "Who could she be talking to?" Jack bolted up the steps two at a time.

He stopped on the open door threshold. Kathy sat up in bed, wearing her pink silk nightgown and talking on the phone. Tears streamed down her face as she said, "It was horrible. The screams were hideous. Why does he have to call me?"

Jack rushed to the foot of the bed and blurted out, "Who are you talking to?"

Kathy jerked her head up. He saw mostly white, surrounding her wide-open, pale blue eyes. "Oh, thank God, Jack's home. I have to go." She slammed down the phone, threw back the covers, and dashed into his arms. "God, I'm so glad you're home. He called. He played the screams."

Jack gripped her shoulders, held her away from him, and shook her slightly. "Kathleen, who were you on the phone with?"

"Blaze," she said. She scrunched her eyebrows together and stared at Jack. "He called to see—"

"You told him before me?" Jack tightened his fingers on her shoulders.

She winced. Red crept into her cheeks as she lowered her long lashes over her eyes for a brief moment.

What else did he know before me, Jack wondered as he ran one hand through his hair. He grabbed a fistful, pulling until he felt pain. The soot felt sticky in his hand. He lifted his other hand from her shoulder, ignoring the reddened imprints.

His skin seared down to his soul and he fought down the burning bubbling up his throat. *Damn, it, Bradley knew before me. Probably knew about the baby before me, too.*

Jack spun around and marched out, calling over his shoulder, "Better throw on a robe. We have guests." He brushed by the stunned detective and fire marshal who stood in the hallway.

"Jack, wait," Kathy yelled. "I can explain."

He heard her footsteps scurrying after him. Halfway down the stairs, he turned around, one hand clutching the banister, the other pointing a shaking finger at her. Jack's tension bubbled over. Before he could stop himself, he asked, "Can you explain why he's the first to know everything, Kathleen? He knew about the calls, but I didn't.

Jack hurried down the rest of the stairs and stomped to the kitchen.

At the oak table, he grasped on the chair back so tight his fingers ached. Kathy rushed over to the other end of the table, gathered up a stack of papers and stuffed them into a drawer. She turned around and looked at Jack, then at the counter. She asked, "Want some coffee? George didn't drink it all."

"Oh, that's just great." Jack lifted up the chair and slammed it back down. "What was he doing inside instead of watching the house?" He released his grip on the chair, walked over to the coffee pot, and poured himself a mug of black coffee. He sniffed. "Folgers?"

A slight cough came from the doorway. Jack almost forgot about the men. He said, "Detective Burns, Fire Marshal Lovell, this is my wife, Kathleen."

A twinge of guilt hit Jack when he noticed her flinch at the use of her full name. But how could she have done this to him? He was her husband, yet she told Bradley first.

"Gentlemen," Kathy said, motioning toward the pot. "Would you like some coffee? I can offer cinnamon rolls if you're hungry." She looked at Jack. "George came in when he heard me scream."

Jack stopped drinking and stared at his wife. "Scream?"

Kathy grabbed two more mugs from the cupboard and poured coffee for the detective and Lovell. "When our arsonist called and played the screams again early this morning, I screamed. George heard me and rushed to the door to see if I was all right.

"He came in and calmed me down. Offered to call a doctor to make sure the baby was okay. He's a good friend. Your friend." She placed the coffeepot on the counter, turned, and handed the men their mugs. Then she leaned back against the tile counter.

Jack shifted from one foot to the other. He hated the way he acted after a fire—such a short fuse. The mere mention of Bradley sent him off. He knew Kathy was afraid. He feared for her and the baby. He felt pathetic, acting like a jealous husband.

He sipped from his cup. Too soon to tell her whose house burned and that she lost a good friend, he said, "I'm sorry. I shouldn't have snapped at you." In a soft, throaty voice, he said, "He's close, Kathy, too close. Are you all right?"

She walked up next to him, nodded and said, "I'll be fine, as long as you're here to keep me safe."

Burns cleared his throat. "Good coffee, ma'am. You said this guy called you earlier. Was this the first time since the fires began?"

Kathy bit her lower lip, looked at the two men, then turned and gazed up into Jack's face. "No, he called twice the other day—the day when Blaze came by and ate with me. Later, I went shopping with Joanna. I'm sorry. I was afraid... I didn't want to tell you because of the baby."

The only thing that would have made Jack feel worse—if a landslide had hit him, with rocks tumbling down non-stop. He exhaled.

"Mrs. Hellman, can you tell us what happened?" Lovell asked.

Jack studied his wife. She inhaled deeply before she answered. She always did those yoga breaths whenever she was upset or tense. Her shoulders dropped.

"When I picked up the phone, there was silence," she told Lovell. "Then, a man said, 'Hello, Kathleen. Did you enjoy the fire?' For one crazy moment, I thought it sounded like Darrell. But my brother is dead." She turned to Jack with pleading eyes.

"Yes, he is," Jack agreed.

"Then Blaze and I realized the voice must have reminded me of him, because he's the only one who ever called me Kathleen."

The detective cleared his throat, glanced at the fire marshal, and glared at Jack.

Kathy smiled up at Jack, and continued, "Except you, when you're angry. But that doesn't count."

"I don't lose my temper too often." Jack shrugged.

"Anyway," Kathy said, "then Blaze called and came over. Before he arrived, I received another call. This time, silence and heavy breathing." She held up her hand and before Jack could say anything, continued, "Blaze wanted to tell you about the calls. I wouldn't let him. He made me promise I'd tell you if I got anymore. I just did."

"Bradley knew—"

"I didn't have a chance to tell you he called a little after one-thirty this morning and played screams. Just as you came in, the telephone rang again. You answered it and rushed off. The fire, it wasn't—"

"Excuse me, you said for the second time?" Burns scribbled a note on his notepad. "What happened this morning after your husband left for the *second* time?"

"Gentlemen," Jack said, "let's sit down." He pulled out a chair for Kathy and settled into the chair beside her. The two men sat across the table. Sheba jumped into Kathy's lap, peering over the table edge. As Kathy stroked the tabby's fur, the cat watched the two men.

Kathy pushed a stray hair behind her ear and continued. "Well, Detective, after Jack left, I got up, checked each room, and made some tea.

"Jack, I saw the fire out the upstairs window. When the phone rang, I tried not to answer it." She stopped petting the cat. "But I thought maybe it would be you. The flames were so close. Oh, Jack, I hope—"

"I'm sorry you have to relive this, Mrs. Hellman," Lovell said, interrupting. "But it's important. Please continue."

"When I brought the receiver to my ear and said 'Hello,' a tape recorder played screams." Kathy shivered. "I should be used to them by now, but they're horrible."

"I understand," Lovell said. "We've got to catch him this time. We don't want the two of you to move away."

"Thank you."

Jack noticed her lower lip was bruised where she continued to chew on it.

"He's been after us for so long," Kathy said. "And no one seems able or willing to help us. Oh, Jack, this time he said I was next."

"You won't be next, Mrs. Hellman," Burns said. "We'll get him." The corner of the detective's mouth turned up into what Jack surmised was his attempt at a sympathetic smile. Then Burns' face hardened as he turned and sneered at Jack. "No matter who he is."

"Well," Lovell said, "we better go, Detective. Thanks for the coffee, Mrs. Hellman, and your cinnamon rolls are delicious." He scraped back his chair and stood. His serious look bore into Jack's soul. "Why don't you stay here with your wife? We'll see you at the office about one o'clock this afternoon for a briefing."

Under the fire marshal's steady gaze, Jack shifted in his seat. "I really should get back and check out the fire."

Lovell held up his gnarled hand. "Don't worry. I'll handle the Thompson fire. You can check it out later."

Kathy's face paled. She stared wide-eyed at Jack. "Oh, my God!"

"I'm so sorry, Kathy. I didn't want to tell you."

"Joanna?"

Jack nodded and pulled her against his shoulder. Great racking sobs wrenched her body.

"You knew these people?" Burns asked.

"Joanna and Kathy shopped antiques together," Jack said. "She was helping the Thompsons redecorate and turn their Queen Anne into a bed and breakfast."

"I'm sorry, Mrs. Hellman. I didn't know," Lovell said.

Kathy took a deep breath, looking at the detective and fire marshal. She wiped away her tears and stared up into Jack's eyes. "I shouldn't have been with her the other day. I never should have involved... He was getting closer. He picks people we know. It was my fault."

Jack shook his head. "No."

"If I'd only told you about the telephone calls. Maybe you could have saved them." Tears rolled down her face. "It was all my fault."

"No, Mrs. Hellman," Burns said in a harsh voice. "It was not your fault. The fault lies with the arsonist." He scowled at Jack.

Lovell reached out and grabbed the detective's arm. "We better go. Again, I'm so sorry for your loss, Mrs. Hellman." He tugged Burns toward the doorway. "Jack, we'll show ourselves out."

"Yes, Sir, and thanks."

Burns shook off the old man's grip. "Thanks for the coffee, ma'am. Our condolences." He set his mug on the counter and followed Lovell.

The front door closed. Sheba jumped down from Kathy's lap. Jack helped Kathy to her feet. "Let's get you up to bed. Then I'll take a shower and wash off this soot." He kissed her forehead. "Wish I could make you feel better."

He put his arm around her and together they climbed the stairs, Jack steadying Kathy as they went up. Sheba padded along behind.

As he gazed at his wife, her eyes flooded with tears. He hoped she'd see the warmth in his own eyes. "I'm sorry about Joanna, but remember I love you and need you."

"Oh, Jack, I love you, too, but I can't make love to you right now," she said as they walked into their bedroom.

He stopped. "Nobody asked you to!" He dropped his arm from her shoulder. "Why do you think I have to have sex after a fire? Do you think after seeing charred bodies I'm in the mood? All I want from you is to hold you, Kathleen. Not screw your brains out. Why can't you understand that?"

Kathy opened her mouth, but before she could utter a word, Jack said, "Forget it. Go to bed. I'm going downstairs."

He hurried from the room, not waiting for her comment. She looked hurt and confused. He rushed down the stairs into his study and slammed the door behind him.

CHAPTER 22

When I hear Kathleen's voice, tingles and warmth course through my body filling me with joy. Her pleading excites me almost as much as the screams. I feel ecstasy in my heart.

I put her through the pain because it's her turn.

Careful. Careful.

Mistakes. I can't afford any. Not now. Detective Burns and that fire marshal—I have to stay out of jail. They're smart, but not smart enough. They tapped the telephone; I'm sure, Kathleen doesn't know. But it won't make any difference.

Time is running out.

Earlier in the day, I removed the map from my old car's glove box and placed it on my desk. Now, I spread it out. The paper crinkles when I lean on it to study the city streets. I glance toward the closed door, and hold my breath. I hear nothing but the constant ticking of the clock. I exhale slowly. The map draws my attention again. What will be my next move?

The Thompson fire had been three blocks away from her. That old lady and she were becoming quite close—almost like mother and daughter. I can't allow anything like that to happen. Not to mention the fact Mrs. Thompson was smart—might have helped Kathleen figure everything out.

I tap the map. Thank you, Carsonville City for pinpointing all of your Victorian homes. Makes it easy for me to find my next target. I trace over different routes.

I love my job. It allows me access to homes and people. They trust me. Gullible. If they only knew what I did after hours. Laughter rumbles up through my chest and bursts out, making me sound like a laughing hyena. I clap my hand over my mouth.

Do I have enough time to burn one other place? I look at the date on the calendar circled in red—five years to the day.

I close my eyes, picturing the woman I love and hate. Her face lights up when she sees me. She runs her tongue across her luscious lips and her blue eyes sparkle as she beckons me into her loving embrace.

The image fades. Everybody who really loves me dies. They die in fiery deaths. When Kathleen dies, they will all be dead, including the little one growing inside her. It would have loved me as much as she had.

I run my hand through my hair, thinking about the Carsonville streets. If I do two back to back it will work!

CHAPTER 23

Jack pushed away from his cluttered desk in the study and stood. *Man, what a jerk.* Kathy and Joanna were close—must have been a shock to hear about the Thompsons' death. How could he have gotten so angry?

His muscles felt wadded up. *If only… No use going over it again.* He should go upstairs and apologize. He headed out of the study. Kathy put up with so much from him. He wasn't good enough.

This arsonist frustrated him—got on his nerves. He'd been so afraid of solving this and losing her. The pressure at times was unbearable.

Instead of heading upstairs, he left the house and drove back to the Thompson scene. Maybe this time he'd find some evidence to convince him one way or the other who the maniac was. He had to solve this.

As Jack climbed out of his car, he spotted Farley, Lovell, and Burns standing over by the ladder truck, staring at the emptiness where once a home had stood. They turned and watched his approach.

Farley exploded. "Crimeny, we've lost every structure this bastard's torched!" Sweat poured down the captain's forehead. He removed his glasses, cleaned them with a bandanna, and then wiped his nose. "Why didn't Kathy tell you about the calls?"

Jack swallowed hard, not liking the way the captain eyed him. Couldn't blame him though for the anger in his voice.

Burns smoothed down his slacks. "Appears she was afraid to tell him, supposedly because of the baby. Doesn't sound right to me."

Before Jack could respond, Lovell said, "Jack, you're frustrated not being able to solve this case."

"Yes, Sir, very," Jack said.

Lovell spit tobacco juice out. It landed close to Burns' black, sooted shoes. "You think you'd react different if it was your wife, Detective?" The fire marshal wiped his mouth with the back of his hand.

Burns glared, but said nothing.

"Come on, Jack," Lovell said. "Since you're here, let's sort through this smoldering mess and look around. Maybe we missed something."

"Not if Jack's as clever as he's been in the past," Burns said.

Jack wanted to punch the detective and took a step toward him. Farley put his hand on Jack's chest.

"Stop." The captain looked at Burns. "There's no proof Jack's involved. Until you give me concrete evidence, keep your trap shut." He lowered his voice. "Especially in front of any of my firefighters. Is that clear?"

"Sir," Burns said, glaring at Jack. "He was out when his wife received the arsonist's phone call. You've got to suspect this guy."

"No, Detective, I don't," Farley said. "But I am curious as to why you're so convinced."

"Me too," Jack said.

Burns banged a fist into his open palm. "I know about people like you."

"People like me?"

"One's with multiple personalities," the detective said, clenching his jaw.

"And you think Jack has this?" Farley asked. "What would you know about it?"

Burns' fist turned white. Through gritted teeth he said, "A lot. My sister's dead because of one."

The captain stared. Lovell grimaced. The vehemence in those words.

"Jack," Farley said. "Go with Lovell. We know where the good detective is coming from."

Burns shrugged, and stood near the captain as Jack and Lovell headed toward the ashes.

After Burns had a conversation with Farley, Jack watched him walk towards Lovell. He called out over his shoulder to the captain, "Seems Mrs. Hellman and the female victim here were close friends. Too bad."

Jack couldn't believe the detective. He drove thoughts of Burns away and walked around the perimeter of the foundation. Farley depended on Lovell and him to find an overlooked clue.

He took more photographs, used his pocket recorder, and continued searching, recording locations of what little evidence he found. Lovell and he found the twisted, melted, plastic gas cans. Next to them, laid a balled-up piece of burned plastic that must have been used for the igniter, just like the other fires.

Burns leaned over and inspected the area where the steps used to be. "Is this the point of origin?"

"Yeah," Jack said. "Same MO as before. My pyro."

"Or—"

"Or nothing, Detective," Lovell said, interrupting. Jack glanced back at Farley, too far away to defend him.

As the fire marshal leaned over and sifted through the debris, he said, "Until you have proof, keep your thoughts to yourself."

"Come on, Lovell," Burns said. "You even suspect Jack. He's had plenty of opportunity. He knew these people, for God's sake."

Jack continued his work. Maybe he had an ally with the fire marshal.

"Yes. But it's hard for me to..." Lovell glanced around. "Right now I'm more suspicious of this Zilence character. I'll keep an open mind." He wrote something on his legal pad. He looked up. "Jack, did you do this?"

"No." Jack scrunched his eyebrows together.

"Until I have proof otherwise, I believe him," Lovell said, turning to the detective.

"Well, you better find some," Burns said, "because I'm worried about Mrs. Hellman."

"We all are," Jack said.

"What about the tapes from the wire tap?" Lovell asked.

Before Burns could answer, Jack caught movement out of the corner of his eye. Farley waded toward them through the ashes.

"Sorry, Ted," Lovell said before Burns answered his question. "Nothing new so far."

For the next hour, they all sifted through debris, checking for any other clues they could find. Like all the other fires, they found no real evidence. Jack grew more discouraged.

Burns and other officers spread out and questioned neighbors. Later, Lovell would canvass the neighborhood.

As Jack hung around the scene, Farley came over and told him Burns' sister's story.

"No wonder the guy suspects me."

"Watch your back." Farley walked away. With the other firefighters, he checked on hotspots, making sure no smoldering embers would ignite after they returned to the firehouse. At the engines, he oversaw the rewinding of hoses. When they finished cleanup, Lovell walked over to the fire engine and asked, "Ted, are you heading back to the firehouse?"

Farley nodded.

"Good, I'll follow you. There's nothing here. The detective has questioned some of the neighbors. So far, no one saw anything suspicious or remembers hearing anything."

Farley climbed on the engine, and said, "Jack, you go on home. Lovell, I'll see you back at my office."

Back home, Jack trudged upstairs, walked across the bedroom floor, and stood near the edge of the bed next to Kathy. She was propped up on pillows against the iron headboard, reading. Her eyes were glassy. Moisture stained her cheeks.

"I'm sorry," he said. He ran his hand through his hair. "I don't want anything to happen to you, or the baby."

Kathy nodded.

"Can you forgive me?"

"I'm trying. But, can you forgive me?"

"Maybe we should try and forgive each other," Jack said, "and not let this creep ruin anything between us—no matter who it is."

Jack went to the end of the bed, looked at Kathy and shrugged. He crossed to the bathroom. The soot and grime felt toxic on his skin. He needed the warm embrace of the hot water. His wife's behavior left him chilled. He stepped into the shower; the running water cascaded over his head. He scrubbed his body almost raw in places. All he wanted to do was crawl in bed and hold Kathy close. *I need to, but no loving arms for me now.*

At the sink, he stared into the mirror and shaved. Wrapped in a blue towel, he walked into the bedroom, straight for Kathy, not taking his gaze away from hers. She'd slipped under the covers. He dropped the towel and slid in beside her. She sighed and rolled away from him. Jack turned out the light.

The telephone rang.

Kathy stiffened beside him and Jack cursed under his breath as he reached out to answer the phone.

"No!" Kathy clutched his arm. "Let it ring."

"I can't." He snatched the receiver. "Hello?"

"Oh, hi, Jack. Is Kathy there?"

"What the hell are you calling so early for now, Bradley?" Jack glared at his wife as if she'd planned this telephone call.

"To check… check on Kathy."

"Yeah, well she's fine and so's the baby. I'll tell her you called." Jack slammed down the receiver. He plopped down on his back. "His timing's perfect!"

"Forget about Blaze." Kathy leaned over, kissed Jack's naked shoulder and ran one finger down his chest to his thigh.

He pushed her hand away and turned on his side facing her. "How do you think it makes me feel that he knew about the baby before I did?"

"I'm sorry," she whispered. "But I was afraid of your reaction. I didn't want to put more pressure on you. Besides, Blaze, he guessed," she added.

"I don't understand how he knows things." Jack rolled onto his back again and stared at the ceiling, lost in thought. He shut his eyes.

"Forget, Blaze!"

The bed moved. Jack heard the swish of silky fabric. She rolled on top of him. He inhaled the scent of lilacs; her soft, cool breasts brushed against his hairy chest, tickling him. Nose to nose, she said, "Please, Jack, I need you, too." She kissed him long and hard.

Jack threw the covers over them and grabbed Kathy, hugging her body close. Her warmth crept into his soul. He rubbed her back and felt the tension seep out of his muscles.

She lifted up her mouth to his. Jack devoured her sweetness, pushed them over so he lay on top, and kissed his way down her body.

When they finished making love, Jack gazed into her loving eyes and kissed the tip of her nose. *What would I do without this woman?*

CHAPTER 24

Sated and drowsy from love, Kathy wasn't ready for the attack of crippling guilt and niggling doubts. She'd lied to her husband. She'd snuck behind his back. *I've pried.* But he hadn't told her everything either. Maybe she should tell him what she'd done. Would he approve of her help or be mad because she'd read the files?

Earlier he'd taken the original files from the house. She figured the fire marshal and maybe even the detective had wanted them. It's a good thing Joanna and she copied them.

Tears flooded her eyes. *If only I hadn't asked Joanna for help. Maybe she'd still be alive.*

Kathy took a deep breath and looked at her husband. "I have to tell you something." Would that loving look disappear?

He stroked her arm and smiled. "That I'm the greatest lover you've ever had."

"Besides that." Kathy tried to smile. She reached out and put her hand on his arm, and then said, "Now be serious. I don't want you to get mad."

Mad? Would that be the extent of it? What if he was the arsonist? She felt bile rise in her throat. One hand automatically went to her abdomen while the other remained on his arm. She inhaled deeply.

His body tensed beneath her hand.

"Jack, I want to help you with this investigation."

"Nothing—"

"No, listen. Another pair of eyes going over your reports wouldn't hurt."

"True," Jack said. "But the files on these fires are with Farley. You don't need the aggravation." He reached over, moved her hand, and rubbed her tummy. "Especially now."

"I can handle it. Joanna and I copied the files," she blurted out.

"What?" Jack balled his hand into a fist, gritted his teeth, and stared at her. "You what?"

"I knew where you kept them." Kathy rubbed his arm, trying to soothe him. "I found the key after searching around a bit. I'm tired of running. So, Joanna and I were trying to figure everything out."

"And you got her killed."

Tears welled up. It was true, but did he have to be so cruel about it. "How would that maniac know?" Kathy asked. "Did you?"

"I suspected something when I found the folders out of order. Did you two come up with anything?"

Kathy didn't like his sarcastic tone. "Yes, I think Joanna did."

Jack didn't say a word. The silence grew between them. Finally he said, "Well, you going to enlighten me?"

"Why are you mad? We wanted to help."

Jack ran his hand through his hair. "You snuck into my locked files, behind my back, and lied about it. Why shouldn't I be angry?"

"Because, I was only trying to help not only you, but me and the baby. You've looked and looked, Jack. I thought a new set of eyes might see what you've missed. I'm not running anymore."

"Well," he drew out the sound. "You're right. I need all the help I can get. This does affect you, too. As long as it doesn't cause you too much stress, I guess I'd welcome your insights."

"Thanks. I'm not sure what Joanna found, but stay right there, I'll go get my copies."

Kathy snatched her pink robe off the end of the bed, raced down the stairs and grabbed the papers out of the drawer.

Back in the bedroom, she sat next to Jack, laid out the papers and turned to the ones on Jack. *Would he tell her now,* she wondered.

"Do you really think you have a split personality?"

Jack shook his head. "I had to check. I've been at each victim's home one week before the fires."

"Even Joanna's?"

"Yes, remember I told you about it last week."

"Oh, Jack," Kathy said, "don't you think I'd know if there were two of you. You're not doing this."

"Dr. Madison and all the other doctors tend to agree with you. Unfortunately Detective Burns doesn't."

"Well, he's wrong."

"He has good reason. His sister was killed by her husband, who had a split personality."

"Oh, my gosh, how do you know this?" Kathy settled back against the iron headboard.

"Farley told me. I guess Burns and his friend Nick went to the police academy together. Nick became a sergeant and started dating Burns' sister Debbie. They fell in love and married. Burns was happy for her, but then his sister was killed."

"How did they know it was her husband?"

"If it hadn't been for a passing paperboy, there would have been no evidence to prove Nick had done it. Farley said he'd been so clever, so sincere. He'd stalked her, terrified her and eventually killed her. No one knew he had more than one side? He'd told Burns he hadn't done it, his other personality had." Jack put his arm around Kathy and drew her near. Her heart raced, just like Jack's.

"That's why he suspects me."

"Poor, man. But I don't care what Detective Burns thinks," Kathy said, pulling away. "Any other reason he might suspect you?" She tapped Jack's papers.

He lifted an eyebrow. "Did you read all my reports on me?"

She lowered her lashes. "Yes."

"Then you know I left a lit lantern in the barn, which started the fire. My parents were killed because of me."

"But it was an accident and you were just a boy."

"True. But it still eats at me sometimes."

"Oh, Jack, why didn't you tell me?"

"I try to forget. It's too painful. Maybe Burns has reason to suspect me."

"No! Let's prove you're not doing this." She gathered some insurance forms. "How long have you known about Blaze's family?"

"A long time."

"And you couldn't tell me?"

"I don't have conclusive proof. Anyway, it's up to Bradley to tell you, not me."

"Thanks for that." Kathy squeezed her husband's hand. "I'm not sure why he's never said anything. Maybe he wants to forget like you. And, he's seen the victims, too."

"Yes," Jack said. "That's why my file's so thick on him. But I've never caught him at anything nor have the police."

"Well, whatever Joanna found, it was in Blaze's file. Here," Kathy said. "You take this stack of insurance forms and I'll take these."

After five minutes of reviewing the forms, Jack said, "I don't see anything in these."

Kathy leaned over, picked up one form and then another. "Look at these two forms. What do you see?"

"Nothing unusual," Jack said, after reviewing them.

Kathy pointed to the bottom of the pages. "These initials—R.N.—are on each form."

She flipped through several more. "See. Same initials no matter where Blaze works."

"So?" Jack asked.

"He's worked in different states."

"Yes, I know." Jack pointed to the initials on his form. "Those are just some secretary's."

"All the same?" Kathy asked.

Jack rubbed his chin. "I asked Bradley if he had a secretary. Told me her name was Roberta Nesselbaum."

Kathy frowned. "Did she move with Blaze? I find that hard to believe."

"No," Jack said, "he had other secretaries. A Rachel Nelson, Rene somebody—"

"All with initials R.N.?"

"That's what he said." Jack tilted his head. "I see your point. I'll check further."

The telephone rang.

Kathy straightened, muscles tensed. Jack reached over to the nightstand and yanked it up. "Hello!" he answered gruffly.

After listening for a second, Jack smiled at Kathy. "Yes, Cap, all's fine."

Kathy exhaled. A girlish grin crept across her face. She leaned over, grabbed a few chest hairs, and twisted them within her slender fingers. Jack mouthed, "Ow!" and clasped her hand.

"Sorry to bother you," Kathy heard the captain say. "I'd like you to come down to the station. The detective, Lovell, and I have been studying your files. We should go over them all together. We have questions."

Jack released Kathy's hand and sat up on the edge of the bed, turning his back to her. "What did you find?"

Kathy couldn't hear what Captain Farley said.

"Let me grab a bite to eat," Jack said as he turned and looked at Kathy. "I'll be down after."

Kathy watched him as he listened, then he said, "No, she should be okay at the house for a few hours. This pyro has never struck during daylight."

Jack hung up, turned around and enveloped Kathy into his arms. "Sorry, I hate to leave you, but I've got to get to the firehouse." He kissed the top of her head. "Hey, you want to go with me?"

"No, I'll look at these reports while you're gone. I'll be fine." She hesitated. "You going to tell them what we found?"

"Yes."

"Did they discover something else?"

"Don't know. I'll call you."

"Don't be gone long. You need some sleep." Kathy pulled back and gazed into his eyes.

"I think you have more than my rest on your mind. You're insatiable, but I love you all the more for it." He brushed his lips against her cheek and stood. "While I get dressed, can you fix me something to eat?"

Sheba jumped up on the end of the bed. Her yellow eyes stared at them, as she kneaded the comforter, purring. Jack patted the tabby's head as he walked past.

He threw on his faded blue jeans and a red polo short-sleeve shirt. They went downstairs. He ate the fried eggs and sausage Kathy cooked, and rushed off to the station. Kathy closed the door behind her husband and entered the alarm code.

CHAPTER 25

Jack walked into his captain's office.

"Glad you could make it," Farley said. "Have a seat."

The only chair left vacant was between Burns and Lovell. Jack sat down. The arm rests on the leather chair felt cold. Stacks of papers were strewn all over the desk.

"Cap, this is the closest this guy's ever been to our house. We have to move."

"I thought we'd agreed that you'd stick it out this time," Farley said.

"I'm scared. What if by not moving, I put my family at greater risk. I want to get him—but he's hitting too close to home."

"You don't have a choice this time," Burns said. "You're not leaving town. These guys don't think you're doing this. You act like you're in love with your wife. But you'll have to prove it to me."

Before Jack could answer the detective, Lovell said, "There's another man involved here." He tapped on a report in the middle of a folder that sat in front of him. "This Bradley Zilence."

"Yes," Jack said. "As a matter of fact, Kathy and I were going over some of his insurance forms."

"Thought you turned those over to us," Burns said, raising his eyebrows.

"Joanna and my wife made copies."

"Bet that made you mad." Burns scribbled in his notepad.

Jack shrugged. He felt a twinge of guilt that his wife had involved Joanna. Had she gotten killed because he couldn't solve this?

"Think that's why the arsonist went after the Thompsons?" Lovell flipped through a few pages he held in his hand.

"Not sure." Jack didn't want to express his opinion out loud.

"So what did Kathy and you discover?" Lovell asked.

Jack paged through Bradley's file and grabbed some reports. He handed them out. "Each one has initials of R.N. on the bottom."

"So?" Burns asked. "What's that have to do with anything?"

"I don't know," Jack said. "Bradley told me they were his secretary's."

Lovell tapped his form. "This one's from Southern California." He picked up another one. "This is from Colorado."

"How can that be?" Farley asked, leaning forward in his chair.

"That was Kathy's point," Jack said.

"Big deal," Burns said. "So he had a secretary with the same initials."

"That's what I said." Jack shrugged. "I'm not sure about him," he muttered.

"Why not?" Lovell asked.

"He's like a brother to Kathy."

The fire marshal perused his notes. "I see. But you have considered him?"

"Of course. Why am I here?" Jack glanced at the captain. "I suspect him half the time. The other half..." He scrunched his shoulders together. "Others besides me have watched and questioned him. I'm sure I've even been kept an eye on too. Nothing leads to either one of us. Besides, why would he do it?"

Farley studied all three men. "This Bradley character appears to be a prime suspect."

"Among others," the detective said.

"Answers." Farley pounded on his desk. "Dang it, we need answers." He sat back in his chair and glared at Lovell. "We don't want the Hellmans to move or to be hurt in any way."

"Maybe we could lock Jack up," Burns suggested. "See if the fires stop."

Jack jumped up, fists clenched. "I'm not burning these houses, Detective. I won't put up with—"

"Sit down, Jack," Farley said. "And shut your mouth, Burns. Knock it off, both of you. I want answers, not fights."

"Jack, calm down." Burns shook his head. "Didn't mean to get you so riled up."

Farley focused on Lovell. "Can't you add something here?"

"Those initials need to be checked out. Zilence is my concern at the moment. Maybe if we brainstormed. Possibly there's someone else overlooked in these files."

"Then study them some more," Jack said, acid dripping from his words. "I have to call Kathy. I told her I'd keep in touch." He walked out the captain's door and into the secretaries' area. Christina stood behind the front counter, helping a citizen fill out some sort of paperwork, probably a burn permit. He didn't know where Gloria had gone.

With his back to the captain's office, Jack sat on the corner of Christina's desk, pulled out his cell phone, and punched in some numbers.

CHAPTER 26

The telephone!

Kathy sat up straighter in bed and turned over another insurance form. She stared at the ringing phone. The tingling began in her toes and crept up the rest of her body until she trembled. With a shaking hand, she leaned across Jack's empty space and picked up the receiver. She cleared her throat and said, "Hello."

"Hi! Man, I can barely hear you. Must be a bad connection on this cellular. You okay?"

"Oh, Blaze," Kathy said, clearing her throat again and speaking louder. "I'm fine."

"Your voice doesn't sound like it. It's happened again, hasn't it?"

"Look, I'm fine. I don't want to talk about it."

"You got another call. Is Jack there?"

"No. He went down to the firehouse. Captain Farley wanted him in his office for something."

"Are you moving again?"

"No, not this time."

"Really?"

"I don't think so. I hate moving hassles."

Kathy didn't want to move this time. The arsonist was nearer than he'd ever been before, but she felt they were closer to figuring out his identity. For the first time, they'd bought the house instead of renting. She loved it here.

"I know what you mean about moving being a pain," Blaze said.

Of course, Kathy thought. Blaze settled in either the same town or nearby whenever Jack and she moved. Even though it pleased her, she once had asked him how he'd managed to end up near them. He'd shrugged and told her he was just lucky. His insurance office transferred him all over. He would be promoted or transferred to a new district, requiring him to change locations, sometimes even before she and Jack.

Blaze knew her so well. He always sensed when the pyro grew too close to her. She and Blaze tuned-in to each other. Every once in awhile, he would even tell her before she told him they were moving. *Why was that?* She pushed a loose strand of hair behind her ear and shifted the phone to the other side.

"I like living in Carsonville, even with all its fog and rain. Besides, I've got more to do on the house."

"It's looking great."

"I'm being selfish, I know, but I don't want to have to sell our first house we've ever owned outright. I don't want to give up my plans for the baby's room."

"But you have to take care of yourself, especially if this maniac is getting close."

"Oh, God, Blaze, last night he burned Joanna Thompson, her husband and grandkids over on Celeste. That's only three blocks away. I can't believe they're gone."

"Joanna? Oh, Kathy, I'm so sorry. You two were like... almost like mother and daughter, although I know that no one could replace your mom."

Kathy fought back sobs that threatened to burst forth. "Joanna was so kind-hearted. Poor Max."

"You mean the old guy with the Carriage Company downtown? Was he there, too?"

"No. He was going to help them out around the place. His room wasn't quite ready."

"The Thompsons were just around the corner from you. This guy has never been that close. Want some company? I'm almost finished here. I'm between appointments, so I can come over. Actually, I'm only three houses away from you. Allen's folks are just signing some papers. I'm leaving in a few minutes."

Kathy looked at the insurance forms and at the initials R.N. "Perfect. Come over. You always know when I need a friend."

"What are brothers for? I'll be right over. How long will Jack be gone?"

"He just left. I'm not sure how long he'll be."

"We don't want to tick him off."

"Don't be silly. He won't be angry because you're here." Kathy bit her lip. *Well, maybe he'd be a little angry*. Sometimes he did act jealous, but Blaze and she were like brother and sister. "He'll be glad I have the company."

"Sure he will." Blaze didn't sound convinced. "I'll be over shortly."

Kathy figured that would be plenty of time to put the papers away and get ready. "You said you were at Allen's?"

"Yeah."

"Would you cancel our cooking lesson for today? I'm not up to it."

"Sure, no problem."

"Thanks. See you in a bit."

She threw back the covers, struggled into her ever-tightening jeans, and threw on a baggy T-shirt.

She made it halfway across the room toward the bed when the telephone rang again. Kathy figured Blaze was calling back like usual and hurried to the phone on the nightstand.

When she picked up the receiver, screams erupted.

"Stop it!" she yelled. "Just stop it!"

"I'll be there soon. Now you'll prove to me you love me and no other."

The phone went dead.

Kathy held out the receiver and stared at it as if it was a rotted fish. He'd never said anything like that to her before. The screams. The silence. The "I'm coming after you soon." *But proving love?* She shivered and hung up.

The phone immediately rang again. She yanked it up, yelling, "Who are you? Why are you doing this to me? Leave me alone."

"Kathy, you all right? What's wrong?"

"Oh, Jack, he called again."

"Calm down. Take deep breaths. What did he say this time?"

"He told me he was coming for me so I could prove my love to him." Kathy paused. "What did he mean by that?"

"He's crazy. I don't know what he meant. Could you recognize his voice?"

"No. It sounded muffled. I couldn't tell you if it was a man or a woman."

"I'll be right home." Jack didn't give her a chance to reply and continued, "We're just reviewing the files for the hundredth time. I wanted to let you know I'd be awhile, but I'll tell them I can't stay."

"I'm sorry. It's the stupid call. He gets to me." Kathy inhaled deeply and slowly let her breath out. "Don't worry about me. Blaze called, before I received that other horrible one. He's at Allen's. Said he'd come over and keep me company."

"Bradley? He's three houses down from you? Please, don't let him in. Not right now. Tell him you have to go out or I'm on my way home. Anything. But, Kathy, don't let him in."

Kathy frowned. The urgency in his voice frustrated her. "Jack, don't be ridiculous."

"Kathy, do what I say."

"Oh, there's the doorbell. I have to go. I can take care of myself. I'll see you later." She hung up.

So I lied about the doorbell, Kathy thought as she grabbed the papers from the bed and went downstairs. Sheba followed in her footsteps.

In the kitchen, she put the papers in the drawer, and shoved it part way closed. As she put on a kettle of water for tea, the doorbell really did ring.

Kathy hurried to the front door and checked the peephole. Blaze stood on the other side. His brown hair was cut short and his handlebar mustache curled neatly. His grin gave her a warm feeling. She thought about what Jack had said on the phone. Was he just jealous? Kathy opened the door wide, and said, "Hi, Blaze. Come on in."

She admired the way he dressed. Today he wore a gray tweed sport coat with black twill pants. The burgundy tie offset his gray silk shirt.

Blaze stripped off his leather driving gloves. "You look pale. Everything all right?" Concern laced his voice. "Did you get another call after we talked?"

"How'd you know? You always know when I get his calls." Kathy turned around and headed down the hall. "I'm glad you're here. How about a cup of coffee?"

Blaze caught up to her in the kitchen, grabbed her arm, spinning her around. "Don't pretend with me. I know you're scared." He pulled her close, inhaling deeply. "Hmm, you smell nice," he mumbled.

Kathy felt safe and hugged him. "Thanks, Blaze, for being here for me."

"I'll always be here for you, Kathleen. Maybe we can figure this out."

She pulled away and smiled.

"Jack will."

"Why doesn't he stay then?"

"He's afraid for me."

"Was that a question?" Blaze held up a hand to silence her. "Is he afraid for you or himself?"

"That's not fair!"

"You know he's involved somehow."

Kathy took a step back. Blaze gripped her shoulders. She scowled at him. "I know you don't like me to bring this up," he continued, "but it's time you faced this."

Blaze glanced down at her abdomen, then back into her eyes. "We should think about it. After all, doesn't he move on because the fire department gets a little suspicious of him? Don't they start to mistrust him?"

Kathy pulled away, avoiding his gaze. "That's not true. He's good at his job. Why would he start fires?"

"You tell me."

She shook her head and remembered Darrell's voice on the recorder in the study. She thrust the idea aside. "No, no, it's not possible."

She studied Blaze. He'd sold many of the victims some form of insurance. Maybe this wasn't a good idea having him over. She should have listened to her husband. Would he see the partially open drawer and spot the papers?

"What's the matter?" Blaze shrugged, loosened his tie, and unbuttoned the top button of his silk shirt. "You're looking at me funny. I'm sorry if I stepped out of line." He plopped down in the kitchen chair and crossed his legs.

Kathy shoved the drawer closed with her foot. She said, "I found a tape recording of Darrell's voice. It started out, 'Hello, Kathleen.' It was the recording he'd made right after Mom and Dad's funeral. Jack must have kept it for me."

Blaze planted both feet on the floor and leaned toward her, eyes wide, mouth agape. "And you didn't know he had it?"

The first telephone call she'd received the other day had started with, 'Hello, Kathleen,' but she would not tell Blaze that. "Well," she said, "I knew we had some tapes from Darrell." She grabbed the freshly brewed coffee, filled Blaze's mug, and sat down in front of her teacup. "You remember he used to send us each a tape at Christmas time."

Blaze settled back into the hard-backed chair. "Yeah, I have a few of those."

Kathy tilted her head and lifted the tea bag out of her mug. Her hand froze. The tea bag dangled in mid-air. "He used to send us those corny homemade Christmas tapes. Darrell loved dabbling in electronics—you both messed around with it."

Blaze sipped his coffee. "How's the baby? Have you felt it kick yet?"

"What? It's too soon to feel the baby, Blaze."

Blaze had Darrell's voice on tape, too. Jack said not to let him in. Kathy felt cold—cold as death.

"Look, maybe you should go. Jack will probably be home any moment."

"I thought you didn't know how long he'd be at the fire station?"

"He called right after you. I told him you were coming over. He said he'd be right home."

How come she hadn't thought of those tapes before? She swallowed some tea. Jack? Blaze? Had she waited too long to start her own investigation? She couldn't think with Blaze here. She glanced at the closed drawer with the copies safely tucked away. "Look, I'm a little tired. I need some rest. Anyway, you said you had an appointment to go to."

"No, I just came from Allen's. My next appointment isn't until this evening."

He won't leave, Kathy thought.

"I've got all afternoon," he said, smiling. "If Jack comes home, I'm sure we can be civil. By the way, Allen says he'll miss throwing spaghetti against the wall. Does that make sense?"

"We were going to make seafood pasta today."

"Ah. Anyway, since he won't be coming over, I don't think you should be alone." Blaze smiled wider. "Besides, I miss you."

After Darrell's death, Blaze had grown his mustache. As he talked, Kathy watched the curled ends bob up and down, reminding her of her father's mustache. Whenever she chatted with Blaze, she felt warm and cozy. Their talks reminded her of the ones she used to have with Darrell. Blaze filled the void that her brother had left.

"I miss you, too."

No, she thought, shaking her head. *Blaze can't be the arsonist who is killing my neighbors, taping the screams.*

She pushed those dark thoughts away, back into that safe place in her mind to think about later. All the reports she'd been reading confused her. She prided herself on being a good judge of character, but the initials R.N. invaded her thoughts. It was time to ask about them. Kathy smiled, reached across the table, and patted Blaze's hand. "I'm glad you're here. There's something I need to ask you."

"Sounds serious." Blaze stood up, removed his sport coat, and draped it over the back of the chair.

The cat ran into the kitchen, skidded to a halt in front of Blaze, arched her back and hissed. Sheba then turned and dashed out of the kitchen.

Kathy stared after the cat. The niggling doubts crept out of the dark safe place she had stuffed them into.

CHAPTER 27

Jack looked over his shoulder into the captain's office. The detective waved his arms in an animated discussion with Lovell and Cap. Farley stared into the central office right at him.

Christina still stood at the front counter helping a customer. Jack fiddled with his recorder while he used his cell phone to dial a number.

As the number rang, he observed Farley and Burns. The detective squirmed in his seat and stared at his hip.

Burns jumped up and grabbed his cell off his belt. After dialing and listening for a moment, the detective turned to the outer office window, glaring. He replaced his phone back in its clip.

Jack hung up and dialed. After talking a bit, he slapped his cell phone shut, shoved his recorder in his shirt pocket, and rushed back into Farley's office.

"He's at my house. I don't want her to be there alone with him."

"Who?" Farley asked, glancing from Jack to the other two men.

"She got another crazy phone call," Jack said, smoothing his hair with his fingers.

"We know," Burns said, pacing back and forth. He stopped, addressed Farley and continued, "That's what my cell phone call was about. We weren't able to trace it. We haven't had any luck with those calls." Burns sat back down in his chair and stared at Jack.

"I told you before, you wouldn't be able to. I don't want her alone with him."

"May I see your cell phone?" Detective Burns asked, holding out his hand.

"What?" Jack asked. He took his phone from his pocket and threw it at the detective. "You'll see I called her. I don't want her to be alone with him."

"Alone with whom?" Farley asked again.

Jack clenched his jaw and balled his hands into fists. "Bradley. Zilence. I've got to get home."

"You said he never sets fires in the daylight," Lovell said. He glanced down at Zilence's folder and flipped a page. After a brief moment, he said, "However, Zilence sold the Thompsons reconstruction insurance a couple of months ago. Did he know them, too?"

"Probably. I don't know."

The detective handed the cell back to Jack, apparently satisfied with what he had observed.

"Of course," Lovell continued as if he didn't hear Jack. "Not all those policies he sold were for fire."

"I know that. Kathy and I were just discussing him. We both have a hard time believing it could be Zilence." Jack rubbed his hair again. "Some health or life insurance policies were sold several months before the fires, and for those, he didn't need to tour the house. Some even moved after buying their policy from him."

The detective finished scribbling in his notebook and brushed a hair off his jacket sleeve. "Yes, and you inspected them one week before. Pretty convenient, if you ask me."

"Look, that's enough," Farley said, glaring at Burns. "Maybe Zilence became a friend, and revisited them again. Not necessarily on business."

As Jack paced, Lovell said, "About those initials. What connection would they have with anything?"

"I don't know," Jack said. "Maybe I could go home and ask him." He started for the door.

"Wait," Farley said.

"What for? We need answers, Cap. Bradley's there with Kathy. Let me go."

"We have more questions," Burns said.

"Like what?" Jack asked.

"I checked with your former Captain Ramirez in Rancho Verdes," the detective said.

Jack raised an eyebrow, waiting for Burns to finish.

"When I told him about these arson fires and the calls, he seemed concerned for your wife."

"Captain Ramirez and Kathy were friends," Jack responded, his voice flat.

"He said you moved on after your co-workers suspected you of setting the fires."

"I talked with Captain Ramirez before I hired Hellman," Farley said. "Those were just rumors. Nothing ever proven and Captain Ramirez himself didn't believe Jack was the arsonist."

"Then," Burns said, "why'd he let him go?"

"Because I gave my resignation," Jack said. "I had to get Kathy to safety. The last fire down there—six blocks from my home. Last night—three."

"Yet," Burns continued in a triumphant tone, "Captain Ramirez said the chief wanted you gone and that those blazes stopped when you left."

"Yes, and did he tell you that some of my co-workers, besides the police and others, investigated me as well as Bradley. And they couldn't prove a thing," Jack said.

"He said your wife came to the firehouse and cooked sometimes. He thought she was wound too tight," Burns said.

"All the more reason for me to get home to her when Bradley's there."

Farley cleared his throat. "Detective, don't you have officers at Hellman's house?"

"Yeah. McAdams and Trenton," Burns said.

"I think it's time Jack confronted this issue," Lovell spoke up.

The captain waved Jack toward the door. "Go."

Jack didn't wait for the detective to object again, and hurried out the door.

CHAPTER 28

I can't believe I'm doing this in daylight. But, if done right, they won't even know it's me.

I leave the inside doors ajar, amble down the sidewalk and around the corner, just a neighbor out for a stroll. I look back toward the house, my finger poises over the detonator. The anticipation burns through me. I drop my thumb onto the button. Sparks fly. In moments the entire house is ablaze. I have my recorder ready. I can hear the screams and push record.

The anguish and pain only last minutes, but the best is still to come. I laugh and take out my cell.

Soon—too soon it'll be over.

CHAPTER 29

What's taking Blaze so long? He said he was going out to lock his car and use the bathroom. That was eight minutes ago, Kathy thought.

She heard loud crackling and sirens.

"What the...?" She jumped up. Smoke smell permeated the air. "Is the house on fire?" she yelled.

Blaze ran into the kitchen. "Check the front," Kathy called over her shoulder, "I'm checking the back."

The phone rang.

She rushed over, yanked it up. She heard the horrible wails and slammed it back into the cradle. She stared vacantly through the back window clutching her chest. The paralyzing tightness began to take her over. She slumped against the wall.

Kathy saw Jack run out of the garage carrying his cell phone. The back door banged; Jack charged past her as the house phone rang again.

He reached out to lay the cell phone on the table, but jammed it into his pocket and seized the phone on the wall. "Yes?"

Kathy knew what the dispatcher would tell him. She could see the blaze through the side window. She bent over and gasped, "It's Allen's house! Help them! Oh, Allen. My student, my student."

Jack hung up, grabbed her before she fell to the floor and pulled her to him. She struggled in his arms.

"Kathleen, stop! I have to go help, but I can't worry about you. Promise you'll stay here—no farther than the porch."

"I have to save them."

"No!" Jack grasped her chin and made her look at him. "That's my job. You have to trust me. I can't do my job if you're right there."

Tears rolled down her cheeks, her stomach clenched and she felt Jack's muscles tense. *Can I trust him?*

"Stay here!" Jack kissed her and hustled out the front door. She followed him to the porch railing where Blaze stood, mesmerized by the fire three houses down. They both gawked at the chaos as Jack ran down the street.

The flames engulfed the house. *Wrong time,* Jack thought as he ran toward the burning inferno. *It can't be him.*

At the curb, Davidson dragged a hose off the engine. George rode the ladder bucket toward the blazing second story.

Jack helped Davidson with the hose; the firefighters battled the blaze.

Farley yelled, "Jack, go get your turnouts. We can handle this 'til you get back."

Jack dashed back toward his house and around the corner to the garage. He took his gear from the trunk, grabbed his camera and climbed into his turnouts.

Back at the fire, all he could think about was saving Allen and his family. He forgot about snapping pictures of the crowd as he and the firefighters worked their way inside, spraying a swath of water, making a path. In every room, flames leaped toward the ceiling, lapping at the furniture and walls. They found Allen's mom at the foot of the stairs, like she was trying to climb up, not escape.

Her blackened corpse sickened Jack, but he left her there and struggled up the stairs. He had to save Allen.

A back draft hit the firefighters and knocked Jack on his ass. The lead man yelled, "Head back down, the floor's collapsing."

They barely made it down when a part of the second story crashed down on top of the first floor.

Outside, the firefighters fought the blaze. They turned the hoses on neighboring shrubs and houses, knowing this house was lost, keeping the fire from spreading.

Jack broke away, dug out his camera and snapped pictures. The grim look on his neighbors' faces made him feel like he'd let them down. His leg ached and so did his heart. He shot Kathy through his telephoto, standing at the porch railing next to Bradley. She looked so pale. At least she stayed on the porch as he'd asked.

Farley walked up to him. "Is this your guy?"

"Too soon to tell. Timing's off." Jack hoped it was something different. "This is too close, Cap."

"I know. Let's concentrate on this fire right now."

Burns stood across the street, arms folded, glaring. He lifted his shoulders as if to ask the same question.

Jack shook his head and shrugged. Burns walked toward him.

"Well?" the detective asked.

"Don't know yet. Kathy's on the porch, ask her if she received any calls, unless you already know. I'll check to see how this started."

The flames weakened. Water poured from the hoses and smoke rose into the air.

Another hour raced by. When the fire crew stomped most of the fire down, Jack went into the melee and searched for the point of origin.

He found it in the burned out shell of the kitchen; not where he expected to find it. As he knelt down to inspect what was left of the wall socket, Lovell came up behind him and asked, "The kitchen? This isn't your arsonist's MO. A coincidence that this place is so close to your house?"

"I don't believe in them," Jack said. He traced the burn pattern.

"Did your wife receive a call?" Lovell asked.

"Burns went to my house to check."

"Here he comes now." Lovell leaned over and said, "An electrical fire that started in the kitchen."

"Yes," Jack said. "Allen's mother was remodeling."

"Allen?" Lovell questioned.

"Kathy's summer cooking student," Burns said as he walked up.

"Oh, no!" Lovell groaned.

"Yeah," Burns said. "And before Jack charged into the house carrying *his* cell phone, she received her usual scream telephone call." The detective glared at Jack.

"This doesn't make sense." Jack couldn't believe this fire had been set in their neighborhood. He had to think. "The MO doesn't match. There's never been an electrical fire with my guy."

"Maybe the call was him, but the fire's not?" Lovell scratched his chin. "Any trace on the call, Detective?"

"No. Jack, hand me your cell."

"Don't have it on me." Jack turned to Lovell. "Why switch MO's now?"

"Not a clue. Let's investigate."

"I want your phone, Jack." Burns grabbed his arm.

"Later. Lovell and I have a job to do. Take your hand off me and let me do it. I'm not going anywhere."

"That's for sure," Burns said.

CHAPTER 30

Kathy turned to Blaze. "I didn't like telling the detective about getting the call. Especially about Jack not being there and his racing in with his cell phone in his hand."

"You had to tell the truth."

"He's not the arsonist." She didn't sound convincing to her own ears. She shivered, not from the cold air. *Was he?* She hated her doubts. She loved her husband and was having his baby. He wouldn't... he couldn't...

Stop this!

She squirmed under Blaze's stare.

"If you're not convinced, why should I be?" he asked.

"It's not him," she whispered. Kathy squeezed the railing, spun around, and walked into the house toward the kitchen. Blaze closed the front door and followed.

"My God, Allen, his family!" Kathy's innards felt queasy. She kept the tears from flowing. "The fires have never been this close."

"Maybe it's not him," Blaze said. "Houses do catch on fire for other reasons."

"But the phone call..."

"Let's wait to hear from Jack."

Kathy clutched the back of the kitchen chair, and felt her fingernails digging into her palms. No longer fighting them, tears flowed.

Blaze came up and enveloped her in his arms. "It'll be okay, Kathleen."

"We'll have to move now. We can't take the chance."

"It might not be him," Blaze said as he patted her back. "You might not have to go."

"You're right," she said, pulling away from Blaze's embrace. "I will not run from him—whoever he is!"

With new resolve, she wiped the tears from her cheeks and turned to Blaze. "I'm going down to see if there's anything I can do."

"Jack said to stay here."

"You can, but I'm going." She marched out.

She spotted Captain Farley, the detective, the fire marshal, and her husband. They looked like they were arguing. When she got closer, they stopped talking and all turned toward her and Blaze.

"Allen?" she asked. "His family?"

"I'm sorry." Jack shook his head. "No one made it out."

"Oh, God. Is it him?"

"Burns said you received a call," Jack said.

"Yes, but it's a different time." Kathy scrunched her eyebrows and brushed away more tears.

"I know," Jack said.

"And," Fire Marshal Lovell interjected, "the MO is different."

"How?" Kathy asked. She was tired. How long could she survive this happening over and over? *Is this my fault?*

"Kathy, it's an electrical fire." Jack reached out his hand toward her, but then dropped it by his side. His hand balled into a fist. "Our pyro uses accelerants and starts at 1:30 in the morning. Looks like the wiring caused this one."

"Are you sure?" Kathy asked, eyeing each man, searching for verification.

Detective Burns cleared his throat. "Sure it's a different MO, yes. But, you *did* receive that—"

"Unfortunately," the fire marshal interrupted, "we can't rule your arsonist out. Maybe he changed his MO for a reason?"

"Why would he do that?" Blaze asked.

Kathy had almost forgotten he stood beside her. She tilted her head and contemplated her husband, waiting for his answer.

Jack lifted his shoulders, looking defeated. "Can't say one way or another for sure. Not enough to go on."

"What about the calls?" Blaze asked.

"Could be screams from the other fire," Detective Burns admitted. "Jack, hand me your cell now."

Kathy inhaled sharply. "Why?"

"You said he charged into the house carrying his cell right after you received the call."

"It's not Jack, Detective." Kathy placed her hand on her husband's arm. "Show him!"

"When I got my turnouts, I think I left my cell in the trunk."

"Then let's go get it," Burns said.

Kathy watched Blaze take out his cell and dial a number.

A phone rang. It came from Jack's pocket.

"I can explain," Jack said as he answered his phone.

Blaze sneered and hung up.

Jack gritted his teeth. "Damn, Bradley," he muttered.

Detective Burns reached out and took Jack's phone. The detective searched through the numbers. "Your husband didn't call you when you thought he did. He tried earlier before he came home."

Kathy expelled a long sigh. "I didn't believe it was him in the first place."

"I have to go to the station." Jack turned to Blaze. "Bradley, why don't you head out?"

"If that's what you want?" Blaze started to walk away.

"No," Kathy said. "You stay with me! Jack, he stays, or *you* stay."

"Burns has two men watching the house."

"Jack, leave it alone," Captain Farley said, making it sound like an order. "Your wife's scared."

"Thanks, Captain," Kathy squeezed her husband's arm. "Do your job. We'll be okay. Come on, Blaze, let's go."

They walked back to the house, and into the kitchen.

Blaze sat at the table; Kathy busied herself making tea. *Am I really safe?*

CHAPTER 31

The perfect, dreaded day finally dawns. Looking at my calendar, on this day, so long ago, everything started in motion. The pain—I go through it every year on July 10th.

I cradle my pounding head against the cool leather of my car seat.

Screams reverberate through my scull. Pictures, like on a movie screen, flash. The pressure feels like my head will burst open. Make it stop! Make her prove she loves me. This pain in my head—I can't concentrate on what I must do.

From my vantage point, I can see two officers, watching the house like me. But for a different reason. I'll have to be extra careful now. The electrical fire—a classic. She's rattled. The police are unsure. They won't expect anything more.

What's going on inside? I bend over and with my gloved finger, flip on the toggle switch. Tiny voices fill the confines of my car. Kathleen's voice stands out. I know what they're doing. I hate them. I will destroy those adoring looks that cross her face whenever she looks at him.

I slide further down in the seat, not wanting to be seen or recognized. Won't have to worry about the neighbor kid Allen—definitely a pest—but no more.

My face feels hot; my skin tingles as I sit this close to danger. The police officers don't bother me. They're too intent on wondering what is happening inside the house to notice me. But being this close to them thrills me.

Soon the woman I love will fulfill her destiny. The love Kathleen has for me will be complete. Dying for me—her final act of love. She must burn.

CHAPTER 32

Jack sat in the old Coupe, the engine idling. He drummed his fingers on the steering wheel and watched the house. Bradley and Kathy were inside his home together—laughing, sharing secrets.

From the moment he'd met Kathy, he'd sensed that she had a special kind of love for Bradley—a kind of love that Kathy and he would never have. His stomach tightened every time he thought about them together.

At the station, Burns had grilled him some more about his phone. Then they reviewed the insurance forms. A waste of time.

Jack gripped the steering wheel. He pictured big-lettered initials "R.N." from those forms. The letters faded and a fuzzy picture of him appeared.

Burns thought I was like Nick his brother-in-law. Could he be right? Do I have an identity I don't know about?

He shoved the car into gear, pulled into the alley, and parked parallel to the garage door. He took a deep breath and let it go, trying to calm down. To relieve some of his frustration, he walked out of the alley and around the corner. Instead of going through the back yard, he went to the front, staring at his house as if he could see through it with X-ray vision.

Suddenly, he heard, "Hellman, time to answer some questions."

Jack spun around and glared at the young reporter. He should have used the back door. The reporter held his recorder out toward him and asked, "How do you know this arsonist?"

Jack wanted to answer, but Farley had given an order. "No comment."

"Come on, the public needs to know if they're in danger from this pyro. Why so closed-mouth?"

"We're still investigating. Go talk with Detective Steve Burns. He's in charge, or contact Fire Marshall Lovell. I have no comment."

The young reporter stepped too close, shoved the recorder under Jack's nose, and asked, "How come you can't solve this case? Don't you want to?"

Jack grabbed the man's shirt. "Get off my property before I call the police." He shoved the reporter hard enough for him to land in a rose bush and hurried up the walkway, yanking his front door open. "I said, no comment," he called out over his shoulder.

Laughter drifted down the hall. His stomach cramped and his temples throbbed. He shut the door with a soft click. He'd put this unpleasant confrontation off too long for his wife's sake. *This stops today. I'll settle this one way or another.*

He glowered down the hall toward the kitchen where she entertained her guest. Instead of heading in that direction, he rushed up the stairs to their bedroom. If Bradley was their arsonist, he was crazy and dangerous. No second chances.

Jack never packed a gun unless he was about to face a suspect. He pulled the .38 revolver from the nightstand drawer, gathered the loose bullets as they rolled forward, and loaded it. Kathy hated guns, didn't want them in the house. She'd compromised, permitting the weapon in the bedroom, if it remained unloaded.

He'd tried to explain how ludicrous the scenario of a nighttime burglary would be.

"Excuse me, Mr. Burglar, but could you wait 'til I load this gun."

Kathy still had insisted.

With the chambers now filled, Jack snapped the cylinder shut with a satisfying click. He tucked the gun into his pants under his shirt, and retraced his steps downstairs.

The happy duo sat at the kitchen table. Their talking and laughter ceased. He walked behind Kathy, leaned over and kissed the top of her head.

"Hi, honey," Kathy said. "I thought I heard the car." She reached around, grabbed the back of his leg from her seated position, and squeezed it tight. "I know you won't mind Blaze staying for dinner. How'd everything go?"

"Bradley," Jack said as he stared into the man's dark eyes.

Bradley squirmed. "Hello, Jack. Kathy says you're going to stick around this time. No more moving."

"Yes, we'll stick it out to the end." Jack glanced at his wife. She nodded.

Papers were strewn about on the table. Jack sat down next to Kathy and cleared his throat. "What are all these?"

Kathy said, "I was just about to ask Blaze about those—"

"First," Jack said, interrupting. "I have a question. Where were you last night, Bradley?"

Kathy frowned. "I thought you were going to ask—"

"Later." Jack held up his hand. "Let him answer." He didn't want her to bring up the initials until he'd had this out with Bradley.

"Last night?" Bradley asked. "Home I guess. Why?"

"Because I have to clear you from these fires."

Bradley pointed his finger. "Have you cleared yourself?"

"Have you both lost your minds?" Kathy's voice cracked. "I'm sick of your jealousy." She covered her ears with her hands, turned her head back toward Bradley and said, "This is ridiculous."

Jack gently took her wrist and pulled her hand away from her ear. He clasped her hand. "I'm sorry; he's a suspect, Kathleen. It's my job."

"I know," she said.

Jack focused on Bradley, and said, "I know his life story, way before he met Darrell."

Bradley broke out in a sweat. His face paled and he clenched his teeth. "Jack, please..."

Jack continued, "My file's three inches—"

"—I know, Jack," Kathy said. "I've read it."

"You've read my file?" Blaze asked.

"Yes," Kathy said.

"There's no proof, just my suspicion about Bradley," Jack said. "But we have to discuss all of it."

"Kathy, I don't care what Jack's file says." Bradley jumped up. "He's crazy; I don't trust him either. Kathy, leave with me right now." He held out his hand. "Even the fire departments he's worked for in the past, including this one, suspect he's the arsonist. Why do you think he leaves?"

"No." Kathy shook her head. "That's not true."

"Your denial will get you killed," Bradley said. "I can't help you, Kathleen, if you won't help yourself. I'm out of here." He took a step away from the table.

Jack reached under his shirt with his right hand, withdrew the thirty-eight, and pointed the gun at Bradley's chest. "Sit down! You're not leaving until we get answers."

Kathy reached to grab his arm. "Jack, put down the gun!"

He slapped her hand away. "Stop it. This is my job and I'll do it my way. Don't reach for my gun again, Kathleen," he warned.

Bradley put his hands in the air and eased back down into the chair. "Kathy, shut up, sit still, and listen. Jack's in control here."

"That's right, I am."

"You want to know where I was last night. Let me think." Bradley slowly lowered his arms and placed them on the table. His hands balled tight into fists.

"Sorry, Kathy," Jack said. "But we have to settle this one way or another. Let me do it my way. Trust me." *Don't let her trust Bradley more than me,* he thought. The evidence pointed to Bradley or himself. "I love you, Kathy. I'm doing this for you."

She chewed on her lip, but nodded.

"Because of you, I've refused to believe that my investigation points to Bradley," Jack said. "Now it's beyond time we found out."

"I don't know what evidence you have," Bradley said. "You're the expert, not me. I just sell insurance." He held up his hand to cut Jack off. "Let me finish. Yes, I sold insurance to the victims. Does that make me a murderer? This is ridiculous. Some policies were sold way before their fires."

"How do you know that?" Jack asked.

"I'm their agent, and I'm not stupid. Besides, Kathy could be hurt," Bradley said, "and I've investigated on my own. You think I'd let you handle this all by yourself?"

"I'm sorry, Kathy," Bradley said, "but my file's quite thick on Jack, too. Some people believe he's your arsonist, but can't prove it."

"You're both wrong."

Bradley scowled at Jack. "Even Frank Davidson and George Everett at the firehouse suspect you. Some buddies. You were there exactly one week before all of the victims' demise. You knew the home layouts." He turned his gaze toward Kathy and said, "Some of them were your friends."

"We know, Blaze." Kathy reached down and caressed her abdomen. "But I know it's neither one of you."

"Kathy," Bradley said. "You told me that when your folks and Darrell died, Jack had been gone for awhile." He hesitated, then asked, "Long enough for him to have started the fires?"

Kathy gasped. "How dare you!" She glanced at Jack. "You're both thinking one of you is after me?"

Bradley nodded.

Jack said, "Yes, I know, it's scary." He still gripped the gun tightly in his right hand aimed at Bradley. "Look, Bradley sold them insurance. He's always around. I don't know his motive—other than maybe, he's jealous."

"No way," Kathy said.

"Hey, I don't want to believe Bradley's the arsonist," Jack said, "but this has to end."

"Well, even I've suspected you, Blaze."

"Kathy, you really think I could be doing this to you?" Bradley asked.

She shook her head. "No more than Jack."

"Uh, Jack, could you put that gun down? Makes me nervous."

"No." Jack turned to Kathy. He hated the anguish in her eyes. "I'm sorry, until I'm sure, I keep it."

"You know how I feel about guns." Kathy muttered, "Neither one of you are involved."

At that moment, the cat jumped up on the table, eyed Kathy, and then Jack. The tabby paraded by Kathy, strolled over to Bradley, and sat right in front of him. Sheba lifted her paw and groomed herself.

Bradley reached out to stroke the feline's fur. Sheba stopped licking and hissed. Bradley withdrew his hand. "You want a detailed itinerary about yesterday? Fine. I'm going to reach down inside my coat pocket for my daily planner. Okay, Jack?"

"Fine. Do it slow." He tightened his grip on the revolver, the barrel pointing toward Bradley.

After digging in the pocket of his sport coat hanging over the back of his chair, Bradley slowly pulled out a book. He twisted around, facing Jack. "See." He held it up. "Just my appointment book."

He flipped through the pages. "Yesterday evening at six o'clock I had an appointment two doors away from your house. Allen's folks turned me on to them." He looked up. "I stayed until about eight-thirty. I drove home, ate a Domino's pizza, and went to bed."

Kathy bit her lip and raised an eyebrow. "You were in the neighborhood and didn't call or stop by?"

"I try and visit you when your husband's not around. He hates my guts."

"Oh, he does not." Kathy waved her hand in dismissal.

"Hate? No, Bradley," Jack said. "Kathy wants to understand why you were only a few doors away, and you didn't call or stop by." This could be his first mistake. No way would he be that near Kathy and not contact her, not unless he was up to no good. Bradley squirmed under both their stares. "Well?" Jack asked.

Looking at Kathy with a grimace on his face, Bradley shrugged. "I'm sorry. The meeting took longer than I thought. I was late."

Kathy furrowed her brows and cocked her head. "I don't understand. Late for what?"

"A date."

"A date?" she asked. "Why wouldn't you tell me you had a date? I don't believe it."

Bradley blushed and said, "It's true. I think you'll like her. I didn't have time to stop by."

"You expect us to believe that?" Jack asked. "What's her name?"

"Lisa," Bradley said. "Lisa Moore is her name."

"She'll verify you were with her?" Jack asked. "What's her telephone number? What time did you drop her off?"

"Oh, Jack, quit it." Kathy smiled. "Blaze said he had a date with Lisa Moore. I believe him. It's too easy to check out." She shook her head. "Besides, he couldn't be involved. I'm sure that other fire was an accident."

Jack sneered at Bradley. "Was it, 'Blaze'?"

Bradley turned pale. He coughed. "Jack, don't."

Kathy glanced from one to the other. "That was a long time ago."

"What?" Bradley questioned.

Kathy softened her voice. "Must have been horrible when you lost your family, Blaze." She pictured her own parents' home's burned shell. The sadness brought an ache to her heart.

"You know about the fire?" he asked.

Kathy nodded. "I read the entire file."

"I didn't mean to kill my family," Blaze said. "The kids at school knew I played with matches. They suspected me. That's why they started calling me Blaze." He eyed her. When she didn't say anything, he covered his face with his hands. "I'm so sorry. I've never told anyone that story."

"So," Jack said, "he does know how to set fires."

"Yes, accidentally, years ago," Kathy said. "I'm sure Blaze hadn't meant to burn anyone. He must feel awful living with something like that. And *you* know what he's going through.

Jack opened his mouth.

Kathy held up her hand. "No! You both watched your parents die. I didn't see mine die, but we've all lived through that." All three men that she loved had seen their folks go up in flames.

She couldn't stand Blaze's dejected look. It broke her heart. Before Jack could stop her, she jumped out of her chair, nearly knocking it over, and rushed around the table. Blaze stood and she threw her arms around him and squeezed. "Oh, sweetie, you should have told me." Blaze hugged her tight.

The cat stretched and strutted across the table over to Jack and sat down in front of him.

"Kathy, get away from Bradley!" Jack slammed his hand down on the table. The tabby jumped straight up in the air. The hair on Sheba's back looked like spikes as she darted off.

"Jack," Blaze pleaded, holding up one hand. "I swear, that's my only house fire. I'm not your arsonist. I love Kathleen too much to hurt her." With his one arm, Kathy felt glued to him.

She heard the pain in his voice and realized for the first time how much Blaze did love her. She let go and tried to back away. He put his other arm around her and clung on. "Please, let go," she said, pushing on his arms.

He tightened his grip and pleaded, "Kathleen, don't leave me. The car accident wasn't my fault."

She twisted in his grasp, shoving harder on his broad shoulders. "I believe you, but let me go!" Her voice raised an octave. She glanced over at her husband.

When Blaze refused to release her, Jack cocked the hammer on the revolver still aimed at him. "Let her go."

Kathy stared down the black hole. "Jack, don't. Blaze, please."

His arms slackened and he sunk down into the chair. "You're my last link to family," he whispered. "My lifeline."

She didn't move, but stroked the top of Blaze's head. "You haven't lost me. You were just holding me and the baby too tight. I know it's not you."

"What car accident?" Jack asked.

Blaze scrunched his eyebrows together. "What?

"You said the car accident wasn't your fault. What car accident?"

Kathy hadn't seen anything in Blaze's file about a car accident. She waited for him to answer Jack's question.

After a few seconds ticked off, Blaze said, "When I moved from Denver, my foster family died in a car accident. I'd left the car. I had nothing to do with it.

"We'd already crossed two state lines. No one knew about my connection, I sort of vanished." Blaze looked at Kathy. "That's why no one ever met my parents. I lived alone. Darrell never even knew."

"Blaze, you've been through so much," Kathy said. "I know you couldn't hurt anyone."

"For God's sake, Kathy, make up your mind. Do you think it's me then?" Jack asked, waving the gun barrel around, his thumb still on the hammer, making her nervous. He ran his free hand through his hair. One section remained standing in a dark tangle.

"Thanks for believing in me, Kathy," Blaze said. "Jack, of course she doesn't think it's you." He shrugged. "It's probably not, either."

She strode over to Jack, gently lowered his gun arm to the table, and gazed down into his dark eyes. She reached over and smoothed his wild strand of hair. "I love you too much. I know it's not Blaze, or you."

"But—"

"Sh." She pushed back another stray hair that had fallen onto his forehead.

Blaze's chair crashed to the floor and he dived for the gun. Jack yanked his hand away. The gun went off; the bullet going into the table and floor. Jack jumped up and leveled the barrel at Blaze's face.

Kathy watched in horror. Jack cocked the gun again and held the hammer back with his thumb.

"No!" Kathy screamed.

Blaze held up both hands. "Can't blame a guy for trying." He looked at the hole in the table. "Sorry. Stop pointing that thing at me."

"Sit down," Jack said. "Don't try that again. This gun has a hair-trigger. No more accidents."

Blaze settled back down in his chair. Kathy placed her hand over her heart, feeling it racing. "Blaze, please don't do that again. Promise me."

"But, Kathy..."

She stared, wide-eyed at him.

"Okay, I won't."

"Oh, God." Kathy inhaled deeply. "My heart's going to explode. Jack, watch the trigger." His hand quivered slightly.

Slowly she lowered her hand as the pounding in her chest slowed, and gently rested her fingers on his gun arm. As he gazed into her eyes, she said, "I know you're not sure about each other, but I am. That's why you're at each other's throats all the time. Blaze, fired by jealousy and fear of losing a family. You, afraid he wanted to burn us."

Jack lowered the hammer. His Adam's apple bobbed up and down. "Guess I was a bit jealous, too," he said.

"You, jealous of me?" Blaze asked. "What on earth for?"

"You love Kathy a little more than like a brother."

"But—"

"Maybe not now," Jack said. "You two share something she and I never will. You understand her moods better."

Kathy stroked her husband's face. "I love you, no one else."

"At first, I did love her more than like a sister." Blaze coughed. "But she only had that kind of love for you."

"Yeah, I kind of figured the way you looked at her," Jack said.

Kathy knew this was hard for him. Jack slid back into his chair, keeping the gun closer to his body, and resting his thumb on the hammer. He pointed the barrel at Blaze.

"You still think it's Blaze?" Kathy asked as she sat down next to her husband.

"Who else could it be?" he asked.

"What about those initials?" Kathy asked, digging through the forms on the table.

"What initials?" Blaze questioned.

"These," Kathy said, holding up an insurance form and pointing. "I was about to ask you about them when Jack came in."

"Those initials on the bottom of your insurance forms," Jack said. "They're always there. I assumed they were your secretary's. Remember Roberta Nesselbaum?"

"Yeah, my secretary in Colorado. I haven't thought of her for a while."

"Who's your secretary now?"

"Nancy Ingram. Why?"

"The initials R.N. appear on every one of your forms." Jack reached down and grabbed a different form off the table and handed it across. "Aren't they your secretary's?"

Blaze studied the sheet, fidgeting in his seat. "No. You're talking about my boss, Richard Newman. He took a keen interest in me. Newman's my mentor. He made sure I did well in the business."

"Your boss?" Jack asked.

"Yeah. He checks up on me. Each time I moved, well, most of the time he suggested I relocate. Anyway, Richard insisted on remaining my boss, no matter where I went. I report to him."

"Richard Newman?" Kathy asked. She leaned over and studied the insurance form.

"Yeah, why?" Blaze asked. "Do you know him?"

She looked to Blaze, then back to Jack, and blinked several times. "I'm sure... Well, it has to be a different Richard Newman."

"What do you mean?" Jack asked as he laid the gun on its side, but his knuckles still looked white.

"Well," she said, "I used to date a Richard Newman before I dated you. I'm sure it's not the same person. Richard couldn't have anything to do with these fires, could he?" Kathy placed a stray hair behind her ear. Both men stared at her with open mouths. She chewed on her bottom lip.

"Does Newman ever ask about Kathy or me?" Jack asked.

"Yes, as a matter of fact," Blaze said, and cleared his throat. "But I never realized he was acquainted with you personally. He knew about my closeness to Kathy. Always asked me how you were doing and where and what you were up to."

"And you told him?" Jack asked.

"Of course. Why wouldn't I? Didn't understand he knew either one of you." Blaze turned to Kathy. "Before Jack, I never paid attention to the guys you dated. Besides, weren't you seeing some guy named Dick Mann?"

Kathy laughed. "I forgot Darrell nicknamed him that. I could never get Darrell to quit calling him, 'the Dick Man.' Don't think he liked him very much."

"Darrell didn't like any guy you dated."

"He liked Jack," Kathy said. She felt a twinge of sadness.

"No..." Blaze coughed, and then said, "Anyway, Richard never told me he'd dated you. He said any family of mine, he'd like hearing about." Blaze hesitated.

"What?" Jack asked.

"Well, he did insist on anonymity. Didn't want me to discuss him with anyone. Said it would affect our working relationship. It'd be our secret."

"You didn't find that odd?"

"Are you kidding? Newman makes six figures or more, and he's very high up in the company. I'll overlook weirdness if the man can make me rich."

Jack released his grip on the gun handle and drummed his fingers on the table.

"Well, how was I supposed to know?" Blaze asked. "Besides, Newman lives in Illinois where the corporate insurance office is. How could he be involved?"

Kathy turned to Jack and asked, "Why would my old boyfriend set fires, trying to scare or burn me?"

"Good question."

Kathy cringed and bit her lip. If Richard turned out to be the arsonist, then Jack and Blaze were totally innocent. She hated Jack's vacant look—lost deep in thought. She shuddered.

"Blaze, where was your boss last night?" Jack finally asked. "Do you know?"

Blaze's face paled. "In Carsonville," he whispered. "He came out to check on me."

"When?" Kathy asked.

"He flew out yesterday morning."

Jack leaned forward. "Is he still here or did he leave last night?"

"He had an early flight this morning," Blaze said. "I can call Illinois. See if he's back."

"You didn't see him this morning?" Kathy asked.

"No."

"Is that usual?" she asked.

"Sometimes he doesn't see me the next morning." Blaze rubbed his chin. "Come to think about it, guess he does that quite a bit. I offer to buy breakfast or take him to the airport, but he says it's too early. Not to bother."

Kathy glanced at Jack and then turned back to Blaze. "Think real hard. This is important," she said. "What about the other fires? Was he near you?"

CHAPTER 33

I hunch down on the seat on the passenger side, peer at the house, and avoid the unmarked police car by parking several cars behind it.

Before long, another car with two men in suits turns the corner and pulls up alongside the already parked vehicle. The men roll down their windows, speak to one another, and a few minutes later, both cars speed away.

I laugh. The police think the arsonist has already entered the house they watch and that they won't have to worry about tonight. That Detective Burns, the arrogant buffoon, is wrong—they're all wrong.

I whack the dashboard when I think about Kathleen's betrayal—she married that firefighter.

The gunshot sounds loud over my speakers. If I wasn't listening to their conversation, I might have been afraid that Kathleen was shot.

Too bad the cops left. Might have been interesting to see what happened if they'd stuck around and heard that shot.

After several deep breaths, my heart rate lessens, and I eye the house once again. Patience. Let them talk, have their last meal.

Let them stay together.

Die together.

She wants her own family. I have to stop that!

I'm clever, careful.

This moment has traveled through my mind in many different scenarios for so long. This chase will end today. The sound of my heart pounds in my ears. A lump in my throat threatens to block my breathing. Slow down. More deep breaths.

The neighbor in the green two-story glances out the window. Too long in one spot. Scooting over into the driver's seat, I turn on the engine, shift into gear, and drive around the block to park on the side street.

Just as I turn the corner, I glance in my rearview mirror. A car pulls up and parks next to the curb a couple of houses down the block from the Hillmans'. No one gets out.

Well, well, well. Detective Burns isn't so dumb after all. The good detective sent someone back to watch the house. That makes my job more difficult, but not impossible. I'll just have to take more precautions. I can still get inside without anyone seeing me.

My heart races thinking about the future rendezvous with my victims.

Calm down!

No mistakes, not now.

CHAPTER 34

Kathy stroked Sheba as the cat now sat next to her, twitching its tail. Jack drummed his fingers on the tabletop, while Blaze pondered whether Richard Newman had been around during the last fire or any others. Little beads of sweat popped out on Blaze's forehead.

"Richard's been out to visit me here quite a bit," he said. "On those specific nights, maybe. There've been too many—too much time."

"In Carsonville, last week, when Dr. Graves's home burned?" Jack asked.

"Yes," Blaze nodded. "I think so, but Richard couldn't be involved. I'm just not sure about any of the others."

"Think. It's important."

"I know it's important!"

The tabby jumped up at the sound of Blaze's voice.

Blaze tapped on the form in front of him while he stared off into space.

Kathy squirmed in her seat. "Why don't you look at your calendar?"

"He never let me know when he was coming, so I wouldn't have it written down. No," Blaze said, sighing. "Can't place Richard at all of the fires. Maybe some." His face looked like he'd lost his best friend. "I'm not sure. Of course, he could have been there and not checked in with me."

"And you never made the connection?" Jack asked.

"Why should I? I didn't know he even knew Kathy."

She rubbed her forehead and bit her lip. Her stomach rumbled, feeling like she'd eaten plain yogurt that had turned sour.

"Why Richard?" she asked.

"Jealous?" Jack rubbed his chin.

"We dated a long time ago. He took it well when we broke up and I told him about you. He was happy for me."

"Maybe not. Maybe he held a grudge." Jack reached across the table and snatched the form from underneath Blaze's tapping fingers. He brandished the paper. "How'd I overlook this?"

"You didn't," Blaze said. "You've asked me several times about my secretaries. I've had Roberta Nesselbaum, Rachel Nelson, Rene Niederhoff." He stopped talking for a minute, and scrunched his eyebrows together. "I guess when you think about it, Richard picked all my secretaries with initials R.N."

"Richard hired all of them?" Kathy asked, wondering why a boss would do that.

Jack ran his hand through his hair. "I can't believe it."

"Usually he hired my secretaries," Blaze nodded and continued, "except this time. Her name's Nancy Ingram. I hired her." He leaned forward. "Come to think of it, he got upset, but she's a great secretary."

"Can you call and see if Richard's at the office?" Kathy asked. "Think of a reason to check on the other fires." She couldn't believe Richard might be the answer they searched for.

Blaze turned around and looked at the wall clock. Out in the hallway, the old grandfather clock bonged the half-hour loud and clear as if laughing at them. "It's too late," he said. "Office is closed. Time difference. Doubt anyone would be around."

"Well, we have to do something," Kathy pleaded.

"I could call his home." Blaze got out his cell phone. "Jack, do you have the dates?"

"They should be here somewhere in these papers," Kathy said as she shuffled them around.

Jack helped sort through the reports and handed Blaze a stack. "These are dates to check on."

"What do you think about Newman hiring Blaze's secretaries," Kathy asked. "All with Richard's initials. Was it a coincidence?"

"I don't believe in coincidences," Jack said.

"If Richard's not the arsonist—"

"Kathy, let's wait and see." Jack rubbed his temples.

Blaze flipped to the back of his black book and punched in a number.

While he talked on the phone, Jack said, "I should have checked on these initials."

"You did," Kathy said.

"Not far enough. I'm smarter than that. Should have picked up on them in the reports."

"Jack," Kathy said, squeezing his hand, she held it tight. "These fires are not your fault. You couldn't have stopped them."

Blaze shut his phone and said, "Edith Tussey, Richard's housekeeper, said she's not sure when he'll be in. Said he'd called and been delayed. He should be back later this evening or early morning. Also said this was the second inquiry about her boss."

"Lovell was curious about this R.N. Bet he called after I left." Jack stared at the form in his hand, and then crumpled it slowly, balling it into his fist.

"So Richard might still be here in Carsonville," Kathy said. "At least we know it's none of us." She grasped Jack's arm and rested her head on his shoulder.

"Maybe I better call and cancel my next appointment." Blaze opened his cell again.

"Probably a good idea," Jack said. "I have several more questions I'd like answers to. We should go over them now."

When Blaze finished his call, Kathy pushed back her chair and got up. "I don't know about you two, but I'm getting hungry. Let's fix something to eat." At the refrigerator, she opened the door and pulled out a flank steak. She gave Blaze a package of lettuce, horseradish, and some feta cheese to crumble over a salad.

"Maybe I should call Farley," Jack said.

"Shouldn't we gather some more information first?" Kathy asked.

"Okay," Jack said. "I'll ask questions while we fix dinner." He stood, put the gun in his pants, and handed Blaze the cheese grater.

Kathy retrieved four ears of corn, put on a pan of water, and shucked the husks.

While Jack took out dishes and silverware, he asked, "This Richard Newman, does he talk about his past?"

"No," Blaze said. "He's pretty closed-mouth about himself. Asks all kinds of questions about me, but doesn't say much about himself."

Kathy and Blaze put together the food while Jack set the table. The kitchen filled with the pungent odor of feta cheese mingling with fresh acidic tomato smells and strong burning horseradish. Kathy's stomach grumbled. She was hungry, but hungrier for information rather than food.

Jack and she asked Blaze questions and received answers. He answered one of the questions about Richard, and then Jack said, "I don't know. Something about all of this just doesn't sound right."

Does Jack still believe Blaze is the arsonist? Kathy wondered. What was it about Blaze that kept him suspicious? His perfect answers for everything? The way he looked at Kathy? Or was her husband just jealous and secretly hoped it was Blaze? She hated those thoughts, but they kept popping into her mind.

"He's never been married," Blaze said. "Never found the right girl. Richard told me, 'I'm still trying them all out, if you know what I mean.'"

"I guess it's possible he never got over Kathy," Jack said.

"Oh, we weren't in love," she said. "After I met you that was it. Richard and I just weren't that serious about each other."

"Maybe he was more serious than you thought," Jack said as he watched Blaze.

What was he looking for? Kathy wondered. None of Blaze's expressions changed. Was he telling everything he knew?

"I really don't know how he felt about her," Blaze said. "Like I told you before, he never let on he'd known Kathy."

"That sounds suspicious." Kathy tilted her head. "Didn't you know where he came from?"

"Kathy's right," Jack said. "How could you be that close to your boss and not know something more about him? Even if the man didn't talk about himself... Doesn't ring quite true with me."

"Well it is." Blaze wiped sweat from his brow. "I don't know where he was born. I did ask him one time. But, when I asked, he just said, 'Everywhere.' One day I pressed him further and he said, 'It's none of your business.'"

"You didn't find that odd?" Kathy asked.

Blaze swallowed. He reminded Kathy of a little kid caught opening a present before he was supposed to. "Some guys don't like to talk about personal stuff," he said

"What about when he sent you to work near us?" Jack asked.

"How many times do I have to say it, sometimes I moved before you did. The orders always came from Corporate."

"Isn't that where he works?"

"Well, yes, but—"

"But, what?" Jack asked.

"I didn't think he had that much clout. I mentioned it once. Richard just said, 'You're a lucky man.' He told me he didn't have anything to do with it."

"And you believed him?"

"Sorry," Blaze said, grinning. "I felt too lucky to complain. I wanted to be near Kathy."

"And Richard just happens to be in the same town when there's a fire," Jack said.

"You're the expert." Kathy placed a hand on her hip. "Does Richard fit the profile?"

"Has he ever been arrested that you know of?" Jack asked.

"No," Blaze said. "I doubt it, unless it happened before Edith. His housekeeper is a blabbermouth. We've become close over the years. She kind of mothers me. I think she would have mentioned it."

Jack ran his hand through his hair, a nasty habit Kathy didn't like. He saw her staring and reached down and rubbed his neck. "Most arsonists have been in trouble before for petty crimes or something," he said. "He might not quite fit the profile, but that doesn't mean he couldn't be our maniac."

"I guess you don't remember him," Kathy muttered. "He showed up unexpectedly at our wedding."

"What?" Jack closed his eyes for a brief moment. Then he eyed Kathy. "And you never mentioned it."

"I didn't think it important. Remember Betty, from my college days? She had red hair and brought a date? Anyway, she told me later that he'd insisted that she bring him to our wedding. She liked him, so she was excited to be with him. She asked if it upset me, but why would I care? I married you, not him. I think I only danced with him once."

"You mean this guy crashed our wedding? Did he make a pass at you?" Jack asked.

"No, at least I don't think so. If he did, I don't remember. He wasn't important. Just an old friend."

"Farley will be interested in this," Jack said. "Maybe this will get Burns off my back."

"So you think Richard is our arsonist?" Kathy asked.

Jack shrugged. "Who knows?"

"Hey, Jack, don't study me that way," Blaze said. "I'm not your pyro!"

Kathy's nerves felt like cat gut on a newly strung tennis racket. Was Richard stalking them?

"You know, I bet Richard hasn't changed all that much. If he's been watching me, don't you think I'd have seen him at some point?"

"Hard to say," Jack said. "Not if he didn't want you to see him."

Every now and then, Jack made excuses to leave the kitchen. On one of his forays out, Kathy asked Blaze, "Do you know—"

"I've no idea what your husband's doing?"

Suddenly, Jack skidded into the kitchen, startling them, and rushed to the back window.

"What's going on?" Kathy asked.

"I thought I just saw my car. Couldn't be though because it's right where I parked it in the alley. Odd," Jack muttered, wiping the trickling sweat running from his brow.

"Not that odd in this town," Blaze said. "There are lots of old cars here in Carsonville."

"Yeah, but just like mine?"

Kathy had a nagging feeling at the nape of her neck. She remembered that day Allen had said he'd seen Jack's car when she thought he was at work. "Maybe someone else has a car like yours. Not impossible you know."

Blaze mumbled, "Isn't that what I just said." He returned his attention to his task of crumbling cheese for the flank steak salad. "Your car isn't that unique."

"True." Jack looked down.

The cat strolled over to Kathy and wove between her legs, purring loudly.

When the telephone rang, they all jumped. Jack started toward the phone. Kathy stood closest; she reached out and answered, "Hello?"

"Hi, Kathy. Everything okay at your place?" Captain Farley asked.

"Yes," Kathy said, "Everything is fine here. Thank you for not firing my husband. He's innocent you know."

"I think so too," Captain Farley said. "Is Mr. Zilence still with you?"

"Yes, he is, did you want to speak with him?"

Jack took a step closer. She shook her head, glancing at Blaze.

"No," the captain said. "Kathy, do you know a Richard Newman?"

She held up her hand as Blaze approached. "Yes, I do know a man by that name, Captain. We've just been discussing him. I dated a Richard Newman before I became involved with Jack."

"Hmmm, is Jack handy?"

Kathy held the receiver out toward her husband. "He wants to speak with you."

"Yes, Cap?" Jack questioned.

After he listened a minute, he said, "Yes, and no, Cap. Not sure." Jack rubbed the back of his neck. "Did you find out anything on Newman?"

Jack listened. "That's about what we've come up with here. Except, Kathy says they parted friends. I don't think he quite fits the profile. I have no motive."

Kathy kept a close eye on Jack. He smiled, then asked, "You think he's still here... What do you mean you can't find him?"

She gasped. Blaze walked over and stood next to her.

"So you say he hasn't gone back to Illinois. The local airport can't verify his departure. Too many private planes. Maybe he was a passenger on one of them?"

"That doesn't sound good," Kathy said.

Jack shook his head and smiled.

Was he trying to reassure her? she wondered.

Then he said, "Well, you all keep trying to locate Newman. I can't help Burns still thinks I'm the arsonist. I don't think we'll have to worry about a fire tonight."

Jack listened for some moments, and then said, "Hopefully you'll have a complete report on this Newman by tomorrow morning. I'll come in early. Thanks, Cap."

He hung up and put down the plate he'd gripped in his hand during the conversation.

"Well?" Kathy asked, staring at him with both hands on her hips.

"Well, nothing. They can't locate Bradley's boss. I have to go in early tomorrow morning."

"Maybe I should spend the night," Blaze suggested.

"What a great idea." Kathy beamed. Turning to her husband, she asked, "Please?"

"Sounds fine to me," Jack said. "Let's eat, I'm starved."

CHAPTER 35

Hours later, Kathy grew tired of answering and listening to Blaze's answers from Jack's grilling questions about Lisa Moore and Richard Newman.

She yawned. "Jack, can your interrogation of poor Blaze and me please stop?"

"I know it was a long time ago, but—"

"Look, I haven't seen Richard since the day of our wedding. I don't know about you two," Kathy said, stretching her arms over her head, "but I'm beat. I can't keep my eyes open." She yawned again. "I'm going up to bed."

"Good idea." Blaze followed Kathy from the room and up the stairs. Halfway, he stopped abruptly and snapped his fingers. "Wait. I forgot. While I searched through my calendar, I remembered your anniversary. I'd marked it in red. Happy Fifth Anniversary, you two. Hard to believe five years have passed so quickly."

Kathy froze in mid-stride and spun around. "How could I have forgotten?" Looking down at Jack, she gripped the banister until her hands felt cold.

Her husband stood at the bottom of the stairs and looked up. From the look on his face, he'd forgotten, too.

Blaze glanced over his shoulder toward Jack, turned, and gazed up grinning at Kathy. "So, guess I'm the only one here who's remembered your anniversary." He walked up the stairs and kissed Kathy on the cheek. "Good night."

He hummed the tune to "The Anniversary Waltz," and strode on up to the guestroom. The door closed with a soft click behind him.

Kathy plopped down onto the step, gaping at Jack. "I can't believe I didn't remember." She held up both hands. "No, don't say one word. After what happened with Joanna, then Allen, it's no wonder we forgot about our anniversary. I'll fix a special dinner tomorrow."

"Okay," Jack said, beginning the climb up the steps.

Kathy pulled herself up and trudged to the top. She felt heavy, as if she grew older with each step. At the hallway, she looked to the right toward the closed guestroom door.

Jack caught up to her and clasped her hand.

"You don't think it's him, do you?" Kathy whispered.

"Unfortunately, I've always had my doubts about Bradley. But, for your sake, I hope it's not him."

"Thank you." Kathy pulled Jack's hand to encourage him to walk to the bedroom. She caught him limping slightly. His leg must be bothering him.

When Jack rubbed his temple, she figured he must have one of his stress headaches. They came on him more frequently.

As they entered their bedroom, Jack said, "You don't think I forgot on purpose?"

"No, of course not." Kathy smiled.

"All our terror began on this day," Jack said, "or did it actually start a year later, with Darrell?"

Kathy couldn't answer him. She wanted to rid herself of the awful memories. "Wonder where Sheba is?"

"She'll show up soon," Jack said as he stood in the middle of the room.

Kathy undressed, put on her negligee and climbed into bed. "Coming?"

Jack walked over to the nightstand and put the gun in the drawer.

"Aren't you going to unload it?"

"Not tonight."

Kathy nodded, not liking the idea, but Jack was right. She felt cold, uneasy, like she'd forgotten something.

Jack took off his shoes and stripped down. "I'm going to take a shower."

While Jack was in the bathroom, Kathy threw back the covers, crept down the hallway beyond the nursery and stopped in front of Blaze's door. Snores erupted from behind it. She inched the door open a crack and peered in. More heavy breathing and lips sputtering came from within. Convinced he slept, Kathy eased the door closed and came back, going into her soon-to-be baby's room.

She reminisced about Richard Newman. Was being jilted motive enough? She wrestled with the idea of the arsonist being Richard. Jack believed it might be Blaze. He had burned before, followed them, and he'd been jealous. But now he had a girlfriend. Lisa Moore.

What is going on with me? Blaze is not the arsonist. He wouldn't hurt anyone.

Moonlight shone through the windows of the nursery and Kathy found her way around the house with ease.

She walked over to the locked bedroom window and stared out. As she turned to leave, the eerie glow of the moonbeams haloed the room and reflected off one of the Cougar family pictures setting on the old brown dresser.

The photo gave her some comfort as she caressed it with her thumb. Pushing away the intruding memories of her wedding night and the following year, she put the picture back down on top of her meticulously drawn plans for the baby's room.

Satisfied the nursery was secure, she walked out and checked the bathroom. A tingling sensation in her neck irritated her.

She hurried downstairs. Sheba dashed past her and bounded down the stairs. *Guess the cat figures I can't do this without her.*

Passing through the kitchen, the timer ticked on the coffee pot, drumming out a beat like a funeral march. A lingering aroma of the fresh-ground Java and Hickory coffee beans filled her nostrils.

Kathy took a breath, and checked in the laundry room alcove, spotting her permanent note taped on the dryer to clean the lint trap after each load. Jack, usually conscientious about fire, always forgot the lint. *Strange,* she thought, *for a fire person.*

She grabbed the flashlight off the wall, wishing one of these days Jack would get the basement light fixture to work. She slowly opened the door, and after stepping onto the landing, quietly shut the door behind her. With the beam focused on the steps to prevent a fall, she crept down into the dark room.

The cat brushed her leg. Kathy flinched, barely breathing. Her hand trembled as she illuminated the area with the flashlight. The beam wavered and jumped across the nooks and crannies of the basement. Her hand ached from gripping the heavy torch. Her heart hammered in her chest, but she needed to see, to be certain. Steady, she admonished herself. She swung the beam past the heater and along the side wall where Jack built his workbench—nothing out of the ordinary.

She edged a few feet closer and outlined the window above his tools.

"Oh, no," she whispered, placing her hand over her mouth, eyes wide open. She stepped back.

Sheba yowled.

Kathy stared at the slightly open window and felt chilled. For the first time in her life, she thought about guns. *Why didn't I carry Jack's with me?*

CHAPTER 36

I sit in my car and watch as one by one, the lights on the block blink out. One light upstairs in Kathleen's house still defies darkness to enter. A slight cool breeze drifts through my open window. The pulp mill's acrid odor reminds me that soon I'll leave this town and this dreadful stench. Muffled blasts from the distant foghorn interrupt the stillness of the night. It's only announcing the fog is creeping in and covering the city with its eerie gray mist. Covering me and what I must do. My heart races.

I shake my head. Kathleen still loves Victorian homes, which pleases me—they're easy to enter, easy to ignite.

The light upstairs flicks off.

My watch alarm sounds at midnight. The house stands silent. I flip off the toggle switch and picture the layout of each room.

Kathleen never recognized me when I worked on the repairs. Before I finished the job, I found her lingerie. A faint odor of lilac lingered in the drawer—I couldn't resist the red lace panties and snatched them. My memento of Kathleen.

Blaze said the bedroom next to the master suite will be turned into the nursery. The room to the right of the carpeted stairs was the guestroom. Too bad neither Kathy nor Jack had any family left to enjoy it. Even friends desert them like embers popping from a fire.

My head spins with all that I want to do to her. I've outsmarted her and the great firefighter/arson investigator! I'm too clever. No clues, no photos, and no suspect.

Perfect.

No one knows I exist, and I'll keep it that way. I've set up a diversion to protect myself—another arson fire. It will look like my work, which it is, and will send the officer who guards Kathleen's house across town.

I check the street. No one lurks about. No cars drive by. I slip into my gloves and take a bottle of liquid from the glove box, safely placing it in my pocket. I grab a paper bag on the floor and leave my car. From inside the trunk, I remove the gas cans and creep through the thickening fog down the alley.

Near the garage, I set down the cans. Then I slither behind some bushes, working my way toward the street until I can see the unmarked cop car parked out front.

The lights on the car flash on, the engine starts, the officer peels out and squeals around the corner. Right on time.

I scan the neighborhood again. No one. I inch back to the alley, pick up the cans and walk toward Kathleen's garage.

The bulldog darts out from behind a garbage can further up the alley, spots me, and lopes toward me. I open the paper bag, whip out the steak, and whistle softly. The mutt halts, sniffs, and wags. Stupid dog. I toss the meat and he catches it between his strong jaws, and trots over near the fence to chew his snack. The dog keeps a watchful eye on me.

A few minutes later, I hear only snores.

The plastic garbage can works as my stile and I'm over the fence and hurry across the yard. After casing the windows, I jimmy one with an old latch, slip in, and rush to the back door to turn off the alarm code.

I tilt my head, listening. What's that noise? I freeze into a dusky shadow for several seconds. Nothing. Hearing nothing more, I creep across the kitchen floor and out into the hallway near the stairs. I must find Sheba.

The idea of killing an innocent animal sends shivers through my body. I'll make sure the tabby is safely outside. I shudder at the thought of that poor defenseless creature dying.

At the bottom of the carpeted stairs, I grip the two gas cans. This will be my last Victorian.

I smile, turn, and take the stairs one at a time. My foot lifts high over the nasty squeaky step.

I set the gas cans down by the railing and listen. A loud snore breaks the stillness.

I feel only slight remorse about Blaze. My heart pounds. I can hardly wait to see Kathleen's face when she recognizes me. That look will be worth the long wait. Jack is going to be surprised, too. A pity Blaze will never know, but then he's always been a sound sleeper.

I nudge open the guestroom door. A night light barely illuminates the shape beneath the quilt. Another loud snore freezes me.

With the handkerchief and chloroform from my pocket in hand, I tiptoe into the room. Hovering over Blaze, I pour some liquid onto the cloth and gently cover his nose. Blaze will never know what happened.

CHAPTER 37

Kathy stared at the open basement window. *God, my hand is shaking so bad, I can't keep the beam steady. Get a grip!* Jack told her how he felt when he entered a fire—unsure if it might back draft, flare back at him. Why hadn't she insisted he check the house? Jack, and his gun.

She listened intently, not hearing any running water. Jack must be out of the shower. Would he come look for her?

The flashlight beam danced over the window sill and surrounding areas.

She saw no evidence anyone had come through the opening. Her lip ached from chewing on it too hard. She gathered her courage, climbed onto the bench and locked the window. When she touched it, no alarm blasted. She couldn't remember if the window was alarmed. The company had put in wires, motion sensors, and stickers, but some were dummies. Jack would know.

The house groaned. Kathy cringed. After a sharp inhale of her breath, she thought she heard something. Sounded like someone walking around upstairs.

Sheba strolled past the still shaking flashlight beam and sniffed at a box marked "old photos." Then the tabby brushed up against Kathy's leg again. A shiver ran through her body. *Quit it! It's just freezing down here.* Cold from the cement floor seeped into Kathy's bare feet. The house groaned again and her gut knotted. The cat mewled.

Something was wrong.

Very wrong.

At the bottom of the basement stairs, Kathy's dread grew as she listened to the sounds from the house. The creaky noises sounded different—not like the normal cooling of the house. The hairs on the back of her neck stood at attention—like Sheba's. But unlike the cat, Kathy felt her heartbeat thump out of rhythm. She took two steps and froze in mid-stride, dangling one foot over the third step. What were those sounds? She put her foot down slowly. Petrified.

Sheba darted past, bounded up the stairs, and would have to wait at the top by the door. The flashlight beam traced each stair step and Kathy finally found the tabby, the light illuminating her yellow eyes. *Sheba isn't afraid.* Kathy crept up step by step, listening.

She switched off the light and inched the door open. The cat's tail twitched, hitting her leg. When the door opened enough, Sheba raced through and disappeared. Kathy held her breath. Was that muffled voices?

She gripped the flashlight like a weapon and glanced toward the back door. The alarm glowed green! Could someone be in the house? She crossed the kitchen, eased through the swinging door, scurried along the hall, and took the stairs, walking on the edges so none would creak.

She strained to hear, her gaze glued to the master bedroom door. It stood ajar with light filtering through the crack. The lights had been off when she'd left. Had Blaze awakened, walked down the hall, and was now in the room with Jack?

She looked right. Blaze's door stood open.

Muffled voices drifted toward her from the direction of the master bedroom, then nothing.

When she heard the voices, she increased her pace and forgot to step over the third step from the top. Its loud creak broke the eerie stillness. Kathy stopped and listened.

Silence.

While staring at the door opening, she tiptoed to the top of the stairs. A faint gasoline odor wafted by her nose. She froze. By the railing, she spotted two gas cans. Alarm bells blared in her head. Before she could back down the steps, a familiar voice boomed out, "If you don't want Jack hurt, come in, Kathleen!"

She slowly walked forward and peeked through the crack. Kathy couldn't catch her breath.

Jack sat on top of the comforter, naked and still wet, trussed up like a calf at a rodeo. A red bandanna had been stuffed in his mouth.

The man, dressed in black Levi's, a black T-shirt, and a baseball cap, held Jack's gun to her husband's head.

"Come on in, Kathleen. Don't be shy. We've been waiting for you."

Using the flashlight, Kathy shoved open the door and focused on Jack.

Then, she studied the man. "You? It's not possible."

"Have a seat. I'll tell you all about it." Pointing the revolver at Kathy, he said, "Be good and drop the flashlight."

Kathy recognized the voice, but still couldn't believe her eyes. She gripped the handle of the mag-light tighter and thought about using it as a weapon. She took a step forward.

"Don't." The man aimed the gun at Jack's head again.

Kathy stared at the gun—of all the times to leave it loaded. If Jack had only followed her rules, maybe she could have rushed in. She started to take another step.

The man cocked the hammer. Jack's eyes widened and he shook his head.

Kathy held up her hand. "No, Jack says it has a hair trigger. Look!" She released her grip. The flashlight fell to the carpeted floor with a dull thud.

"Move over to the bed."

Kathy walked toward Jack's side.

"Stop. Nice try." He motioned with the gun and said, "Other side."

When Kathy reached the other side of the king-sized bed, the man told her to sit down and put her hands behind her back. With one hand pointing the gun at Kathy, he used his other hand to wind a rope around her feet. Then he pushed her over, bound her hands and rolled her back over.

She turned to Jack and said, "I'm so sorry." He blinked and nodded.

Kathy glanced toward the doorway, hoping Blaze would rush to their rescue. Only Sheba appeared and sat down, tail flicking from side to side.

The man propped Kathy back against the headboard and stuffed a red bandana in her mouth. "Now that I have your undivided attention, and Blaze won't be bothering us, I'll explain what I've been doing for the last few years." He un-cocked the hammer on the revolver and flashed an alligator smile. "Aside from burning houses and chasing after you, Kathleen."

CHAPTER 38

Kathy couldn't stop staring at this man. *He can't be the arsonist!* Her night terror continued no matter how many times she opened and shut her eyes.

This is not happening! Her heart pounded so loud it hurt her ears. Her mouth tasted like she'd swallowed sand.

She squeezed her eyes tight and then opened them one more time. Jack—still trussed up along side of her; the man standing before her—not a ghost. This was no dream. No night terror. This man had loved her. She'd loved him. They'd been so close. At one point, they'd been inseparable. How could he be doing this to her?

She studied his features. His face mirrored hers. A blond ponytail stuck out through a baseball cap with the letter "D" embroidered on it. No scars. Darrell had burned in a fire.

"Kathleen, are you listening to me?" Darrell asked.

She jerked when he poked her in the stomach. "Ah, I see that got your attention. Now, big sister, pay attention. You do want to know why and how, don't you?" Darrell leered at her.

He dragged the rocking chair over closer to her side of the bed, plopped down, and rocked back and forth, back and forth. He drummed his fingers on the wood arm rest. "Well, let's see. First, I should tell you I've always loved you very much."

Kathy nodded.

Darrell continued rocking.

"Sure, you loved me," he agreed, waving Jack's gun from side to side in a haphazard motion. "But only like a brother. My love's more than that."

Kathy stopped nodding. She opened her eyes so wide, they ached from staring. Her stomach flip-flopped. Nausea threatened to overcome her. With her eyebrows scrunched together, she turned slowly to face Jack.

"Don't look at him!" Darrell jumped up, grabbed her chin and whipped it around. "He doesn't know anything. Pay attention to me, for a change."

When the mattress shifted, Kathy knew Jack was trying something. Darrell leveled the gun toward him. "No!" The movement stopped.

Tears spilled over and ran down her cheeks. She moaned, shaking her head from side to side, and searching her brother's wild eyes. She didn't know this person. She cocked her head and studied him. *Maybe this really isn't my brother, just someone who looks like him. My God, how could he have lived through that fire? Why didn't he contact me? What happened to him?*

"Alligator tears," Darrell said. "You think those will melt my heart and make me change my mind?

"Well, forget it!" Darrell's eyes rolled in their sockets. He looked like a madman. "Stop crying. Won't do you any good. Now, where was I? Oh, yes, telling you how much I loved you." He settled back into the chair and rocked.

"Those stupid high school girls. Only you knew me."

Darrell was right, crying wouldn't help. Kathy needed to figure out what she could do. She half-listened to Darrell's rant.

"You promised you'd always be there for me," Darrell said. "We had fun together, but then you ruined it. With him. Why?"

Kathy tried to answer. The bandanna stuffed into her mouth kept her utterances to a low mumble.

Sweat trickled down Darrell's brow. He wiped it away and held up his hand. "No, don't try to explain, just listen. When Jack came into the picture, you didn't have time for me. My world crumbled." He lowered his hand and gripped the armrest until his knuckles turned white. His rocking pace increased.

Kathy shook her head. Her hair whipped about her face. She wanted to tell him, "No, that's not true."

Darrell raved on. "Jack ruined our relationship. Bad enough that Blaze had a crush on you." One side of his mouth drooped. He looked annoyed. "Poor guy, you treated him like another brother."

Kathy nodded.

"But I'm your brother! I loved you more than anyone could.

"I told Mom and Dad you shouldn't marry Jack. They didn't understand—guess they loved him, too. I even suckered poor Blaze into talking to them about it." Darrell laughed. "They thought Blaze's concern came from jealousy. Never knew about me. But you married him anyway."

Darrell stopped rocking and pointed the gun at Jack's forehead. "Pow," he said.

Kathy gasped and threw herself across her husband.

Darrell jumped up and leaned over the bed. He put his hand behind her neck and yanked Kathy up. "Do that again, and I will shoot him. Do you hear me?" His wild gaze darted back and forth between Jack and her.

She nodded emphatically, afraid to look at Jack again. Darrell pulled her over to the edge of the bed. I have to save Jack and the baby. Kathy thought hard about how to do this, but no plan formed. Her mind felt like in a haze. She wanted out of this terror.

"Don't worry, Kathleen. I'm not going to shoot anybody." Darrell smoothed her hair. "I couldn't shoot you. Did you know your eyes turn a different shade of blue when you're scared?"

He ran his fingers down her cheek tenderly, wiping away her tears. "Listen to me. Aren't you interested?"

He popped his finger in his mouth. She cringed. He wore latex gloves. Fear sent uncontrollable shaking through her body. She took a deep calming yoga breath, but all the taped screams reverberated through her mind.

"Now, let's see?" Darrell patted the barrel against his cheek and sat back in the rocker. "Oh, yes, you married Jack and ruined everything," he whined, increasing the chair's pace back and forth. "Mom and Dad died because of you."

What did that mean? Kathy studied her brother and moaned. Memoires of that horrible night rushed her. Was it Darrell?

"That got your attention, didn't it, Sis? I loved that old house. You were supposed to stay home with him." Again he waved the gun toward Jack, and continued. "Mom and Dad should have been at the motel." He stopped the rocker, cocking his head. "Your plans changed. You should have told me!" His voice hardened. He pushed off with his toes and wild rocking started.

Kathy shut her eyelids tight. More tears leaked down her cheeks. Then, she opened her eyes wide. She took such a deep breath; it broke the eerie silence and she almost sucked the cloth down her throat, gagging.

Darrell sprang from the rocker, leaned her forward, and patted her on the back. He pulled the bandana part way out. "Oh, no. You can't die on me this way."

When she quit choking, Darrell sat back down. Kathy squeezed her eyes closed. *My brother killed our parents.*

"That was my first fire." Darrell smiled. "Since you'd married a firefighter, you had to die that way, too. But you even screwed that up!"

Jack groaned, but Kathy didn't dare look at him.

Bile rose in her throat. She fought it down and pictured the baby. *I have to get out of this!* She wriggled her wrists, trying to loosen the binding.

"Mom and Dad suffered for it." Darrell wagged the gun at her. "You should have heard their screams. They should have been your screams. That's who I thought I was listening to."

His face contorted. He rocked harder.

"After your wedding reception, Blaze poured me into bed. But, I sneaked out. Hid the gas cans behind the house. Should have checked on you, but didn't." He lifted one shoulder and sighed. "Anyway, I spilled gas all over the furniture and floors, and then lit the match." He looked at Jack. "I've learned a lot since then."

Darrell frowned, eyes clouded. "I stood and listened, thinking their screams were yours. I hurried back to where Blaze and I had stayed that night. Susan called, said our home was on fire. Blaze shook me until I opened my eyes. He thought I was sound asleep. When we rushed to the scene, Susan said it was Mom and Dad, and that you'd gone to the lake. How I've hated you for that.

"You were moving away with Jack, leaving me. You promised we'd always be together. You lied. You killed Mom and Dad. I had to pay you back."

Darrell's voice turned icy. He paused the rocker, planted his feet on the floor, and leaned slightly forward. "Mom and Dad didn't deserve to die.

He shrugged, settled back in the chair, and rocked again. Then, in a monotone, he said, "But they were there, and you weren't. Even Blaze hated Jack, because his obsession for you drove him crazy."

Darrell laughed at her husband. "Because of that, you always believed Blaze, or should I say, *Bradley,* started the fires. Very funny."

A strange sound emanated from Darrell's throat; Kathy realized he was giggling. This man could not be her brother. He stopped the chair's motion. "But Blaze only burned his family."

Kathy glanced at Jack. With his furrowed brow he looked as confused to hear that as she. Blaze had said he'd never told anyone. Kathy tilted her head. How did Darrell know?

"Oh, don't look at me like that. Blaze never told me. I found that out after 'I died.'"

At the mention of his death, Kathy raised her eyebrows. She wanted to know about that. She'd felt so devastated at the loss of first, her parents, then her brother. *How could he have done this to me? Himself?*

"Ah, I see by the look on your face you're curious about that, too. Well, I'm coming to that." Darrell pushed off and got the chair rocking again. He peered at his watch. "We have enough time.

"When I recovered from Mom and Dad's death, I wanted to hurt you." He gazed into her eyes. Drool ran down one corner of his mouth. "The best way—kill me off first." He rocked faster. "So, I picked the date." He smiled. "Nice touch, your first anniversary, huh. Found a derelict, and WHOOSH!"

He shrugged and stopped rocking. "Sis, you can't imagine what it's like going to your own funeral." He placed his hand over his heart. "It touched me how all of you grieved."

Kathy wanted to scream. She missed her brother so much and had felt so sick the day she'd buried him. And it wasn't him she'd buried. Who was in Darrell's grave?

He smiled, leaned forward in the rocker, and winked. "Thanks, Jack. I learned a lot about setting fires and fooling the arson investigator from you. Had you going in circles." Darrell sighed and settled into the chair again. The rocking increased in momentum.

"Loved the chase." His smile broadened. "Watching those Victorian homes burn... gives me a warm, fuzzy feeling."

How could her brother have turned into this monster?

"When I accidentally killed my first family," Darrell said, "I sat and listened to their screams. They reminded me of Mom and Dad. So I decided to capture those screams just for you, Kathleen. I didn't want to leave you out. Hope you enjoyed them. I did." He grinned like the psychotic killers on horror shows. She shivered.

She wanted to tell him how horrible those screams were. How wrong it was. *If only he would take the gag out, maybe I could reason with him. Get him help.*

Darrell stopped rocking. He scrunched his eyebrows together and his voice grew husky. "It's only fitting you go that way, too."

He glanced at his watch again, and stated casually, "Well, it's time, you know."

Kathy's muscles ached from clenching so tight. She chewed at the bandanna in her mouth and tried to work it out. If she could keep him talking, maybe she could work the gag free. Talk some sense into him. She'd always been able to talk to Darrell. Could this madman still possess enough of her brother to change his mind?

He stood. The chair pitched back and forth, back and forth without him in it, like a ghost sat still watching. Beside the bed, he stroked her cheek, gazing into her eyes. She couldn't believe the love and tenderness she saw. Maybe some of the old Darrell still existed.

"Sorry, but I have to finish this before you have his child."

Kathy stopped chewing on the bandana. How did he know about the baby? Fear seeped into her soul as she gaped at her brother.

"Yeah," he said, smiling. "I know you're pregnant. I walked right by you in this house during your restoration. Even saw you and that old lady down on Second Street. Have you ever chatted with the bag lady? She's weird."

Darrell laughed, and then stopped. "Nobody could take care of you better than I could. That's what you used to tell me."

Did I do this to Darrell?

Her brother reached out and smoothed her hair. Gently, he pushed her back against the iron headboard. Its coldness reminded her that this was reality, and she wouldn't awaken to find that this was all just a bad dream.

Darrell's mouth drooped and his shoulders sagged. She spotted the dullness in Darrell's eyes.

"You really shouldn't have married him." He leaned over and kissed the top of her head. "I loved you so much."

He brushed a stray hair behind her ear. "But now, it's payback for Mom and Dad's death. You killed them, not me."

As Darrell walked away, Kathy tried to mumble, her garbled words a hollow echo in her mind. He turned around, shook his head, and blew her a kiss. "Good-bye, Kathleen."

CHAPTER 39

I turn to leave the bedroom. A flash of orange darts between my legs. I pivot in time to see the cat jump on the bed and race over to Kathleen. Sheba swipes at the bandanna in her mouth. One claw snags and sticks in the cloth. When the cat tries to shake her paw free, the gag comes part way out.

"What the...?" I hurry toward the bed. "You, cat, outside!" I look at Jack. "Still remember that horrible story about your parents burning in the barn with the horse. God, the thought of an animal going up in flames." I shudder and scrunch my nose. "Stench from burnt fur smells way worse than human flesh."

Sheba breaks free from the bandana, spins around, and glares at me with yellow eyes. The cat hisses.

"Sheba, here kitty." I reach out to grab the tabby.

Orange fur spikes along Sheba's arched back. She spits at me, leaps off the bed, and runs out the door.

"Sheba, come here!" I shove the gun in my belt and chase after the cat. Sheba scurries through the next doorway. I reach the room. Moonlight streams through the window through an open patch of fog and lights up the picture frame on top of the dresser. It glows. I can barely see the people in the photo, but I'm drawn to the picture. My hands tremble as I pick it up. The entire family stands smiling: Mom, Dad, my sister, and me.

"Stupid cat." I slam the photograph down. Glass shatters. Shards fall across the dresser and sprinkle onto the floor. I whirl around as Sheba dashes past me and hides under the crib.

The baby's bed. I have to finish what I started. Time is of the essence.

"Come on, Sheba. Here kitty, kitty." As I call the cat, I remember all the animals; I've never killed one yet. "Sheba, come! I'm not going to let you burn." I smile. Of course I won't harm the cat. Couldn't. No, I'll make

Sheba my own pet. It will be a constant reminder of Kathleen. Sheba will love me, not leave me.

Eyes peer out from beneath the crib as I stalk forward and reach out my hands, my fingers inches from the orange fur, ready to grab the feline. Sheba hisses in my face and the tabby darts out the door. I run out of the room. The cat bounds down the stairs.

I scramble after her. Out in the hallway, I lose my footing, and kick over one of the gas cans. "You stupid cat!" The liquid soaks into the carpet.

I right the container, choking on the odor, and hurry down the stairs after Sheba. While searching the living room, I hear a noise. It sounds like a chair scraping across the kitchen floor. The cat must have bumped into it. I run in that direction.

In the kitchen, Sheba crouches underneath the oak table and eyes me. I lock the swinging door into the closed position to prevent the tabby's escape. Her striped tail twitches back and forth.

"Sheba, you're angry, but you'll get over it. At least you'll live." I stroll over to the back door and jab in the alarm code to turn it off. I yank open the door and place the stopper in front so it won't close.

"Come on, Sheba, time to go." On the other side of the table, I pick up one of the oak chairs and shove it at the cat. "Git!"

Sheba jumps, growls, and arches her back, but doesn't budge.

With a broom from the closet, I swing it under the table, and hit a chair. After slapping the floor, I finally get the cat moving and force the tabby outside into the back yard. I shut the door behind her.

"Dumb cat!" I look at my watch. Time's running out, but I had to get Sheba outside. I always free the pets, no matter what they are. Like the snake. I had to spill it from an aquarium onto the back lawn. That gives me the jitters thinking about it. The snake twirled around my arm. Yuck! I don't like snakes.

Dogs are the hardest to deal with, but I manage to get them out without too much fuss. A steak laced with a sedative always works. Probably should have done something like that with Sheba.

I think back to that fateful evening; I'd stood and listened to what later turned out to be my own parents' screams. I'd been so thankful my German Shepherd had been with me. Garth kept me company on the worst night of my life, Kathleen's wedding night. The thought of Jack with her is too much for me.

I smile. Even Kathleen forgot about the dog. It's a good thing no one ever wondered why Garth had never been found in my studio apartment fire. My dog finally died of old age. I cried over Garth, but the tears dried up a long time ago.

I hear a "yowl" from the back yard. "Sorry, Sheba, but your mistress has to go." I whistle as I push through the swinging door into the hallway and lock the door open. I have work to do.

CHAPTER 40

Thumping and yelling. Blaze opened his eyes, but they refused to focus. He rolled over and fell off the bed with a resounding thud. *Where am I?*

Through his dazed mind, Blaze remembered. "Kathy?" he mumbled. Nauseated, he half-crawled, half-stumbled out the door. His head pounded.

Near the stairs, the odor of gasoline fumes burned his nostrils and churned his stomach. He fell to his hands and knees and retched onto the carpeted hallway.

"Kathy?" He sniffed. The odor of gasoline panicked him. "Jack's going to burn us! Kathy, where are you?" He tried to yell, but his voice came out a whisper.

From the kitchen someone cried, "Git." Familiar. Who? He pulled himself along the carpet towards Kathy's bedroom. His right arm tingled and finally, it wouldn't hold his weight. He bumped into the wall as he fell.

Another whiff of gas assaulted him; he threw up, and then wiped the spittle from his mouth.

"Kathy, I'm coming." His speech slurred. He stiffened his right arm, placed it in front of him and dragged his knee forward. He crawled toward the master bedroom, determined to find Kathy.

The room looked miles away. Could he me make it? Fifty extra pounds seemed to weigh him down. He huffed and dragged himself until he reached the open doorway. He blacked out.

When he came to, Blaze had no idea how long he'd lain there. He got up on his knees and squinted. First one, then the other eye focused a little. Everything had a fuzzy outline. He rubbed his eyes and stared into the room. Two shapes formed on the bed, trussed up, and gagged. He peered through the slits in his eyes, concentrating on Kathy. Her eyes looked puffy and red. She shook her head violently. Who sat next to her? Jack? But he was the arsonist!

Blaze vaguely remembered hearing a commotion from downstairs. If not Jack, who had it been? Richard Newman's face floated through his mind. No, couldn't be. The scene in front of him cleared. He regained some control of his thoughts. Hadn't he heard a familiar voice from his past? He shook his head and took a deep breath, trying to ward off the cloudiness. It felt as if a fog had seeped into his brain and blunted his thought processes.

He put one foot on the floor and pushed off with his hand. Halfway standing, he wobbled. Nausea came in waves, hitting him like rolling seas. He steadied himself against the doorjamb. Kathy's eyes widened. She moaned and shook her head from side to side, her blond hair whipping across her face. She chewed on a red bandana in her mouth. Jack uttered a throaty growl. His naked body underwent contortions as he tried to free himself. Then, Jack froze.

The groggy haze slowly lifted from Blaze's brain.

He stumbled to the foot of the bed, eyeing Jack and then Kathy. He took one step toward her side. The whites of her eyes grew bigger. He stopped. "Don't be afraid. I'm here to help," he said, garbling his words.

Kathy just stared at him. Or was it beyond? She mumbled something. She worked her jaw and tried to free the cloth from her mouth. A piece of it dangled below her lip. Jack struggled again with his bonds.

The back of Blaze's neck tingled. Too late, he realized they were trying to warn him. Before he could turn around, something crashed onto the back of his skull. Blackness engulfed him once more.

CHAPTER 41

Kathy watched in horror as Blaze collapsed at Darrell's feet. "Thought I gave him enough stuff to knock him out for the duration. Must have miscalculated a little." Darrell cocked his head and raised one shoulder. Then he giggled a hyena laugh. "Be right back, Kathleen."

He grabbed Blaze by the ankles and dragged him out the door. "You've put on a few pounds," Kathy heard him say.

She caught a sound like beating a pillow and heard, "Sorry, old buddy, but we can't have you running around. Just lie here and sleep. It'll all be over soon."

Darrell strolled back into the master bedroom carrying a gas can. Kathy felt sick at his evil look. Tears slid down her face. She saw Jack grimace and struggle with the ropes.

"Why try?" Darrell asked. "They're too tight for you to get loose.

"Your precious cat is safe outside. Sheba didn't want to go, but you know I don't harm pets. Never have, nor will. Have the highest regard for animals."

He splashed the flammable liquid onto the two dressers and up on the curtains around the windows. The carpet soaked up the gasoline around the bed as he sang, "Smoke gets in your eyes." Grinning at them, he continued humming.

Backing out the door, Darrell grinned wider. "Been a pleasure, Kathleen. Finally, this will be over. And, Blaze," he motioned with his head toward the guestroom, "he's an added bonus. Should've stuck with me, Sis. My love..." he shrugged. "Never should have married him."

Darrell glared at Jack. Kathy had never seen her husband look so angry.

"Nothing you can do now, old boy." He laughed, and backed from the bedroom, tossing gas here and there as he went. "Good-bye, Kathleen. Scream loud and clear for me."

Suddenly, he stopped and Kathy wondered, *What now?* Her brother stroked his chin.

"Hmmm, how are you going to scream for me with those gags in your mouths? That's a dilemma. If I remove them, you'll scream and maybe alert someone." He tilted his head to one side, raised an eyebrow, and continued rubbing his chin.

Kathy chewed faster on the bandanna. She put her chin to her shoulder and pulled the gag out. It fluttered to her lap. She gulped in air. "Darrell, please."

In her soft, loving voice that she used when he'd been little, she continued. "You can't do this. All these years? You're my brother. I love you." Tears flowed down both cheeks.

"I love you, too. I always have." Darrell wiped at his own tears.

"Please, please, Darrell, don't... You can't... It's wrong to love—"

"Wrong! How can you say that?" Darrell rushed toward the bed. "Kathleen, you're everything to me."

"Oh, Darrell, I'm sorry. Oh, God, Mom and Dad. We were so close as brother and sister. Nothing more. It's wrong to love—"

"Shut up! Don't say that," Darrell shouted. "I love you. You promised you'd take care of me." He pounded his chest. "You said you'd love me forever. That changed. You were moving. You must die—just like Mom and Dad."

He stuffed the bandanna back into her mouth. "Not another word. Won't change my mind. I have to do this. I'll imagine your screams. Thoughts of you burning and watching the flames will satisfy me. Bye, Bye."

He waved at them and backed out the door.

An overpowering odor of gasoline assaulted Kathy.

CHAPTER 42

Kathy fought with her bonds and could feel Jack doing the same. Her wrists hurt, but she kept twisting. She spewed at the gag in her mouth.

Jack stopped fidgeting. She worked the gag out again. Jack shook his head.

She whispered, "I love you."

He nodded and turned his back, showing his tied hands. "I'll try," she whispered. She turned her back and scooted closer.

While she struggled to untie their bindings, Kathy heard footsteps running up the stairs. Had her brother heard them?

"Sheba, come here!" he yelled. "How the heck did you get back in?"

Kathy stopped working with Jack's bonds and listened. She felt Jack's fingers picking at her knots.

Darrell hadn't spotted the cat door. She prayed Sheba wouldn't come into the bedroom.

"Got you, you son of a... Ow, quit scratching. This time you're going out and staying out." Footsteps receded down the stairs. Kathy could hear the cat hissing.

Jack still fumbled with her bonds. Finally, he freed her wrists. Kathy quickly untied her ankles, pulled the gag out of Jack's mouth and undid his wrists.

He bent down and unlaced the knots at his ankles. "Go to the nursery," Jack whispered as he pulled on sweats. "With any luck, Darrell didn't find the escape ladder. I'll meet you there with Blaze."

He grabbed a T-shirt and rushed out of the room before Kathy could protest.

Banging and swearing came from downstairs in the kitchen area. Kathy snatched her robe from the foot of the bed and dragged it behind her as she rushed to the nursery.

She hurried over to the window to locate the escape ladder. A stinging pain bloomed under her bare foot and radiated into her leg. Broken glass. The warm spread of blood seeped from her foot as she yanked a piece of glass from her sole.

She raised the window. Sirens wailed in the distance.

The escape ladder was missing. Kathy limped from the room, closed the door, and sped down the hall to the guest room, leaving a trail of blood droplets behind.

The guest door stood ajar. Jack shook Blaze.

"Escape ladder is gone." Kathy whispered loudly, "Blaze wake up!"

"Close the door and get the backup sheets out of the closet before Darrell comes." Jack continued trying to wake Blaze.

A door slammed downstairs.

Kathy threw open the closet door and dragged out a pile of white sheets tied in knots. Jack put these in every room. He took them from her and secured them to the iron bar bolted next to the window on the side of the house.

The stair-step creaked.

Jack rushed over to the closet, ripped a box apart and took something from it.

"What's that?" Kathy whispered.

"A motorized toy car. This is the remote control. Go out the window," Jack said. "We'll be right behind you."

Kathy grabbed her stomach and winced.

"What's wrong?" Jack asked in a voice just above a whisper.

The nursery door banged against the wall. Darrell yelled, "Where are you?"

Footsteps thumped down the hall. The door burst open. Darrell aimed the gun at Jack. In his left hand, he clutched a similar remote control to the one Jack held.

Kathy realized the remote control was used to ignite the fires. *How much time do we have?*

Darrell yelled, "What are you doing? Where's Kathleen?"

Kathy stood motionless. Darrell was staring at Jack and hadn't even noticed her. Blaze stirred.

Darrell reeked of gasoline.

The white's of her brother's eyes darted all around. She couldn't let her brother shoot Jack. "Darrell, I'm right here."

When he noticed her, a smile spread across his face. "You didn't leave?"

"No, I'm here," Kathy said in a soft voice. Darrell still pointed the gun at Jack, but his other hand directed the remote toward her.

"Give it up," Jack yelled. "It's all over."

"I haven't come this far to lose now." Darrell's right thumb pulled back the hammer on the gun.

"No, Darrell, don't! I love you. Let me help you."

"Shut up! You have to die. So does Jack." Darrell's finger slid over the control button.

Jack raised his remote and pointed it at Darrell.

An ear-splitting blast shook the house, rocking Darrell, pitching him forward. As he fell, he fired the gun.

The bullet slammed into Jack's shoulder, knocking him back across Blaze.

Kathy screamed.

Blood oozed from a hole in Jack's shoulder. He grabbed his wound; red liquid trickled out between his fingers. He moaned.

Kathy caught a whiff of smoke.

Darrell pushed up onto his hands and knees, shaking his head as if to clear away a daze.

Still on all fours, Darrell lifted his head. He sneered, lifted the gun, and tried to stand.

Jack struggled to get off the bed, but before he could get up, Kathy rushed over. She kicked the gun out of her brother's hand.

Darrell lunged for it, but missed, skidding his face into the carpet.

Another explosion blew the door from its hinges and smashed on top of Darrell. Grey, acrid smoke billowed in.

Kathy rushed to Jack as he fell back next to Blaze. She couldn't rouse either of them.

CHAPTER 43

Kathy needed to save Jack and Blaze. When she opened the window, the oxygen fed fuel to the fire. Flames swooshed in from the hallway.

"Help!" Kathy screamed. She didn't believe anyone heard her and had to get help. She fought down her panic, scrambled over the sill, and took the homemade ladder in her hands. She slowly lowered herself down, gripping the cotton cloth so tightly her fingers turned white. Entwining her legs and feet around the sheets like Jack had taught her, she descended. A trail of little drops of red blood dripped from the cut on her foot.

Two-thirds from the top, she stopped. She grimaced from the pain, took a deep breath, and then slowly exhaled. Hand under hand, she inched her way lower.

Almost down, she slipped, lost her grip, and fell. She landed with a soft thud on the Algerian Ivy that Jack had planted thick enough to cushion a fall.

A twinge in Kathy's stomach made her curl into a fetal position for a minute, but she used Yoga breathing to lessen the pain. She picked herself up and limped toward the front of the house and pandemonium. Fire hoses extended and crossed the front yard like bare tree roots. Firefighters bustled about from engines to ladder trucks, dragging hoses and shouting at each other.

Kathy spied Captain Farley standing near an engine. She waved and yelled, "Over here."

The captain spotted her. He rushed over, whipped off his jacket and wrapped it around Kathy's shoulders. "Where's Jack?"

Kathy motioned toward the house. "Still inside.

"Did Jack start the fire?" Captain Farley asked.

"No!" Kathy looked around. George and Frank stood not too far away. She spoke louder and said, "He's not the arsonist. Neither is Blaze. Save them!"

"Where are they?" Captain Farley asked.

"The guest bedroom. Around the corner on the side street. Put a ladder up to the open window where the sheet is."

Captain Farley yelled, "George, Frank, take another firefighter and hustle a ladder around to the side."

The men disappeared. Two EMTs followed, each pushing a separate gurney, one piled with medical supplies, stopping at the gate on the sidewalk.

Kathy headed in that direction. Captain Farley yelled after her, "Your foot, it's bleeding."

"I don't care. My, God, if we don't save Jack, I'll die."

Captain Farley ran up beside her. "We'll save him." He motioned for the rescue vehicle to drive around the side of the house.

Kathy and the captain hurried back toward the side yard. The vehicle pulled up alongside.

The top half of the open guest bedroom window exploded. Shards of glass rained down on the firefighters and bounced off their helmets. Three more firefighters dragged over a hose and sprayed the window. When the water hit, flames crackled, popped, and sizzled. Great clouds of smoke billowed into the air.

Captain Farley gently guided Kathy toward the back of the rescue vehicle. While an EMT bandaged her foot, she watched Frank climb the ladder.

At the window, he yelled down, motioning inside. The breathing apparatus and roar of the fire muffled what he said, but Kathy caught "here." Frank scraped away broken glass and crawled through the opening.

George scrambled up the slippery metal steps. Frank passed someone out through the window. George hefted the limp body over his shoulder and backed down. Frank disappeared inside again.

Sheba jumped through the window. The cat made her way carefully down the ladder, step by step. At the bottom of the ladder, Lovell, who'd just arrived, tried to grab the big tabby. Sheba avoided his grasp and raced under the nearest bush.

Kathy couldn't believe the cat had gone back inside the house through the cat door a second time. She knew dogs would try and save their masters, but a cat.

Sitting on the floor in the doorway of the fire rescue vehicle, Kathy dangled her feet over the edge. She twitched her bandaged foot.

"Ma'am, we should get you to the hospital for your foot and check you out. You're pregnant aren't you?" the EMT asked.

"Yes, I'm fine," Kathy said. "I let you bandage my foot. We're not going 'til my husband, Blaze, and Darrell get out."

A sharp pain stabbed her lower abdomen. She gasped. *Were these pains like when I miscarried before?* She shook her head and said, "No!"

"Excuse me, ma'am?" the EMT said.

"Nothing," Kathy said. "We'll wait for Jack. I have to see he's okay."

Captain Farley draped an arm around her as if protecting her from the commotion. She knew he restrained her from rushing toward the house. She sat, her gaze frozen on the side yard.

George, carrying a limp body over his shoulder, hurried through the gate onto the sidewalk. He laid the body down on the gurney and the EMT rushed it toward the ambulance.

Kathy jumped up, covering her mouth, and said, "Oh, my God, is he okay?" Captain Farley's jacket slid to the ground. She limped forward.

Blaze lay on the gurney. "Where's Jack?" Kathy cried out.

Before anyone could answer, she heard the squeal of tires and screech of brakes. Turning, she saw Detective Burns throw open his car door, lights still flashing, and rush over. "Did you catch Jack?" Looking down at the gurney, he blurted, "Who's this?"

Kathy ignored him, and directed her speech to the EMT. "Darrell used chloroform to knock Blaze out. When he came to, Darrell hit him over the head with the gun."

"Darrell?" Detective Burns questioned.

Captain Farley pulled Kathy back a few steps and put his coat back over her shoulders. "Darrell, your dead brother?"

Kathy nodded, still looking at Blaze. "He's alive. She shivered and gripped the coat tight around her neck. "My brother is the arsonist."

Detective Burns and Captain Farley exchanged glances like maybe she'd lost her mind. Kathy wrung her hands and concentrated on Blaze's unconscious form. She focused on what the EMT and paramedic were doing with him. The technicians seemed to be immune to their surroundings of fire, smoke, water, and calls of working firefighters.

An EMT opened Blaze's airway and listened. "He's breathing," the EMT exclaimed. Then he slipped the oxygen mask over Blaze's nose and mouth.

The paramedic inflated a blood pressure cuff on Blaze's right arm. He called out, "BP's one hundred thirty over eighty-five. Pulse one hundred twenty."

Kathy felt her own heart race. "Come on, Blaze, I can't lose you," she pleaded.

"Respirations are twenty-four and shallow," the EMT said. The two technicians collapsed the legs of the gurney and slid Blaze inside the ambulance.

From inside, she heard the paramedic loudly reporting to base. "I'm starting a 16 IV, left A.V., with a normal saline." The radio static prevented her from hearing the orders.

"Make way," Captain Farley said, gently pulling Kathy back a few more steps, and pushing the detective out of the way. She bit her lower lip and gasped. "Jack, is he alive? Someone answer me."

"He's alive," Lovell said as he and Frank pushed the second gurney close to the back of the second van that had just pulled up. Detective Burns' smile widened. Kathy wanted to wipe it off his face. He'd been so wrong.

On the gurney, Jack's breaths sounded loud even against the roar of the fire. He lay so still. "Please, God, let him be okay," Kathy prayed aloud.

Hank, the paramedic at Jack's side, slipped the oxygen mask over Jack's nose and mouth. He wrapped the blood pressure cuff around his upper arm, pumped it up and said, "Pulse is ninety-six. Blood pressure one hundred forty over ninety." Then he lifted a blood-soaked bandage from Jack's shoulder.

"How's his gunshot wound?" Kathy asked.

"Gun shot?" Detective Burns leaned over. "Who shot him?"

Blood seeped out of Jack's wound.

"George," Kathy screamed. "Do something.'

George, who'd also trained as an EMT, grabbed another bandage and pressed down.

Hank yelled over his shoulder, "Ask the doctor if he wants a wide open sixteen gauge started."

Kathy held her breath. When Jack coughed, her muscles relaxed a little. "Is he going to make it?"

"Where is he?" Jack managed to ask, his voice muffled by the oxygen mask.

At the sound of his voice, Kathy broke from Captain Farley's grasp, and hovered over Jack. "You're alive. I was so afraid."

Jack struggled to repeat his question.

The cat scampered forward and bumped against Kathy's legs. She reached down, snatched up the wide-eyed tabby, and hugged Sheba close, wishing she could do the same with Jack. "Blaze is in that ambulance over there," she said, looking down at Jack.

He shook his head and pulled the oxygen mask away from his mouth. "Not Blaze." He moaned. "Darrell," he gasped out. "Where is he?"

Kathy looked at Captain Farley, then George. "Where is Darrell?"

"Darrell, the dead brother?" Detective Burns questioned.

"He's not dead," Kathy yelled.

"What's going on?" the detective asked. "A neighbor described Jack's old Ford coupe in the vicinity before the other fire started. Have I missed something here?"

"Jack's not your arsonist," Captain Farley said.

"How can the brother be alive?" Detective Burns asked.

"Darrell's inside," Jack managed to wheeze before another fit of coughing.

"He's under the door in the same room where Jack and Blaze were," Kathy said, staring back toward the inferno.

George rushed back through the gap in the side hedge. Lovell and Burns ran after him.

Kathy gazed into her husband's eyes, tears streamed down her face. She clung to Sheba with one hand and squeezed Jack's healthy shoulder with her other. The tabby trembled. Kathy felt as terrified as the cat. Sheba, smelling like burnt fur, clutched Kathy's shoulder and nuzzled her head under Kathy's hair.

Hank replaced the oxygen mask over Jack's mouth and nose, and gently pushed him back down to the gurney. "Relax. Get some air into your lungs. Your bullet wound isn't life-threatening. You'll be okay. We're going to load you into the rig."

Jack grabbed Hank's arm. Through the oxygen mask, he mumbled, "I'm not leaving yet. Not 'til I see Darrell."

Coughing came from inside the other EMT truck. "Is Blaze coming around?" Kathy asked.

"Yes, ma'am, he'll be fine," the paramedic sitting inside called out. He banged on the front of the rig and yelled, "Let's get to the hospital." Someone closed the doors and pounded on the back. The ambulance took off.

Kathy watched the vehicle speed away for a few seconds, and then looked at her house. Firefighters, covered with black soot, circled the burning home, continuing their futile attempt to extinguish the fire. Holding on to Sheba, she stared transfixed at the blaze engulfing their Victorian.

Orange flames shot out from every orifice and reached for the sky. Smoke billowed up, disappearing into and mixing with fingers of the fog bank. She choked on the acrid smell and muttered, "Darrell, is he still alive?" She sighed. *Do I want him to be?*

Captain Farley leaned over, placed his arm around Kathy and whispered, "I'm sorry. We'll try our best, but the house..." He shrugged and glanced over at her husband.

She followed the captain's gaze. Jack breathed deeply with the oxygen. Dressings now covered his burned hands. Also, his dark hair had been singed, just like the poor cat's fur.

Kathy's abdomen cramped. She bit her lower lip and counted to ten, blowing her breath out with each number. Closing her eyes tight, she willed the pain in her gut to go away. *This will not happen now.*

"Here, make way," George said.

Kathy opened her eyes. George carried another form out, laid it on the awaiting gurney, and pushed it toward them. Another EMT, Detective Burns, and the fire marshal followed behind.

After biting harder on her lower lip, Kathy clenched her hands into fists. She inhaled deeply, and then forced the air out of her lungs.

Jack struggled up onto his elbows and looked around.

A third ambulance turned the corner and screeched to a halt. Two EMTs jumped out and opened up the back of the rig.

The form on the gurney did not move. One of the paramedics said, "No respiration. Need the intubation kit." With assistance, the paramedic slipped a tube in a quick movement down into Darrell's throat. "He's breathing. Start the ambu bag."

While one EMT did, Kathy watched as George pumped up the blood pressure cuff on Darrell's arm. "One hundred two over sixty-four, but his pulse is rapid with an irregular rhythm at one hundred."

"He's unconscious," the paramedic said, relaying the information. "Lots of smoke and extensive burns. He's in shock. I'm starting two wide-open IVs with normal saline."

Digging in the kit, George and the paramedic placed burn bandages and sleeves over Darrell's arms and legs.

They collapsed the legs on the gurney, slid it into the waiting rig, and the paramedic climbed inside. George slammed the door. The van raced down the street, tires squealed around the corner, with sirens piercing the dawn. Detective Burns climbed into his car and sped after the ambulance.

Fire Marshal Lovell turned to Kathy. "They'll take good care of your brother. The hospital team will stabilize him, and then airlift him to the closest burn unit. I'm sorry."

Captain Farley and George loaded Jack's gurney into the rig. "George, go with him," the captain said.

George hustled around the side of the vehicle. The passenger door slammed.

"Here, take the cat," Kathy said, thrusting the tabby into Captain Farley's arms. She looked in the back of the vehicle. The knife twisted in her gut again. Her knuckles turned white as she gripped the sides of the door. It felt like she'd been hit in the abdomen by a karate kick. She doubled over.

Captain Farley grabbed her with one hand. "Kathy?"

"Oh, no," she said, moaning. "Not now. Not again. I can't lose this baby."

Jack yanked off his mask. "Get her in. She's had two miscarriages."

Captain Farley helped her into the ambulance, slammed the door shut, and pounded on the back. The van lurched; she gripped the bench so she didn't slide off.

Inside the rescue vehicle, the paramedic laid Kathy down on the seat. He called in and told the doctors to expect another smoke-inhalation victim with a minor gunshot wound to the shoulder. He also said, "And I have a pregnant woman..." He held his hand over the mike and asked, "How many months?"

"Three, almost four," Kathy said.

He removed his hand and said, "Four months pregnant with abdominal cramps. She's had two miscarriages before."

Yes, Kathy thought, *but there's no way I'm going to this time.*

Jack looked terrified.

Kathy tried to smile and said, "I'm okay." She yoga-breathed and closed her eyes. *God, please don't let me lose this baby.*

CHAPTER 44

When the rescue vehicle stopped, the back doors burst open. The emergency team helped Kathy step down and into a wheelchair. They slid out Jack's gurney, let down the legs and rushed him inside.

George pushed Kathy's wheelchair behind the gurney, hurrying into the ER. As they passed two curtained-off cubicles, Kathy wondered if Blaze or Darrell were inside.

The EMTs and ER team transferred Jack to the third emergency room bed, removed the gurney, and left. George stayed in the ER room next to Kathy.

A nurse helped her on to the available bed near Jack and started to close the curtains.

"No," Kathy said, feeling like her world had turned upside down. "He's my husband, I want to see him."

The nurse left the curtain open and hooked up monitors to Kathy's abdomen. Kathy watched the ER team work on Jack. By their ID tags, she noted a doctor, a couple of RNs, and a respiration therapist surrounded him.

They cut off her husband's clothes, taped some pads with electrodes onto his chest and arms, and put a thing in his nose, giving him oxygen.

Standing next to Kathy, George leaned over and said, "The nurse is putting a pulse oximeter onto Jack's index finger. They'll put a noninvasive blood pressure cuff on his arm. Don't worry; they're taking good care of the lad."

Kathy squeezed George's hand; thankful he was a good friend and was explaining the care her husband was receiving.

"Someone insert tubing in the IV pump and plug in the machine," one of the techs said.

Constant beeping, not only from the machine hooked up to Kathy, but Jack's machine made her want to cover her ears and scream.

On the other side of Jack, Blaze called out, "Kathy, are you here? Everything okay?"

A twinge cramped her abdomen and she took a deep breath. "Yes."

"Please be quiet," someone said.

Kathy stared from one monitor to the other. A continuous barrage of chatter emanated from the ER team. "BP is..." "Excuse me." "We need another number sixteen stat." "Can you try...?" "Move, labs here."

A man in green surgical garb hurried in. "How's it going in here?"

Kathy looked at his name tag and asked, "Doctor Martin, how's Darrell? He was brought in minutes before us, badly burned."

"Who are you?"

"I'm his sister." She pointed to Jack. "That's my husband."

Dr. Martin looked at the nurse. "How is she?"

"Almost four months pregnant with previous miscarriages. Has some slight cramping and an injured foot."

"Her OB doctor been called?"

"Not yet."

"Vitals good? You're monitoring her?"

"Yes, Doctor."

"Check her foot and re-bandage. Call her doctor, and keep track of the vitals." He looked at Kathy and smiled. "You're doing fine. Let me oversee these patients and I'll check back."

"But," Kathy said, "Darrell—"

"We'll discuss it later," Dr. Martin said as he examined Jack. "Did anyone contact a surgeon?"

"Yes, Doctor, he's waiting," another nurse said.

"Good. Close the curtain." The doctor turned toward the next cubicle. "Get bed two admitted and bed three to surgery."

As the nurse grabbed the white curtain and started pulling it across the metal rod, causing a scraping noise, Kathy spotted the detective. She waved and struggled to get off the bed, but George put his hand on her shoulder and restrained her. After the nurse finished closing the curtain, she lifted Kathy's foot and took off the bloody dressing.

"Detective Burns is out there," Kathy told George. "Please, ask him if he knows what happened to Darrell."

"Let's take care of you first, lassie. The doctor said he'd be over in a wee minute."

The nurse put some ointment on Kathy's foot and redressed the wound. "When was your last tetanus shot?"

Kathy stared at the closed curtain. *Please, God, let Jack be okay.* She didn't care when her last shot was.

The nurse repeated the question.

"Over seven years ago," Kathy said. A few seconds later, she felt a pinprick in her arm and realized the nurse had given her a shot.

The monitor with the baby's heartbeat beeped steadily.

Twenty minutes later, the ER doctor entered Kathy's cubicle with Detective Burns who stood just behind him.

"Darrell?" Kathy asked.

"How's your cramping?" Dr. Martin asked.

"They're almost gone. What about my brother?"

The doctor shook his head. "I'm sorry; there was nothing we could do."

Kathy closed her eyes. Tears streamed down her cheeks. "Oh, God," she cried out and then covered her face with her hands. "Darrell's really dead."

CHAPTER 45

The day after Darrell's funeral, Kathy, Jack, and Blaze picked up Sheba at the vets, where the cat was boarded, and then drove to the firehouse. They walked into Captain Farley's office where everyone had been asked to come.

"Please, sit," Captain Farley said.

Kathy let Jack settle into the middle leather chair in front of his boss's desk while she took the one to his right. She clutched the tabby to her chest. Jack nodded to his captain sitting across from him.

Blaze sat on the other side of Jack. Fire Marshal Lovell placed himself onto a metal chair next to Captain Farley. At the other end of the desk, dressed in a black suit, Detective Burns cleared his throat. *He looks like a funeral director,* Kathy thought.

The fire chief leaned against the doorjamb with his arms crossed and didn't say anything.

"Thank you all for coming," Captain Farley said. "I know we've been over this, and I'm sure it's upsetting to you, Kathy, but I'd like to clear up the details."

Jack patted Kathy's hand, gazed into her eyes, and said, "I'm sure this won't take long."

Fire Marshal Lovell cleared his throat. "Yes, Mrs. Hellman, we'll try and be brief. Losing your brother was hard," he said, "but to lose him twice, knowing he'd tried to kill you... I can't imagine how you feel."

Kathy chewed on her lip. No one knew how she felt. The pain that her brother had become a madman was unbearable, yet she felt relief that their ordeal was over. Sheba nuzzled her neck.

The fire marshal looked down at his notepad and continued. "Your brother told you the truth. The exhumed body everyone thought was Darrell Cougar turned out to be a young man named Jerry Watkins. He was about the same age, similar in build and size to your brother; an alcoholic who'd run away.

"The autopsy report had revealed he'd been drunk, drugged, and his upper body had traces of alcohol on it. Darrell must have dressed him in his own clothes and splashed alcohol over his face. Since Blaze removed your brother's jewelry from the body, everyone assumed it was Darrell.

"The drugs and alcohol were consistent with Darrell's usage. He even lucked out. The blood type was a match. No DNA was done because of Blaze's statement.

"We reviewed the fire investigation report and I talked to the investigator. Darrell set it up like he'd tipped over a candle. With the alcohol next to his bed, everything went up fast. You can imagine the Watkins family's sorrow and relief, finally knowing what had happened to their boy."

"If I hadn't been so sure it was Darrell, they would have checked dental records," Blaze said.

"Several witnesses had seen Darrell stagger into his apartment and swore he'd never left," Fire Marshal Lovell said.

"Well, at least some good came out of this," Kathy said. "The Watkins family has closure." She rested her head against Jack's uninjured shoulder. *I have closure, too.*

Sheba squirmed loose. The tabby walked across laps and settled into Blaze's.

Jack smiled as Kathy reached down and caressed her abdomen. "Yes, and thank God, you didn't miscarry."

Kathy sighed. With proper care, the doctor told them she would carry to full term.

Detective Burns cleared his throat, and said, "We found Darrell's car parked around the block from your house. An old Ford Coupe like yours, Jack. Same color. Appears he was setting you up for arson."

"I've seen that car around town," Jack said.

The detective glanced down at the floor. "Your brother-in-law knew what he was doing. In Darrell's car, we discovered some sophisticated electronic equipment and tape recordings taken of you from inside your house."

"After Darrell burned his family home," the fire marshal said, "he received a degree in electronics, and even studied fire science. His arson career began."

"He worked for Eureka Electricians," Detective Burns said. "We found disguises in his home. And, he was in your house when you did your restoration work."

Kathy gasped. "He told me that, but I never recognized him." She looked at Jack. "What kind of sister doesn't recognize her own brother?"

"He was good at disguises and he'd changed," Jack said. "No one would have recognized him."

"Darrell also worked for Dr. Graves," Detective Burns said, "and the Thompsons, as well as your neighbor's kitchen remodel, and all the other places he set fire to." The detective shook his head and continued, "He bugged your car and your home. That's how he followed you. Darrell knew where you were going, sometimes before you even got there." Turning to Blaze, Burns said, "Thanks to your permission, we swept your car and house and found listening devices there, too."

Kathy shuddered and turned to Jack. "And you suspected Blaze."

"That's okay, I thought it was Jack," Blaze said. He stroked Sheba who lay curled in his lap. The tabby was a little singed, but otherwise fine. Sheba purred and twitched her tail.

Kathy couldn't believe they'd all made it. *All except Darrell.*

Blaze broke into her thoughts when he asked, "Jack, how did the house go up in flames if Darrell was upstairs with us?"

"Darrell used a controller," Jack said, "like the ones in remote control cars." He explained how he'd bought a toy replica as a present for the baby and how he'd tried it out in the store.

"You are happy about the baby," Kathy said, smiling. "You bought a present."

Jack's grin matched Kathy's. "Anyway, I hid it in the guestroom." He told them what happened. "I'm not sure whether Darrell pushed his button or I hit mine, but the place exploded. I must have passed out next to Blaze." Jack stopped, went to rub his hand through shorter hair and stopped. "Thanks to my fearless wife, Frank, George, Cap, and all the firefighters, we made it though."

He reached out and rested his arm on top of Kathy's. "Man, I'm sorry, but I never suspected... God, Darrell was supposed to be dead."

"I know." Kathy thought a minute about what Jack had just said. "Wait. You just called Bradley 'Blaze'."

"I guess it's about time," Jack said.

Blaze nodded.

Fire Marshal Lovell interrupted the moment when he said, "Who would suspect a dead man?" He hesitated, glanced over at the detective, and said, "Darrell fooled us all."

"Guess I owe you an apology, Jack," Detective Burns said. "I figured you for the arsonist. No doubt in my mind. I'll try to be more objective from now on." He pushed out of his chair, walked over, and reached out his hand, with a slight smile on his face.

Jack glanced at the outstretched hand, and then reached out his own bandaged one. Detective Burns' hand closed over it. "No apologies," Jack said. "Guess it looked like me. Darrell set it up that way."

Blaze rubbed his chin. "He had me convinced. Jack, I have one more question. Where were you when the fires started?"

"Yes," Kathy said. "I'd like to know, too." She waited for his answer.

"One-thirty," he paused, shaking his head. "Always a haunting time for me. I'd wake-up sometime after midnight and couldn't sleep. So, I'd sneak out and watch the heavens, asking God that there be no more fires. Part of me still listened for explosions." He looked out the window and took a deep breath. "Sometimes I'd put on headphones, listen to music, and work on the car."

"Even on your wedding night?" Blaze asked.

"Not that night." Jack chuckled. "I needed to slow myself down and say thanks for having Kathleen in my life."

"Well, I'm just glad it's over," Blaze said. "Can't believe it was Darrell. I know it will take time, but I hope we can be a family."

Sheba stood and stretched. The orange tabby left Blaze's lap, walked across Jack's, and sat in Kathy's.

Jack put his arm around Kathy's shoulder. "A close family sounds good, Blaze."

Kathy sighed. "Darrell was sick. It'll take time, but, yeah, sounds perfect to me, too."

ABOUT THE AUTHOR

J. A. Winrich lives and writes in Northern California. A member of the Mystery Writers of America, Sisters in Crime, and Redwood Writers branch of the California Writers Club.

See website: www.writerjaw.com

Made in the USA
Coppell, TX
26 February 2026